Praise for Ray Keating
and his Pastor Stephen Grant Thrillers...

"In this, Ray Keating's sixth novel featuring Pastor Stephen Grant, we discover that the always intriguing former Navy Seal and CIA operative is also a world class wine aficionado. This comes in handy as the pastor is once again forced to divide his time between his understanding wife, the needs of his church and congregation, and what some describe as his 'hobby' of joining the fray to assist colleagues from his past life when called upon. Grant is a wonderful character and *Wine Into Water* is a great read."

> - *David Keene, former chairman of the American Conservative Union, former president of the National Rifle Association, and opinion editor at* The Washington Times

Murderer's Row was named KFUO's BookTalk "Book of the Year" in 2015.

The River was a 2014 finalist for KFUO's BookTalk "Book of the Year."

Marvin Olasky, editor-in-chief of WORLD magazine, lists Ray Keating among his top 10 Christian novelists.

The host of KFUO radio's BookTalk calls Ray Keating "a great novelist."

"What Ian Fleming's 007 series has probably done for ex-MI-6 agents and Tom Clancy has done for retired CIA officers, Mr. Keating has done for the minority of former CIA agents who have served their country by working in the intelligence community, but now wish to serve God... Mr. Keating also allows you to discover how each of his characters ticks in a style and tone reminiscent of some of the best-loved books of all time."

- Kenneth V. Blanchard
The Washington Times review of
The River

"Ray Keating has a knack for writing on topics that could be pulled from tomorrow's headlines. An atheist mayor-elect of NYC? I could envision that. Pastor Grant taking out a terrorist? I could see that."

- Lutheran Book Review on An
Advent for Religious Liberty

"This novel is a fascinating read with a murder mystery, unique and exceptional characters, and wit... With multiple layers and a complex plot, the novel moves forward with a smooth and even pace."

- SeriousReading.com on Murderer's Row

Lionhearts

A Pastor Stephen Grant Novel

Ray Keating

Stay strong and keep the faith!

Ray Keating

This book is a work of fiction. Names, characters, places, events and incidents either are the product of the author's imagination or are used fictitiously. Any resemblance to actual persons, living or dead, events or locales is entirely coincidental.

For more information:
Keating Reports, LLC
P.O. Box 596
Manorville, NY 11949
raykeating@keatingreports.com

ISBN-10: 1548964182
ISBN-13: 978-1548964184

Author's Note

On the stylistic matter of whether or not to capitalize "he" or "his" when referring to God the Father or Jesus, I have used the *Lutheran Service Book* for various parts of the Divine Service, which capitalizes. In terms of Bible passages, my choice of *The Lutheran Study Bible (ESV)* does not capitalize. In other parts of the book, I generally have followed the lead of the *Lutheran Service Book*.

As always, for my family,
Beth, David and Jonathan

Previous Books by Ray Keating

Wine Into Water: A Pastor Stephen Grant Novel (2016)

Murderer's Row: A Pastor Stephen Grant Novel (2015)

The River: A Pastor Stephen Grant Novel (2014)

An Advent for Religious Liberty:
A Pastor Stephen Grant Novel (2012)

Root of All Evil? A Pastor Stephen Grant Novel (2012)

Warrior Monk: A Pastor Stephen Grant Novel (2010)

Discussion Guide for Warrior Monk:
A Pastor Stephen Grant Novel (2011)

In the nonfiction arena...

Unleashing Small Business Through IP:
The Role of Intellectual Property in Driving
Entrepreneurship, Innovation and Investment
(Revised and Updated Edition, 2016)

Unleashing Small Business Through IP:
Protecting Intellectual Property, Driving Entrepreneurship
(2013)

"Chuck" vs. the Business World: Business Tips on TV
(2011)

U.S. by the Numbers:
What's Left, Right, and Wrong with America State by State
(2000)

New York by the Numbers:
State and City in Perpetual Crisis (1997)

D.C. by the Numbers: A State of Failure (1995)

"Greater love has no one than this, that someone lay down his life for his friends."

- John 15:13

"Even though I walk through the valley of the shadow of death, I will fear no evil, for you are with me; your rod and your staff, they comfort me."

- Psalm 23:4

"Jesus answered them, 'Do you now believe? Behold, the hour is coming, indeed it has come, when you will be scattered, each to his own home, and will leave me alone. Yet I am not alone, for the Father is with me. I have said these things to you, that in me you may have peace. In the world you will have tribulation. But take heart; I have overcome the world.'"

- John 16:31-33

Prologue

25 Years Ago

"This isn't the way I was supposed to hit the beach in Cancun," declared Lieutenant Mike Leonard to the other seven members of his Navy SEAL squad.

Leonard believed that as a mission grew closer, it paid to try to keep his squad members at ease – well, as much as that might be possible. After all, they were professionals and knew what had to be done. Besides, the exact details of this assault were still to come. He added, "Crystal and I keep saying that we're going to leave Richard with her parents or mine for a long, get-away weekend. Cancun's on the list of possible destinations."

Freddie Pederson replied, "Lieutenant, maybe you can grab some brochures after we take care of business."

That drew laughs from seven of the eight men seated in the Seahawk helicopter. They were being transported from their base of operations in Virginia to a Landing Helicopter Dock amphibious assault ship heading toward the east coast of Mexico's Yucatan Peninsula.

Leonard looked at Stephen Grant, the youngest member of the team, sitting next to him. Grant had only smiled at Pederson's jab.

Leonard leaned in close, and asked, "Hey, Grant, you sure you're okay?"

For the past two-and-a-half weeks, Grant had been working very hard to push away the still-raw pain from the death of his parents.

Douglas and Samantha Grant had been traveling home on I-75 late in the night when a drunk driver in a large sedan lost control at 80-plus miles per hour. He plowed into the side of the Grants' Pontiac Grand Am, and drove the couple into the concrete pillar of an overpass. Doug, who operated a Coca-Cola delivery truck for nearly three decades, was at the wheel, but never had a chance.

Stephen journeyed home to Glendale, Ohio, after receiving word. For a man who had graduated from Valparaiso University in three years and become a Navy SEAL, he felt like a child again, overwhelmed making decisions about the joint funeral for his parents. While greeting family members and longtime friends, he tried to hide the fact that his head was swimming. People told him time and again how "Doug and Sam" had helped others, and how much they were loved and would be missed.

Stephen also had to decide what to do with the quaint home in the historic village where he grew up. He loved Glendale. From first grade through high school, he was active at school and church. His passionate interests – such as reading, the Cincinnati Reds and Bengals, playing golf and baseball, and practicing archery – were born and grew in that village. And even when he left for college, Valpo wasn't all that far away. But the loss of his parents made clear that it wasn't Glendale itself, but what his parents had created there that really mattered.

At Valpo, Stephen expanded his interests, especially studying history and using time to discipline his body. He then went on to the Navy SEALs, and its enormous challenges and responsibilities. But throughout, the close family life of the three Grants stood at the center of Stephen's life. Ever since his earliest school days, he loved telling his parents what he was doing, and enjoyed listening to their lively conversations about church, their interests and work. And suddenly, it was all gone. The anchor broke away, and he was struggling not to drift.

After his parents were buried, Stephen decided that he needed to get out of Glendale, and back to the SEALs. He pressed the lawyer on estate matters. Grant lied to a cousin, claiming that he had to get back to the Navy immediately, and asked if he would mind packing up the non-furniture contents of the house, putting it all in storage, and letting family and friends take any of the furniture they might want. Grant had rented a storage facility, and hired a real-estate broker to sell the house.

A mere ten days after heading home due to the deaths of his parents, Grant had returned to his SEAL team. Now, a week later, he was part of a squad being sent to rescue 11 young Americans held captive by Marxist guerillas in a small hotel on the beach in Cancun.

Grant responded to Mike Leonard's question, "I'm fine, Lieutenant."

"That's bullshit. But I'm trusting that you're okay for this mission."

Grant looked Leonard straight in the eyes. "Don't doubt that, sir."

They sat in silence for several more minutes, and then Leonard, still talking quietly to Grant, said, "I've been there. I know what you're going through."

Grant just simply listened.

"Did you hear any assholes at the church or the funeral say something about your parents' deaths being part of God's plan?"

Grant replied, "Sure enough."

"I heard that when my sister died. I thought it was the strangest thing to say. The pastor at our church overheard the comment, and must have seen my reaction. So, he pulls me to the side, and tells me something that I'll never forget."

"What's that?"

"He said that shit happens."

"What?"

"Well, those weren't his exact words. But his message stuck. He told me that we live in a fallen world, a place where suffering exists and death is inevitable, and sometimes these things come in big, unpredictable ways."

Grant shook his head. "Is that supposed to be comforting?"

Leonard smiled, and added, "I asked him the same thing. The comfort, he said, comes from faith. He gave me this quick rundown on how things ended for each of the Apostles. Hell, it wasn't pretty for those guys. But they understood that Jesus was with them throughout it all, and that their reward would be found elsewhere. That made sense to me. Like I said, it stuck."

Grant thought about what he was being told.

Leonard added, "So, my philosophy on life kind of comes down to seven points. Do you want to hear them?"

"Sure."

"Shit happens. Have faith. Stay strong. Love and take care of your family. Pursue excellence. Help others. And enjoy the gifts."

"Not bad, Lieutenant. For now, I'll take it."

About an hour later, the Seahawk touched down on the amphibious assault ship. After another three hours of planning and moving into position, the squad of eight SEALs were moving under the cover of darkness in a RHIB, or rigid-hull inflatable boat.

The limited intel received from the local Mexican police said there were about a dozen guerillas. They were demanding freedom for a handful of their leaders who recently had been captured by the government. If that freedom was not forthcoming, they threatened to execute the hostages one by one.

At the highest levels of government, the Mexican president let his U.S. counterpart know that he didn't think any prisoners would be set free. Given that reality, the U.S. administration didn't trust the Mexicans to get the job done correctly. Meanwhile, the government of Mexico wanted the issue of guerillas in their international resort area to go away as quickly as possible. For good measure, if the rescue mission was botched, Mexico could blame America.

As the RHIB moved forward, Leonard received a message from the ship. He listened, and finally replied, "Thank you, sir."

He relayed to his team, "We've got a couple of CIA spooks watching the hotel. They're telling us that the guerillas have most of their eyes on the streets and what the police are doing. Apparently, only two seem to be watching the beach side, from a third-floor balcony."

Pederson commented, "I like that. It's about time the CIA stepped up with something useful."

Leonard commanded, "Once your feet are planted, Freddie, you need to take the two guerillas down."

"You got it." Pederson was a marksman, and the best shot among the group.

As the RHIB approached the beach, Pederson stepped into the water. The waves were gentle. As the tide went out, he trained the scope on the M16A2 rifle, with suppressor attached, on the third floor of the hotel. Pederson quickly found his two targets, and eliminated both. One guerilla fell backwards, while the other staggered and went over the side railing, dropping to the concrete below.

Leonard gave a thumbs-up, made sure everyone in the unit saw him do a time check with his watch, and then signaled for the team to advance up the beach as planned. They split into predetermined teams of two, with each unit assigned a point of entry.

Each pairing entered the building at the same time. The element of surprise was complete.

*   *   *

Grant focused on two of the guerillas standing against the wall, who were watching the 11 hostages on the floor. He squeezed off a few shots at the first hostage taker. Blood hit the wall, followed by the man's body. As the second guerilla raised his rifle, Grant switched his targeting, and the second hostage taker succumbed in the same way as the first.

*   *   *

As the SEALs moved in, two guerillas were tucked away, out of clear lines of fire.

With comrades dying around him, one of those guerillas screamed, raised his gun, and shot a hostage. Mike Leonard finally gained position, and riddled the man with bullets.

On the other side of the expansive room, the eyes of the second partially hidden guerilla moved frantically. He dropped his rifle, pulled out a knife, and lunged forward to grab one of the female hostages by the hair. He tugged her close, let go of her hair, and slipped his arm around her neck.

Speaking Spanish, one of the SEALs – Miguel Ramos – warned, "Don't do it."

The guerilla replied, "Get back."

Ramos slowly lowered his rifle.

The guerilla, though much taller than his hostage, hid behind her. But as Ramos lowered the rifle, the guerilla eased his grip on the woman, and stood a little taller.

Ramos then dropped the rifle. The guerilla said, "Good." He now towered over the woman.

In one quick motion, Ramos pulled his Beretta M9 semiautomatic pistol from the holster, aimed, and pulled off two shots. One projectile entered the guerilla's forehead, and the second entered via the left cheek. The guerilla's body fell back, and the hostage stood quivering. Ramos moved forward, and caught the woman as her legs gave out. "It's alright. You're okay."

*   *   *

Pederson knelt to check on the young hostage who lay bleeding on the floor.

Leonard screamed out orders. "Confirm that this was all of them! And make sure they're all dead ... or incapacitated."

A minute later, one of the team members called out, "Ten dead!"

Pederson looked up at Leonard from his position on the floor where he was working on the young lady who had been shot. Grant and his partner spoke with the hostages, trying to calm them. The other four SEALs checked the remainder of the building.

Leonard radioed to the two Seahawk choppers hovering in the distance. "Guerillas are down. We've got one hostage shot. She needs medical treatment ASAP. Other hostages secure."

Pederson looked up, and shook his head. "She's gone, Mike."

Leonard clenched his teeth.

Within ten minutes, the two Seahawks were spraying sand as they lifted off from the Cancun beach. In one helicopter, weeping was heard from the college students who had been kidnapped, threatened at gunpoint, and lost their friend.

In the other, there was silence among the SEALs. The mission would later be praised as a success. None of the men in the SEAL unit, however, would ever fully consider it a win, given that a hostage was murdered.

Grant stared across at Lieutenant Mike Leonard, whose eyes were closed, with his head tipped back. Grant thought about their conversation hours earlier. *Help others. Shit happens. Stay strong. Have faith. I'm still working on all of that.*

Chapter 1

Present Day

Pastor Stephen Grant's mind actively reviewed key points of a sermon that he already had delivered during the Saturday night service. It was rare for Grant to preach on the Old Testament, but on this day, he chose Psalm 23 for his text. After all, here was a psalm of trust and a confession of faith.

People struggle with death – both the idea of death and the reality when it arrives. On some level, the mind understands death's inevitability, but that same mind works to fight off or delay death as an unwelcome – indeed, even unnatural – intruder. Unnatural? But since all living things die, how can death feel unnatural? Such musings rank as but a sliver of mankind's ongoing effort to somehow make sense of death, particularly brutal, senseless deaths inflicted via nature, or at the hands of our fellow human beings.

As a Navy SEAL, then a CIA operative, and now a pastor, Stephen Grant saw many different kinds of death, and found himself reflecting upon it more often, and from more perspectives, than the average person sitting in a church pew. In a few minutes on this early Sunday morning at St. Mary's Lutheran Church on the eastern end of Long Island, Grant was supposed to ascend the pulpit in order to help his parishioners make sense of what can seem senseless.

Only Christianity could provide answers or true comfort. In Jesus, God became man, not only experiencing life and death, but through His particular death, taking on the sins of all mankind. And in conquering death via resurrection, He offers eternal life. It is the ultimate truth and hope, and the only answer that, through faith, provides true perspective, comfort and confidence.

This would be one of those days when evil would put faith, hope and confidence to the test.

After a hymn opened the Divine Service, Grant led the congregation in Confession and Absolution. Following the words in the *Lutheran Service Book*, he said, "If we say we have no sin, we deceive ourselves, and the truth is not in us."

Those in attendance replied, "But if we confess our sins, God, who is faithful and just, will forgive our sins and cleanse us from unrighteousness."

Silence followed during a short time for reflection.

Grant said, "Let us then confess our sins to God our Father."

The congregation joined Grant in declaring, "Most merciful God, we confess that we are by nature sinful and unclean. We have sinned against You in thought, word and deed, by what we have done and by what we have left undone."

As this confession was being spoken, a man staggered through the front doors of St. Mary's. One hand, in futility, pushed against a hemorrhaging wound below his stomach. Blood emerged from another hole just below his left shoulder. He looked around wildly, with one eye swollen shut. Indeed, much of his body was swollen, bruised and cut. Blood leaked from his nose and mouth. He stumbled toward the doors leading into the nave.

Unaware of the nearby developments, Grant and his congregants continued, "We have not loved you with our whole heart; we have not loved our neighbors as ourselves."

The man burst through the doors. He built up speed moving up the center aisle. While reaching out in the direction of Grant on the altar, he lost his balance and started to fall.

Grant moved forward, followed by the second man on the altar, Pastor Zack Charmichael.

While a few started to notice the disruption, most of the congregants continued to read the response: "We justly deserve your present and eternal punishment. For the sake of your Son, Jesus Christ, have mercy..."

The voices trailed off, and shifted into shouts and cries of fear and shock.

The man's face struck the end of one of the pews, and he crashed to the floor.

Grant arrived, dropped down next to the man, and looked at the face. Even through the bruising and blood, Grant knew him from years earlier. He leaned down closer, and said, "My God, Freddie, what happened?"

The man worked to focus. He grabbed Grant's chasuble, pulled him closer, and whispered, "Attacks ... today. Not sure where..."

Grant raised his voice. "Freddie, what attacks? What are you talking about?"

Grant could see the energy, the life, draining from the man. Death was close.

Pederson shook his head slowly. He summoned some final strength, and said, "Leonard ... the kid. Help the kid..."

Grant could see that was it.

Dear Lord, please take Freddie into your arms.

Fred Pederson exhaled. His breathing stopped. The eyes went lifeless.

Amidst the crying, shouting and 911 calls in St. Mary's, Stephen Grant kneeled next to the lifeless body of someone he'd considered a brother when both were SEALs.

What happened? What did he mean?

Grant looked around at the friends, members of St. Mary's and guests who were pressing in close. "Please, I need a phone."

Several hands immediately thrust cell phones in his face. He grabbed one and punched in the number for the person he knew best at the FBI.

The call, however, would come too late. Sin, evil and death were about to rain down. It would appear senseless to some, but it actually possessed unmistakable purpose.

Chapter 2

Forty-five minutes earlier...

Where did it go wrong?

While doing deep cover work, it was possible to lose perspective. Living an entirely different life – a lie, but another life nonetheless – for any extended period of time came with consequences.

Losing perspective, however, was not a problem for Fred Pederson. While in his fourth month of deep cover work for the FBI inside the world of Islamic terrorists, Pederson walked a fine, sometimes even blurry, line between earning the trust of terrorists and not undertaking endeavors from which there could be no return. But Pederson, who operated under the name Rob Highsmith, managed to infiltrate a terrorist group on U.S. soil. Or, at least, that's what he was led to believe.

I blew it. Shit.

As Highsmith, Pederson was working to find out who was leading an undetermined number of terror cells in the country. He relayed to his FBI contact that he was getting close.

And then he received the call just past midnight on Sunday morning. It came from one of the men in his cell. Pederson was to proceed immediately to the house the man was renting in Wading River on the eastern North Shore of Long Island.

Before leaving his own small rental house, Pederson woke his FBI contact with a call. He said, "This might be it. They've been talking about meeting our leader soon. And this is how they'd do it. Unannounced and at the last minute for security purposes."

How could I've been so wrong?

When Pederson arrived, he was ambushed immediately upon entering the house.

For six hours, Pederson endured both physical and mental torture. The instruments of physical torture included fists, brass knuckles, knives, clubs and a bat. His tormentors did not yet get to their guns.

The mental torture occurred between physical blows. The terrorists actually had never accepted him. They told him the story of how they learned very early on that he was FBI, and how they misled him the entire time.

Pederson tried to keep his mind focused on not making his errors worse. He remained silent throughout the hours. His mind, however, offered up accusatory questions.

How could you be so inept?

And then came a revelation from these terrorists that made it all unbearable.

Pederson noted that of the six who were in the house when he arrived, he had only seen two of them for the past few hours. One leaned in, and said, "Best of all, Pederson, your failure played a significant part in what will happen today. The blood will be on your hands."

Pederson finally spoke, "What the hell does that mean?"

The two men smiled. The one standing several feet away said, "He finally speaks."

Pederson's training never really could be fully turned off. Throughout the hours of torture, he almost subconsciously had been working to loosen the rope that secured his hands together behind the chair.

The man leaning in close raised the knife in his hand, and drove it into Pederson, just below the left shoulder.

Pederson growled in pain.

The terrorist yanked the knife out, and said, "What do I mean? I mean that jihad will be brought against Christian infidels this very morning. As you FBI-types like to say, they are 'soft targets.'"

Pederson sucked in air through gritted teeth.

The terrorist continued, "Ah, you don't like to hear this. Think about this: Your months with us were wasted. The planning went on, and you had no clue. You people do not have an answer for us. Do you know why? Because we fight for Allah." The man stared into Pederson's eyes. He added, "Yes, and one more thing. I believe you know one of the infidels we have the honor of eliminating today. Richard Leonard. You committed atrocities with his father." He leaned in closer. "See how much we know, Pederson. At least his father was something of a soldier. But his son leads people away from Islam, and deserves nothing less than death."

His hands finally came free. Pederson reached up, and grabbed his torturer's hair. He pulled the man even closer, turning the terrorist's head while doing so. Pederson's mouth found the man's ear, and he bit down hard. Blood streamed forth, as did screams from the terrorist's mouth. The knife dropped to the floor.

With his teeth secured to the ear, Pederson quickly moved his hands down onto the terrorist's throat. The former SEAL summoned his strength, and pushed. The airways were crushed. This terrorist would die in a few minutes due to asphyxiation.

Pederson released the neck, and used his teeth to rip part of the man's ear off. The terrorist's screams were now little more than gurgling sounds. Pederson then shoved the body into the other terrorist who was hurling himself forward while swinging a bat. The severity of the blow

16 Lionhearts

from the bat to the side of Pederson's head was reduced somewhat.

The three bodies crashed to the floor. In the chaos, Pederson's feet finally worked free. But his effort to stand up only made it as far as one knee. The second assailant had picked up the knife, and drove it into Pederson just below the stomach. For good measure, he dragged the blade sideways.

Fred Pederson fell back, with the knife still in his body. He didn't look down at the wound. Instead, he spotted the bat. He grabbed it off the worn wood floor, and swung it wildly at his assailant. The blow landed on the man's temple, and he fell to the floor.

Breathing heavily and feeling dizzy, Pederson finally looked at the wound. He knew the end was very close.

What the hell do I do now?

He pulled the knife out, tossed it aside, and slowly rose to his feet, trying to control the spinning in his head. As Pederson took a few steps forward, the second terrorist stirred.

Pederson declared, "Shit."

He exited the large bedroom that had been used as a torture chamber. With hands on each wall, Pederson moved quickly down a hallway into a living room. He went toward the front door, and saw the keys on a shelf.

Pederson pushed the door open, and gained a small bit of energy after hitting the dry, cold, late-January air. The pickup truck was parked in the driveway. He climbed inside, and struggled to get the key into the ignition.

The terrorist stepped out the front door of the house, and pointed a gun. He fired.

Glass shattered as Pederson slipped down to use the surrounding vehicle as cover, while still trying to focus in order to insert the key.

The terrorist came down the steps and walked slowly toward the truck.

Pederson finally managed to start the vehicle. The terrorist bolted forward, and began firing shots once again.

Pederson slipped the pickup into drive, and dared to raise his head slightly. He hit the accelerator and turned the pickup at his opponent. More bullets flew. The truck slammed into the terrorist. Pederson didn't let up on the accelerator, crushing the gunman under the passenger side front tire and then the rear wheel.

Pederson continued to push down on the accelerator, and turned the truck across the dormant front lawn and bounced onto the street.

What do I do? ... Get to Grant...

Freddie Pederson had not seen Stephen Grant, his fellow Navy SEAL, in years. But when his undercover work brought him to the area, Pederson made a note of where Grant lived and worked.

With his left hand pressed against the wound below his stomach, Pederson made a left onto Sound Avenue, and then a right onto Wading River Road.

Straight shot to his church. Hang on.

The pickup moved along the bumpy, wooded road at better than 60 miles per hour, weaving more with each bend in the road. Pederson fought to stay conscious and to keep the truck on the pavement. He knew he was fighting to just stay alive.

Pederson finally slowed and made a right turn. That was followed by another right, and an acceleration up the driveway leading to St. Mary's Lutheran Church.

Pederson stopped the truck in front of the church steps. He practically fell out of the cab, moved around the vehicle, grabbed the railing and pulled himself up the stairs. He opened the door to the church where his SEAL brother was now a pastor.

Chapter 3

Tina Costello looked at herself in the mirror hanging on the back of her bedroom door. She turned sideways, and ran her hand down the growing "baby bulge," as her husband, Nico, called it. Since learning she was finally pregnant a few months ago, Tina felt a joy previously unknown to her. It also seemed easier to get up for Mass on Sunday mornings. She was still working on her husband. Getting Nico to church this Sunday morning, though, was not going to happen. He had worked late on Saturday night. But she was, nonetheless, pleased that Nico was trying. There was real change in his behavior, and he was going to Mass with her every other week now.

Tina went over to the side of the bed, leaned down, and kissed her husband on the forehead.

Nico barely opened his eyes, and smiled.

Tina said, "I'm heading out to Mass."

"Alright, are you okay? Warm enough?"

"Yes, I'm fine."

"And our son?" He reached out and touched her stomach.

"Good, too."

He smiled, and added, "Say a prayer for me, and I promise I'll get to Mass next week."

Nico returned to sleep, while Tina got in the car and drove to St. Francis of Assisi Catholic Church in East Meadow in Nassau County on Long Island.

As she entered the brick, modern-styled church building, Tina stopped to speak with a friend or an acquaintance here and there, each asking how she felt and how the baby was. She sat next to a friend from high school.

There were nearly 200 people in attendance at the 9:00 AM Mass – all ages, from an unborn baby in a mother's womb to some with gray hair and stiff bodies in their eighties, along with two that were north of ninety. As the priest led the liturgy toward the first reading, a nondescript dark midsize car sped into the parking lot, jumped the curb, and stopped at the front steps of St. Francis.

Four men with dark hair and skin – three having beards – exited the vehicle. Each held an AK47, and inside their coats, donned a vest with C4 explosives and a detonation switch.

They ran to the doors, and moved inside. There was no one to stop them in the narthex.

The four proceeded into the nave. One went to a side aisle, another to the aisle on the opposite side, a third took the center, and the last stayed just inside the doors.

More or less in unison, each shouted "Allahu Akbar," and the shooting began.

Worshippers at St. Francis began screaming and running. Some prayed. A few moved toward the attackers.

The terrorist in the center aisle sprayed the altar, with the two priests, the cantor, and three altar boys falling to the ground.

Tina Costello moved toward one of the side aisles with tears in her eyes. A side door was not far away. But she ran headlong into one of the terrorists. He stopped shooting. With one hand, he grabbed her by the throat, and stared into her eyes.

She pleaded, "Please, no, my baby."

He looked down at her stomach, and then said, "Tell me that you reject the lies of Christianity and embrace Islam, and you may go."

Tina closed her eyes, and started to pray, "Our Father, who art in heaven..."

Fury grew on the terrorist's face. He dropped his gun, reached for the detonation switch on his vest, and pressed down. The terrorist, Tina Costello and her baby were immediately incinerated.

As that explosion was being unleashed, the other three terrorists detonated their vests as well.

Only a handful of people inside St. Francis of Assisi Catholic Church would manage to survive. Stained glass windows were blown out, pews tossed and obliterated, the altar destroyed, and the walls of the building cracked.

Nico Costello would be awoken an hour later by a phone call.

Chapter 4

Working on cattle ranches in Montana for all of his adult life turned out to leave Gus Weeghan with a bent, pain-filled body at the age of 86.

He used to wake before the sun. But that was no longer the case. Gus slept more now in a week than he used to during an entire month in his younger days. He'd say to himself, "Actually, it wasn't that long ago."

And it wasn't. True old age did not creep up slowly on Gus. Rather, it struck suddenly. Within a year-and-a-half, he went from still working a full day at the ranch to being unable to work at all. Gus had labored on two ranches for almost 70 years – the last one for a half century through three different owners.

Now, the only day of the week that he bothered to set an alarm was Sunday – as was the case on this morning. After reaching over to stop the beeping clock, Gus prayed out loud for strength. He slowly made his way to the bathroom. An hour later, after a great deal of effort, he slowly walked around the large mounds of snow that had been plowed for him by friends. Snow had started to fall almost three months earlier. Gus dropped his weary body into his old station wagon with a thud.

The drive from his tiny two-bedroom cape at the edge of the ranch where he had worked to the Methodist Church in Big Timber would take twenty minutes. This was supposed to be one of the last times Gus would make the trek to the church where he was baptized, married, and raised his two daughters. He finally had relented, and agreed to move in with his youngest daughter in Billings. She and her husband both worked at the state university, and their children – Gus's grandkids – had moved out and started their own families. They all lived nearby – in Montana terms.

As he drove, Gus reflected on what he'd miss after moving. He decided not much, except his church. But he also knew the church that his daughter attended. It wasn't home, but it would be good enough for him. He then smiled thinking about attending services with his two great-grandchildren. When seeing them, Gus felt a little jolt of youth.

He parked the car in his usual spot. It was a small congregation, with only thirty or so worshippers on a typical Sunday morning. But it was doubtful if the old, tiny, white clapboard church building could have held many more for a service. The congregation kept the doors open, but the pastor had to work at the local feed store to make ends meet.

Gus entered the third pew on the right. The spot where he had sat for his entire life.

Just a few minutes into the service, three men entered the church. Almost everyone glanced in their direction. The new arrivals did not necessarily stand out. In fact, they looked very much like typical twenty-somethings in the area. They were Caucasian, on the tall side, and seemed to be in pretty good shape.

A few people kept watching as the three separated. One took a seat in the back of the church, and the two others in pews on opposite sides.

They sat quietly as the service proceeded, until the congregation stood to hear the Gospel. All three men got to their feet as well. One of them, seated just a few feet away from Gus Weeghan, shouted, "God is great!" Gus turned his bent body just in time to see the man reach inside his coat.

All three terrorists took the same action at the same time. The explosions merged into one destructive force, killing everyone in the church.

The combination of the explosive force and the age of the church blew out the walls of the building. The entire structure crumbled to the earth, with the steeple and bell seeming to float on the air for the briefest of moments, before crashing down on top of the rubble, ash, fire, and what was left of the bodies of 28 worshippers, the pastor, and three terrorists. Even small-town America would not be safe on this day.

Gus Weeghan was freed from all of the pains suffered in this life.

Later, his daughters, sons-in-law, grandchildren and great-grandchildren would weep bitterly.

Chapter 5

To say that the life of Bobby and Annie Barnes was busy would be an understatement. Just a day earlier at the Barnes Family Shooting Range, Saturday morning began with Annie's completing the filming of a gun safety and shooting instructional video. Next came Bobby overseeing two high school teams during a clay target shooting contest. And later in the day, Annie continued a multi-Saturday defensive shooting course.

Busy was the way it had been since the two met and started dating in high school. They both were active in sports at Brenham High School, and that continued when they attended Texas Christian University together, just over three hours away from where they grew up. Annie spent four years on the university's rifle team, just missing the Olympics, while Bobby played baseball.

After graduating, the couple got married and started a family back in Brenham. With the help of their families, the two worked to get the business – their shooting range – off the ground. Nearly six years since graduating from TCU, they had two kids, and seven employees.

Bobby and Annie also were active in the Baptist Church where Annie grew up.

The congregation had grown, and moved into a new, much larger building nearly two years ago. It was then that Annie and Bobby approached their pastor about providing security for Sunday morning worship. Given the changes going on in the world and after some convincing, the pastor eventually agreed. Annie and Bobby volunteered to lead the effort, and wound up assembling a six-person team. Two people would be on duty each Sunday. Bobby and Annie were up on this morning. Each had a holstered handgun, club, two-way radio, and cell phone. They were dressed rather nondescript in white polo shirts with the church's name on a breast pocket, black pants, and black sneakers.

*   *   *

While growing up in Oregon, the lives of Lance and Rowan Fryer lacked any structure or guidance. Their mother left when they were in early grade school, and their father subsequently struggled to keep a job, and he drank heavily.

It was success in wrestling that pushed Lance forward in high school. Rowan, a year younger than his brother, attempted to follow in Lance's footsteps, but came up short. Each boy was lazy and uninterested in the classroom. So, when high school ended, and no college scholarships followed, both Lance and Rowan again were adrift. For Lance, whose expectations had been tied to his wrestling skills, disappointment, disenchantment and anger grew. His need to make a mark in life found a purpose in radical Islam. Naturally, Rowan followed, and his accomplishments in terms of training earned much-treasured praise from Lance.

In the backseat of an SUV, as adrenaline flowed, the two brothers smiled and nodded at each other. Lance slapped his brother on the shoulder.

*   *   *

The worship service had been under way for 15 minutes. Annie and Bobby stood in the building's large lobby, natural light streaming through the three-story glass across the front of the building. They had positioned themselves just outside the doors to the auditorium in order to hear the hymns and preaching inside.

Annie was the first to see an old gray SUV pull up outside. Four doors opened, and each man got out holding an AK47.

Annie whispered, "Sweet Jesus."

Bobby looked around, and said, "Annie." He pointed to cover. She moved behind a large stone pot housing a replica birch tree, and he went behind a welcome desk.

The four men entered the building, and Bobby immediately shouted, "Stop! What are you...?"

The AK47s turned in his direction, and the shooting started. It would end in less than 45 seconds.

Annie did not falter on this Sunday morning. While Bobby's shots were off the mark, Annie epitomized efficiency. She only pulled the trigger five times.

The first was a headshot.

The second shot hit a terrorist's chest.

As the other two intruders turned in her direction, their movement only gave her clearer targets.

Another headshot took down Lance Fryer.

Rowan watched his brother drop to the floor. He then stopped firing and reached inside his jacket. The first shot from Annie hit his stomach, and the second went through the neck.

That was it.

Bobby moved forward, and immediately saw the suicide vests.

The couple quickly directed those still in the building to get out via emergency exits, and called 911.

They saved the lives of 300-plus souls. When the building was clear, Annie and Bobby fell into an embrace.

Chapter 6

Kevin Morris came to know the darker aspects of Charleston, West Virginia, for most of his 44 years. Drugs, alcohol, burglary, auto theft, and robbery meant that he had bounced between rehab centers, jail, halfway houses, and seedy apartments. His body had grown weak before its time, along with graying hair and a pale complexion in which life had etched deep lines.

It was two years ago that the pastor of Community Christian Church walked up to him on the street, and offered to buy lunch.

The two men ate and talked. The pastor patiently listened to Morris talking about all of his tough breaks, and blaming others for his lifetime of woes. In fact, the pastor said nothing while Morris spoke for nearly a half hour.

When the one-sided conversation stopped, Morris stared across the small table with a challenging, tired look on his face.

The pastor, a powerful African-American man with a shaved head, met the look with piercing eyes. He wiped his mouth with a napkin, and then proceeded to tell Morris the story of how Saul, a persecutor of the church, became Saul, the believer, and eventually the Apostle Paul.

Morris said nothing in response.

As he sipped his coffee, the pastor then went on to tell how Jesus responded to the scribes and Pharisees who sought to stone a woman who committed adultery, while also trying to test the Lord. He relayed, "Jesus said, 'Let him who is without sin among you be the first to throw a stone at her.'"

Morris finally asked, "What happened?"

"They just left."

"That's it?"

"And Jesus told the woman, 'Neither do I condemn you; go, and from now on sin no more.'" The pastor continued, "Thanks for joining me for lunch, Kevin." He left money on the table for a tip, took the check, and gave Morris his business card. "I hope you'll come to Community Christian. We can talk some more, try to answer any questions you might have."

The pastor shook Kevin's hand, paid the cashier, and left.

The Community Christian Church looked out at the Kanawha River, and sat not far from the Capitol Building in Charleston.

Kevin was now telling the story to a small group during coffee hour between services. He said, "That lunch kept popping into my head over the next few weeks. I eventually showed up here on a Sunday morning. At first, it felt odd. I didn't come back for another couple of weeks. But then I returned, and I haven't left since."

There were smiles on the faces of each person to whom he spoke.

Morris continued, "It ain't been easy. But I found steady, legit work, and I help out around here almost all of the time. Jesus literally saved me, and this is His place."

Responses included, "Praise God" and "Thank the Lord."

A few minutes later, everyone was in the nave for the service.

With hymns being sung, hands were held high in the air and bodies swayed.

No one noticed when four men – two white, two black – entered. It was the sounds of gunshots and bullets penetrating flesh that led to hands being lowered and bodies falling to the floor.

With the pastor and most of the 122 worshippers dead, bleeding or hiding amongst the pews, shouts came of "Allahu Akbar." Then the C4 vests erupted, and extinguished what earthly life remained in the building.

Kevin Morris had been one of the first to die. His eyes had been closed, hands in the air, and a smile of contentment on his face when a bullet ripped into his skull and through much of his brain.

Having survived on the hard streets for decades, death came after Morris had found his way to Community Christian Church. But life had been found there as well.

Chapter 7

Like most cities, certain areas of Chicago were safe and thrived. Many people reflexively called that "the nice part of town."

As for the not-so-nice parts, crime, including homicides, flourished.

On this particular Sunday, though, it was expected that the number of violent criminal incidents would drop notably. Not because of stepped-up police protection, but because even hardened criminals tended to stay home in the bitter cold. However, expectations often are not met, sometimes in horrifying ways.

Some said people were victims of "gun violence." Jean Robinson shook her head at such ridiculousness. She would have none of it. Where she lived in Chicago, the sources of the problems were clear to anyone who wanted to look or listen. Jean spoke about broken families, absent fathers, a city government that failed to keep streets safe, ineffective public schools, and a lack of faith.

Jean's husband had been shot on his way home from work – from a second job – late at night. Their sons were only five and seven at the time. Jean mourned the loss to this very day fourteen years later, but she kept that sadness to herself the entire time. She took on a second job in order to keep the two boys in the local Catholic elementary school. They then went on to attend a Catholic high school. Their attendance at these schools was, in part, due to a private school voucher program. Her sons now attended the University of Notre Dame, each on full scholarship, one a senior and the other a sophomore. Homicide rates in the neighborhood had moved up in recent years. While Jean was able to drop the second job, it wasn't like she had much free time. She volunteered with the school voucher effort, and often spoke about the difference that having a choice made in her family's life, how being able to send her boys to Catholic schools meant a safer environment, greater discipline, higher academic expectations, and reinforcing their Catholic faith.

On this Sunday morning, after each Mass at St. Anthony's on the South Side of Chicago, she was asked to talk briefly to parishioners about the importance of the private voucher program, and how parents could apply for their own children and how anyone could financially support the school choice effort.

Before leaving her apartment, she spoke via Skype with both of her sons. She confessed to being nervous about speaking in church. She had never done so before. They both encouraged her, and said that they would pray for her. Jean instilled in her sons the importance of prayer. Even now, when her boys came home, the family would pray the rosary together.

One son added, "You'll do fine, as always." The other said, "No problem." Each declared, "I love you." After the Skype call ended, Jean Robinson smiled at the men that her boys had become.

The priest that morning worked the importance of Catholic education into his homily. During the second Mass of the morning, he mentioned that immediately afterward, Jean Robinson would speak about a voucher program supporting families seeking to send their children to Catholic schools in the city.

It was then that gunshots were heard from the narthex. Four ushers who had moved toward four dark-haired intruders were now lying in gathering pools of blood.

As the four terrorists pushed through the doors to the nave, they were met by shouts and several men hurling themselves forward in an effort to repel the invasion.

The AK47s were knocked from the terrorists' hands. And two of the intruders had their arms pinned.

While most of the others in the church fled away from the conflict, both the priest and Jean Robinson moved toward the trouble. This was Jean Robinson.

Unfortunately, even with bodies on top of each, two of the terrorists managed to pull a hand free. The men reached inside their jackets, and hit the detonation switches.

The initial two explosions set off the two other vests as well. Destruction spread in all directions. The church's doors and windows facing the street blew outward. Stained glass on each side of the building did the same. The explosion that pushed into the nave incinerated flesh and shattered bone of forty people, including Jean Robinson.

Chapter 8

The blue SUV traveled over the Outerbridge Crossing from New Jersey into Staten Island, going through the EZ Pass lane. The driver worked to draw no attention, moving at just a hair below the speed limit.

The five men inside the vehicle claimed various backgrounds, but now held a unified view that they were called to wage holy war, that is, jihad, against the Great Satan, against Jews, and against the Christian crusaders.

Two were sons of immigrants from, respectively, Pakistan and Iraq. Another had grown up in the affluence – especially by global standards – of American suburbia, and was radicalized thanks to a community college professor who taught how evil the United States was, and to assorted places on the Internet that presented Islam as the answer.

The last two – the man driving and the terrorist cell leader in the front passenger seat – originally came from Afghanistan, but had extensive global travels, engaging in jihad in the Middle East and laying foundations in Europe.

The leader broke a long silence. "Allah has blessed us beyond imagination, brothers. Of all the attacks this morning against the crusaders, we have been assigned the most important. Not far from where the Towers fell, we shall literally cut the head off this Christian perverter who has sinned against the prophet and Allah. We will wipe out his den of vipers, and let the world know that this war shall be won."

This generated smiles from the three in the backseat.

"Be strong! We have been too quiet for too long. We bring America and its crusaders to their knees. And this is a first step in a new direction. I have been assured that the jihad will continue, my friends, against individual leaders of this place overflowing with infidels. We are leading this new battle. We – each of us here, right now – are leading the first salvo this morning. And we will be remembered and, of course, rewarded."

The smiles were transformed into cheers, and shouts of "Allah be praised!"

The SUV pulled up at one of the side doors of the church.

They exited the vehicle with semiautomatic guns and C4 strapped to vests inside their coats. The cell leader also had an Afghan khanjar dagger in its sheath hanging from his belt.

The five moved into the building, past the gym on the right, and then up a small set of stairs leading to a door entering the nave to the side of the altar. Their orders were to kill everyone, but making sure that the pastor was made an example. He would not be far from that door.

*   *   *

Pastor Richard Leonard had been at St. Mark's Lutheran Church on Staten Island since August. He received a call from the church as their pastor and an offer to head up the history department at the Lutheran University of New York, whose compact campus sat right across from the church.

St. Mark's congregation was an interesting mix of New York City police families – after all, this was Staten Island

– university students and staff, and others living in the area.

Leonard's views created some tension with professors outside, and inside, the history and theology departments at the university. He possessed the temerity to defend traditional Christianity; presented scholarship on the Reformation, the Church, Islam and the Crusades; and served as a notable voice on correcting many mistaken assumptions about Church history, as well as the current conflict with radical Islam. Plus, there was his relative youth in terms of becoming a pastor and earning a doctorate in history before reaching thirty.

However, his views – and an ability to present them in a reasonable manner – appealed to his congregation members, while also bringing in a few new congregants. Indeed, Leonard quickly fit in at St. Mark's.

A Bible study and Sunday school were sandwiched between an early service and a late one at St. Mark's on Sunday morning. The late service was about two-thirds full.

After quickly getting to know Pastor Leonard, Frank Godfrey and Mac Baldwin, NYPD detectives, took it upon themselves to serve as non-appointed, volunteer security at least during late Divine Service at St. Mark's. All that meant was that Godfrey sat with his family in a pew near the front-side entrance into the nave, and Baldwin and his family were seated near the back, primary entrance. One night over a few beers at a local bar, the two detectives decided that they liked Leonard for his forthrightness, but that many might not like him for the same reason. They didn't expect anything to happen, but why not be prepared?

Nearly through a hymn, Leonard moved into the pulpit to deliver the sermon. The pulpit in the 80-plus-year-old church was made of stone, with a winged lion, symbolizing St. Mark the Evangelist, carved in front.

Godfrey sat at the far end of the second row of pews. No one sat in the first row. The door in front of the detective was pulled open, and the first man holding a rifle came through it. It took a second for Godfrey to glance up from the hymnal.

Two more men followed. The second was the cell leader with the sheathed dagger.

Godfrey reached inside his jacket and started to pull out his service weapon. While doing so, he yelled, "Down, down!" He shoved his two sons and wife to the floor.

The intruders began to shout, and it was Godfrey who fired first. He pulled the trigger three times. The third shot finally took down the first terrorist.

Three terrorists began firing into the congregation. People screamed. They ran. Some fell to the floor trying to hide, others because they had been shot.

The last assailant through the door tried to focus his shooting on Godfrey. But the detective had dropped behind the pew for cover. He moved a few feet, popped back up, and put a slug in the terrorist's chest. As the man fell back, Godfrey saw what was inside his coat. Godfrey whispered, "Dear God," and looked at his family on the floor. His wife had spread her body across their children.

At the back of the church, Mac Baldwin had pushed his wife and daughter out the back doors, and was now advancing up the center aisle, moving against the flow of people trying to flee. He looked in the faces of three people coming at him. He knew each of them. They were friends. The woman helped run the church's food pantry. The middle-aged couple had come to his house several times. Their faces of fear suddenly distorted into horror and pain, as bullets were sprayed into their backs. They tumbled at his feet.

Baldwin steadied his gun as best he could at the two terrorists standing next to each other in the aisle. Baldwin squeezed off shot after shot.

One of the murderers fell.

Another shot found the shoulder of the other terrorist. The man dropped the AK47.

Baldwin continued to fire, but his shots went awry. While staring at Baldwin, the terrorist unzipped his coat and smiled.

Baldwin saw the vest, held his breath for a fraction of a second, and as he started to release the air, fired off two more shots. The headshots transformed the terrorist's face into a mess of blood, skin and skull. Death descended on the man before he could detonate the vest.

While Baldwin took on the two assailants and Godfrey was looking at his family, the cell leader had bounded onto the altar, coming straight at Leonard.

Richard Leonard was anything but a physical pushover. He was tall – just about six feet three inches – and strong, with blond hair on the long side touching the back of his collar, matched by a rather robust beard and mustache.

Leonard moved toward the man coming at him with gun in hand. But the pastor lacked experience. Leonard tried to tackle him, but the assailant swung the butt of his rifle, which landed on Leonard's left cheek. The force of the blow sent Leonard tumbling to the floor.

The cell leader discarded the rifle, and pulled out the dagger.

He reached down and grabbed Leonard's hair, and pulled the pastor up to his knees. Leonard's eyes swam in the aftermath of the blow.

The terrorist raised the dagger in the air, and yelled out, "Death to the crusaders!"

He then moved the khanjar down toward Leonard's neck. But the pastor regained some control, and plunged an elbow into his opponent's groin.

The terrorist cell leader cursed in pain and anger. As Leonard struggled, trying to push himself up from the floor, the assailant raised the dagger again into the air. He paused to declare, "Allahu Akbar."

But by then, Godfrey was moving to the bottom of the steps leading to the altar. The NYPD detective fired off three rounds into the terrorist, who dropped the khanjar as his body fell away.

Godfrey quickly pushed forward. The terrorist was still alive even with gunshot wounds in his right shoulder, stomach and right calf. Godfrey pinned the man's arms down, making sure that nothing was detonated, and glanced in Leonard's direction. He said, "We could use a prayer, Pastor, that this vest doesn't go off – and for that matter, any of the other vests on these shits."

Chapter 9

In this digital, wireless age of instantaneous communication, the news of the sweeping nature of the terrorist attacks quickly spread. Before noon eastern time, reports online and via television flowed forth regarding what happened in Big Timber, Montana; Chicago, Illinois; Brenham, Texas; Charleston, West Virginia; and in New York, both in East Meadow, and on Staten Island.

Even as the facts became glaringly obvious, various media talking heads appeared to struggle against those facts, seemingly working hard to deny that the attacks were coordinated and questioning if this was Islamic terrorism.

At the same time, the intent and purpose of the attacks were clear to those with common sense, including local law enforcement, the FBI, CIA, and U.S. military officials. Local police mobilized in towns and cities of all sizes across the nation to patrol and guard, as best they could, the churches in their communities. Making matters more of a challenge from a security standpoint was the fact that a not-insignificant number of people reacted to the news by journeying to local churches to pray and stand in defiance.

St. Mary's Lutheran Church was no different.

Freddie Pederson's arrival and death had not yet gained media attention. After Grant's call to FBI Supervisory Special Agent Rich Noack, the Bureau descended on the church – as they did in the case of each church that was attacked. With the help of the local police, the FBI kept quiet the details of Pederson's death. However, soon after news spread about what occurred elsewhere, parishioners at St. Mary's saw that this wasn't mere coincidence, and the media soon would recognize that as well.

After statements were taken and while evidence was still being collected, attempts to send congregants home turned out to be futile, with more church members actually arriving. The FBI and police looked to Pastors Grant and Charmichael for some kind of solution.

This was familiar ground for Stephen Grant. To say that he was a unique second-career pastor would be the grossest of understatements. Prior to becoming the pastor at St. Mary's and before his time at seminary, Stephen Grant had put a unique set of skills to work for the Central Intelligence Agency, and that was after his time spent as a Navy SEAL. To this very day, Grant seemed to cut the image more of a CIA operative – handsome, black hair, green eyes, and a six-foot athletic frame – than a Lutheran pastor.

As for Zack Charmichael, the church's younger pastor seemed overwhelmed at the combination of Pederson staggering into and dying in St. Mary's; law enforcement's deflection of interest as to who the man was; and the news of the terror attacks. Feeling overwhelmed certainly was understandable.

Newly married and moving past 30 years of age, the thin, five-foot-seven-inch Zack had recently made some changes in appearance that Grant suspected were undertaken to achieve a more mature appearance. Zack's thick brown hair, previously a purposeful mess, was now cut neat, and he'd added a well-groomed beard and mustache. Dark, rectangular glasses were replaced by wire-rimmed, oval spectacles. He actually did look a bit older as a result, reflected Grant.

But while Grant spoke naturally and calmly with the FBI and Suffolk County police on the scene, Charmichael remained quiet. His eyes were saucer-like. He gave off a vibe of nervousness, or at the very least, of being highly uncomfortable. Charmichael seemed captivated, though, by watching Grant exchange information with law enforcement.

After taking a deep breath, Zack finally stepped forward in response to the request by law enforcement. He said to Stephen, "Why don't I gather our people outside for prayers?"

Grant replied, "It's cold out there."

"They're out there anyway, just milling about. We can join together now and pray for a few minutes in the cold, and how about I announce that we'll have a service tomorrow night?"

"Good thoughts. Thanks."

Zack left the nave, headed to his office to grab a coat, and went outside.

The lead FBI special agent on the scene said, "Pastor Grant, thanks for all of the information. We'll hopefully finish up here soon."

"Whatever you need to do is fine."

"The Suffolk police will be leaving a car or two around, of course."

This day reminded Grant of another. It had not been long after he graduated from seminary and was ordained as a pastor at St. Mary's. The Twin Towers fell only 70 miles away. That September 11th and for several weeks afterward, Grant seriously questioned his choice of leaving the CIA to become a pastor.

On this day, with the murder of Freddie and terrorist attacks on churches across the nation, Grant wasn't wrestling with his decision to become a pastor. But he was pulling himself in different directions as to the simple, immediate question: *What next?*

On one level, the question was about whether or not there would be more attacks. On another level, it was about his own actions. Stephen wanted to stay with the law enforcement personnel in the nave because this was St. Mary's – it was his church. And he desired to be here the rest of the day for anyone else who might just show up seeking solace, comfort, or even some courage.

He exited the nave, turned right, and headed toward his office.

What Freddie Pederson said before he died in Stephen's arms – "Leonard ... the kid. Help the kid..." – was pulling him in another direction. Freddie was referring to Richard Leonard – the pastor at St. Mark's Lutheran Church in Staten Island, which was one of the terrorist targets.

Grant and Freddie Pederson had served with Richard's father, Mike Leonard, in the SEALs. At that time, Richard was in kindergarten and early grade school. Later, when Mike Leonard died in Afghanistan, Richard had just entered college, with a plan of eventually becoming a pastor. After Stephen heard about Mike's death, he reached out to Richard. Given that Grant both served with his father and was a pastor, he became a periodic sounding board and mentor for Richard, at least during his years in college, and then a friend during Richard's time at seminary and subsequently. Over the last few years, given how life works, they really only caught up at pastoral gatherings and conferences, along with the occasional telephone call and Facebook exchanges.

I need to get to St. Mark's and see how Richard is doing, if he knew anything about what Freddie said, and why his church was targeted. Although I've got a pretty good idea on the "why."

Finally, there was a natural, personal desire tugging at Stephen. Specifically, the longing to simply hug his wife, Jennifer, and for them to go home together.

Grant entered his office. Jennifer was sitting with Zack's wife, Cara Charmichael. They were watching the news on television.

Grant's office was basically split in two. In one section, there was a couch, armchair, television on a stand, and a rather large rectangular, oak coffee table. That was not, however, a typical coffee table. With a lock hidden from the casual eye, it also served as a gun cabinet. Stephen kept a 10 mm Glock 20, a Taurus PT-25, and a Harris M-89 sniper rifle inside it. That not only was convenient for trips to the gun range at a local sportsmen's club, but it also was peace-of-mind security. Indeed, it had served more than peace-of-mind once before, and Stephen was reminded of that fact again today.

The other half of the office centered around Stephen's desk. Two walls featured floor-to-ceiling bookcases; behind his desk was a bay window bordered by two more bookcases, and against the other wall and next to the door was a large antique wardrobe, which housed his pastoral garb.

Jennifer looked in Stephen's direction, got up, and walked toward him.

The desire to take her to the safety and warmth of their home tugged harder at Stephen.

She said, "Dear God, Stephen, the news just keeps getting worse."

Jennifer Grant was an accomplished, attractive woman. While Stephen was over forty-five, Jennifer was eight years younger. She was thin, and a bright smile accented her fair skin, sharp facial features but for a slightly upturned nose, and short, dark auburn hair.

During conversations, her intelligence shined through, backed up by a Ph.D. in economics, her partnership in a highly successful consulting and research firm, and the fact that she was in demand as a speaker, advisor to business and political leaders, and a frequent witness before Congress.

They put their arms around each other, and squeezed a bit tighter than usual. They then moved over to Cara and the reports emanating from the television.

Stephen asked, "How are you holding up, Cara?"

She smiled sadly, and said, "I'm fine."

Cara was a nurse, and somewhat used to seeing ugly things. But as she brushed aside her long, strawberry blond hair, Stephen could see she was shaken.

Dear Lord, we're all shaken.

He added, "Zack should be back in shortly."

Cara nodded in response.

The three turned to the television reporting. Grant's anger grew watching and hearing about the deaths at Richard's church on Staten Island; the devastation in Chicago, Charleston, and East Meadow; and finally, the complete leveling of the church in Big Timber, Wyoming. *My God, was that the entire congregation?*

In response to an update on what happened in Brenham, Texas, Stephen said to no one in particular, "Thank God." He glanced down at the coffee table doubling as a gun cabinet.

Stephen turned away from the screen and walked over to his desk. He sat in the chair, rubbed his eyes, and tried to clear his thoughts.

Jennifer came over, and leaned on the desk. "I assume you're going in to St. Mark's to see how Richard is."

He looked up, and nodded. "I'll call first. But whatever he says, I have to see firsthand how he's doing. Mike was there for me. I should be there for Richard. But what about you, Zack, St. Mary's…?"

"You should go." She continued, "I spoke to Maggie, and I'm going to head over to their house until you get back."

In addition to being Cara's parents, Maggie and Tom Stone were among the Grants' friends. Tom was the rector at St. Bartholomew's Anglican Church. In fact, Tom and Father Ron McDermott, the priest at St. Luke's Catholic Church and School, ranked as Stephen's closest friends.

Stephen said, "That's good. How are they doing?"

"Okay, but Maggie said that Tom spoke briefly to Ron."

"And?"

"He was pretty close to one of the priests who lost his life at St. Francis in East Meadow."

Stephen shook his head. "Madness."

Jennifer replied, "That it is."

"I'm going outside with Zack to see who is still here. After everyone leaves, including the FBI, I'll drive in to see Richard."

Grant still wasn't fully comfortable with this plan, but then an individual moved into the doorway of his office.

Sean McEnany arguably had an even more interesting background than Stephen. He had been an Army Ranger, and he still had the very short blond hair and muscular five-foot-ten-inch frame from those days nearly a decade past. But there was more. McEnany had come to serve as a direct, day-to-day link for Stephen between his current life as a pastor and his past with the CIA. After leaving the Army Rangers, McEnany put his formidable and varied skills to work at CorpSecQuest, a private security firm. That entity was part legitimate business, and part CIA front. Later, it was a CIA veteran who suggested that McEnany go into business with two former Agency personnel who had worked very closely with Grant during his time at the CIA. For good measure, that CIA veteran put forth the idea that McEnany, after moving to Long Island, might want to attend St. Mary's. Grant knew much, but far from all, of this story, and he had moved past some early resentment at feeling like he was being manipulated. In fact, Grant had come to appreciate Sean on multiple levels, including as a friend.

Sean said, "Stephen, what do you need?"

"Sean, I'm so glad to see you."

Chapter 10

The White House Situation Room actually isn't one room. Rather, assorted rooms take up 5,000 square feet on the ground floor of the West Wing. The mayhem dominating the complex for the previous few hours was suddenly calmed when President Elizabeth Sanderski entered the main conference room.

The president was accompanied by her chief of staff, Andrew Russell. The six people waiting at the table stood as she entered.

Sanderski said, "Please, sit down."

Around the table were the Department of Homeland Security secretary, the director of the CIA, the chairman of the Joint Chiefs of Staff, the FBI director, the national security advisor, and Vice President Adam Links.

Russell looked at the various staff members who lingered, either seated or standing by the chairs against the walls. He ordered, "Give us the room."

Everyone exited but for the eight now with seats at the table.

Sanderski said, "Okay, I'm going on television within the hour, and we need to get this right. What do we know?"

The president, along with Russell seated to her left and Vice President Links to her right, listened as assorted facts about the terrorists, along with some speculation, flew around the room.

"Six Christian churches were targeted in five states."

"There seemed to be a total of 24 terrorists, but we can't be sure. There could have been more."

"No one picked up on anything indicating that this was coming."

"We're not sure about the number killed yet, of course, but it seems like we've lost at least 350. That number will likely rise."

"We've got a report of at least one terrorist alive."

"The armed guards at the Texas church took down the terrorists before they could execute their plans. Thank God, at least, for that much."

"No one has claimed responsibility, yet, and we're not picking up any chatter providing indications. All we hear is celebration among Islamic radicals around the globe, and among some who we might not have considered all that radical before."

"Well, now hold on, are we even sure that these were attacks by those twisting Islam?"

After more bits of information were offered from around the table, Vice President Links turned to Sanderski, and said, "Madam President, this was a well-coordinated, well-executed plan carried out against soft targets. Everything we fear. I also have no doubt that whoever organized this is not among the dead terrorists."

Links had graduated West Point at the top of his class. He earned the Bronze Star while serving in the first Gulf War, and then spent a number of years at the CIA. Later, he came out of nowhere to run for a U.S. Senate seat from Louisiana. Given his hawkishness on national security and foreign policy, coupled with being a pro-life Catholic, most wondered what he was doing running as a Democrat. But Links was a kind of old-time political Catholic. He was strong on national defense and socially conservative, but rarely found a government program he didn't favor, and was partial to some populist, class-warfare dabbling on the economy. On foreign affairs and certain social issues, he arguably was the last among a dying breed of Democrats. In fact, coming out of the CIA, Links probably could have run as a Democrat or Republican. But since a Republican held the Senate seat, Links became a Democrat. The incumbent didn't seem too concerned about the race, and was probably as surprised as everyone else when Links won.

When Vice President Links spoke on national security, people on both sides of the political aisle usually listened. That is, except for one very important person – President Elizabeth Sanderski.

The Sanderski-Links ticket was one of those politics-makes-for-strange-bedfellows moments. As a two-term governor of Delaware, Sanderski was adored by the Left. But after winning the Democratic Party's nomination, she needed something to soften her radicalism. Advisors suggested Links as a running mate. Sanderski reluctantly agreed. Links saw it as an opportunity to serve the nation. The Sanderski-Links team won the general election, but there was little subsequent teamwork while governing. Sanderski ignored Links on foreign affairs, appointing a secretary of state and a national security advisor, for example, who were both very dovish, like the president herself. Links expressed his frustration during the few private moments he had with Sanderski, and she merely would confirm that she had heard him.

With the primary season already under way, Links agreed to stay on the ticket with Sanderski. His entire adult life – from West Point and six years in the Army to some seven years at the CIA and then nearly two terms in the Senate and now vice president – was dedicated to the security of the United States. Some thought it became his sole obsession after his young wife, Linda, died just over a year into their marriage. Links left the military once she was diagnosed with pancreatic cancer. He threw himself into the CIA after she passed away.

Sanderski replied to Links, "Thank you, Adam. Who has other thoughts?"

The Secretary of State declared, "Well, like I said before, I don't think we have enough yet to say that this was terrorism carried out by some kind of extreme radicals misappropriating Islam."

The head of the Joint Chiefs sighed, and replied, "What planet do you live on, Mr. Secretary?"

The president broke in, and said, "That was not called for, General."

The General paused to apparently collect himself, and then said, "Yes, of course, Madam President. My apologies."

The CIA and FBI directors both reported that their respective entities were working hard to figure out who these people were, and who might be behind the attacks.

The General added, "The Armed Forces stand ready to carry out your orders, when appropriate, Madam President."

Sanderski did not respond to that particular comment. She finished the meeting by saying, "Keep me up to date."

The president left the room with Russell at her side.

Vice President Links watched her leave, and turned to the rest in the room. His eyes moved between the leaders of the CIA, Joint Chiefs and FBI. "Let's get to the bottom of this, gentlemen. The American people deserve to know who did this. And they need justice."

Thirty minutes later, President Elizabeth Sanderski sat at the Resolute desk in the Oval Office looking into the eye of the camera. Short black and gray hair sat atop a long face with large brown eyes, a narrow, pointed nose, thin lips, and skin that sagged much more than when she took office three years earlier. She wore a gray blouse beneath a black suit jacket.

Sanderski shifted in her seat, and her eyes nervously moved up and down from the desk.

The teleprompter was ready, and the camera light came on. Reading a speech was never her strong point. Sanderski went on to talk about deadly attacks on the American people. She expressed sympathy for the victims, their families and friends, and promised that these "criminal acts" would not go unanswered. The president concluded by saying, "Americans have the right to worship as they see fit. That fundamental right was violated to the extreme today. In the coming days, as we gain more information and identify the perpetrators, we must keep in mind that all Americans deserve respect, and no one should react by lashing out in blind, baseless hatred. Remain calm. Help each other. And allow law enforcement to do their jobs. Stay strong, come together, and may God bless America."

Even amidst such an enormous tragedy, few were kind to her remarks, with most agreeing that it lacked passion, courage and conviction. Many also pointed out that it failed to explicitly note that all of the targets were Christian churches, and failed to declare these to be acts of terrorism, never mind acts of Islamic terrorism. Assorted critics also accused the president of being more concerned about the possibility of Americans lashing out in blind revenge against Muslims, rather than focusing on those who attacked and murdered innocent Americans.

Chapter 11

Within a half hour of President Sanderski's televised comments, a video was posted on various Islamic terrorist-linked websites. The voice of the man in a dark hood, standing in front of a black background, carried no trace of a foreign accent. It was unmistakably American, as well as exuding a confident calm. He said:

We are Jihad in America, and we are responsible for the justified and holy attacks on the American crusaders who are hostile to Allah and Muhammad, his prophet.

We are your neighbors. Most of us were born in this country, and we experience America's decadence. Jihad in America also recognizes that all parts of America – from its government and politicians to its military to its law enforcement to the people – rank as enemies of Allah. You have rejected Allah, so now, you will live in fear of his wrath. Jihad in America is carrying out his will against infidels, just as the prophet did. As declared in the Quran: "And you did not kill them, but it was Allah who killed them."

Make no mistake, jihad is a holy war that must be carried out without mercy on the enemies of Allah, for you truly are, as written, "the worst of creatures." And our tactics will not be limited. You will not rest easy, America, until the nation has surrendered to Islam, until the law of Allah replaces your Constitution and your other man-made laws.

As for your leaders, who are they? Your president? She is weak. Everyone just saw that, given her pathetic response to the opening of our jihad. She will soon pay for that weakness.

We know the history of American imperialism, and many will say that others have mistakenly thought that America was weak and would not fight. But things change. In the past, with evil in your hearts, you still had the courage to fight. That is no longer the case. While the evil has spread, America has lost the will to fight. And even if you fight, it will not matter, for it is written, "O Prophet, urge the believers to battle. If there are among you twenty steadfast, they will overcome two hundred. And if there are among you one hundred steadfast, they will overcome a thousand of those who have disbelieved because they are a people who do not understand." We will make this clear to the world.

Today's attacks were just the beginning. Through your imperialistic ways, and your embrace of Christians and Jews, you have made clear that you reject Islam. That is unacceptable to Allah. We are bringing jihad to your political leaders, your places of worship, your lying media, including the Jews who run it, your homes, and the Muslims infected by your softness who reject the full, true teachings of Allah and his prophet Muhammad. American leaders and the people of this country are lost.

Your young people crave safe spaces. But each of the targets today were selected for a reason, as will each one in the future. Trust us, there will be no safe spaces.

*   *   *

FBI Supervisory Special Agent Rich Noack turned away from the large screen and toward the ten agents who had gathered. A few were scheduled for work in the J. Edgar Hoover Building in Washington, D.C., on this Sunday, but the others were immediately called in, or came in of their own accord as the news broke on the church attacks. Noack declared, "Okay, people, you heard that. The war continues. It was ramped up this morning, and they're promising more to come. Let's stay in contact with those in the field at the churches. Provide them with whatever they need from our end, and let's pull in all of the information they have. As information comes in, I want it shared with everyone. It's our job to track down who exactly these assholes are, and nail those who are left."

Noack started to head back to his office, and was joined by his partner and friend Trent Nguyen.

Not only were the two men formidable in terms of their accomplishments, but in physical presence as well. Noack stood at a weighty six feet six inches, topped off with a completely bald head. He was a leader whose drive for justice was fueled by a compassion for victims.

Nguyen was thinner and a bit shorter, but still came in at an impressive six feet two inches. He also happened to be one of the most highly decorated agents in the history of the FBI. He thrived in the field, was smart and liked by seemingly everyone. For good measure, he had an intense love of country that nearly rivaled the love for his family. Nguyen's patriotism was largely passed down from his parents. Trent was born in Saigon to an American nurse and a South Vietnamese businessman. His parents regularly reminded him what so many Americans, particularly those in the military, were willing to do and sacrifice for the South Vietnamese people.

Nguyen asked, "Do you think President Sanderski will finally recognize that we're at war, and be willing to truly fight it?"

Noack sighed, and shook his head ever so slightly. "Beats the crap out of me. On the one hand, I sometimes cannot believe that this ... yes ... war has been going on since 9-11. And then I see what happened this morning and listen to what various nutcases say, like the one we just heard, and I think this war will be waged long after I'm dead and buried." He paused, and then added, "But until I hear anything different, we're going to fight this to the best of our abilities."

Chapter 12

Driving from the eastern end of Long Island to Staten Island always involved uncertainty, especially upon entering the Belt Parkway, notorious for its traffic jams. With two of the attacks occurring in the metropolitan area that morning, Stephen Grant was even more unsure as to how long the drive would take from St. Mary's.

He was surprised to see relatively few people on the road – well, at least for New York City. Grant rarely touched the brake pedal in his red Chevy Tahoe on the Belt, or while crossing over the Verrazano Bridge.

Grant exited the Staten Island Expressway, and wound his way to the St. Mark's neighborhood, parking a few blocks away from the church. As he walked up, even though it was several hours now since the attacks, he was not surprised to see the building and surrounding area still cordoned off due to the ongoing investigation. There were several New York City police cars, along with a few unmarked vehicles, which came from both the NYPD and the FBI.

Grant had called Richard Leonard to tell him that he was coming to see how he could help. He left a voice message. Leonard texted back a short response a few minutes later: "Thanks. Much appreciated."

Grant walked by the old brick buildings that populated the small university across the street from the church.

When the founders built the Lutheran University of New York, they also erected St. Mark's. The school buildings, church, president's home and the parsonage all followed a brick gothic architectural style. At the end of the campus, Grant came to the St. Mark's parsonage.

He paused on the sidewalk, and looked back at the church. Grant was a stickler when it came to church architecture, appreciating a wide array of styles, except for the churches built in recent decades that lacked any distinction, sometimes looking like office buildings. Grant not only liked the architecture of St. Mark's, but also that this very much was a neighborhood church, surrounded by homes, the university, small apartment buildings and local stores. He then had a passing thought of appreciation that his own leaders and congregation at St. Mary's had chosen a Tudor-style when their new church was built a few years ago.

Grant turned back to the St. Mark's parsonage.

Big house for a single guy. Grant thought back to how the parsonage at St. Mary's had grown too quiet, while also seeming too big, during a time when he felt a creeping loneliness before he and Jennifer got together.

He took two more steps toward the home, when the front door opened, and out came a middle-aged couple leaning on each other and crying. Grant moved forward quickly, and held out a hand as they came down the numerous steps.

The woman nodded. The man saw Stephen's collar, and whispered, "Thank you, Pastor."

Grant replied, "Of course. I'm so sorry."

The couple moved away. As Grant reached the top of the steps, he looked into the house, and saw it filled with people who were crying, angry or both, and several in shock.

Grant stepped in, and tried to assess the situation. He spotted some of the leaders of the congregation helping others. Richard Leonard was on one knee in front of a young woman. They had their heads bowed in prayer. Grant hesitated. Once Leonard raised his head, Grant stepped forward, and patted Leonard on the shoulder.

Leonard looked up, and said, "Stephen."

Grant was reminded how much Richard looked like his father. In fact, Richard was about the age now that his father, Michael, was when Grant served with him in the SEALs.

Leonard stood up and looked Stephen in the eyes. Grant had never seen him so drained. "Richard, how can I help?"

Leonard nodded. "I haven't been able to talk to the people in the kitchen and dining room yet."

Grant responded, "Of course. We'll talk later."

"Thanks, Stephen."

Grant made his way to the back of the home. As he was about to plunge into rooms flooded with anger, sadness, and despair, he silently prayed. *Lord, please give me wisdom and strength to make clear the comfort and confidence these people can only find in you.*

Chapter 13

When word arrived about the attack and death toll at Community Christian Church in Charleston, West Virginia, Governor Wyatt Hamilton immediately left the presidential campaign trail in Iowa, and took the short flight back from Des Moines. Hamilton knew the church and its pastor well.

While Hamilton's closest advisors debated the best way to respond to the attacks, he spoke to his wife, Vanessa, and their two grown children by phone.

After the plane landed, Hamilton jumped into a dark blue Ford Expedition XLT EL with his campaign manager, director of communications, and chief of staff. The communications person was interested in drawing up a statement. The campaign manager was calling for a quick conference call with a few key advisors to determine the best first step forward.

Chief of Staff Ryan Thornton had worked with Hamilton for his seven years as governor and previous two terms in the U.S. Senate. Thornton waited for the campaign people to make their cases. He glanced at Hamilton, who merely said, "Let's go." Thornton directed the driver to head directly to the church.

Hamilton's SUV moved past the security roadblocks, and stopped amidst a group of police and FBI vehicles.

Hamilton got out, walked a few feet, and then stopped when he had a clear view of the devastation. One side of the castle-like brick church building was gone. He clenched his fists and then took a deep breath. Hamilton shook his head, and wiped away a tear as he approached the wreckage.

He was joined by three people on the scene – the lead FBI special agent, and representatives from both the Charleston Police Department and the West Virginia State Police.

The FBI agent declared, "Governor, unfortunately, it appears that there are no survivors. We're not completely sure yet, but it looks like more than 120 lost souls."

Hamilton replied, "Dear God." He asked, "The terrorists?"

"All four detonated their suicide vests, apparently after they first shot many of those in the church."

Hamilton then moved around, taking everything in up close, and thanking the law enforcement, fire, rescue, and EMT personnel, along with assorted volunteers on hand. Rather than going over to the assembled media – a sizeable group now made up of local, statewide, and campaign press – he pitched in to help carefully move and pick through the debris.

Thornton joined Hamilton in the effort, while the two members of the campaign and the SUV driver stayed at a distance.

With a police officer, Hamilton picked up a large piece of a church pew, revealing a body underneath. The police officer whispered, "Jesus," at the sight of the back of the man's head. The skull had been ripped open from a bullet, exposing mangled brain matter. Hamilton swallowed hard, and called over to one of the groups with the grim assignment of photographing, inspecting, and gathering evidence with each body discovered.

After more than an hour of doing this tragic work, Thornton finally came over to Hamilton, and said, "Wyatt, you're gonna have to go over and talk to 'em." He indicated the waiting press corps.

Hamilton replied, "Yeah, I know." He looked around, and added, "I think I'm ready now."

Hamilton continued to encourage people as he walked. His suit jacket had come off some time earlier, and he now left it behind. It was hard to tell if his round face was red due to the work he had been doing, or because of emotion.

Once clear of the ruins, Hamilton's pace quickened. Thornton worked to keep up. While both men were in their late fifties, Hamilton was in reasonably good shape, while Thornton was overweight, sweating profusely at the slightest of physical activity.

As Hamilton approached a microphone stand that had been set up, his tie was still askew. The sleeves were rolled up and the top button open on his now dirty white shirt. His tightly cut white hair was partially matted with soot and sweat, despite the cold temperature.

Hamilton declared: "Our nation has been attacked in a horrific, cowardly way. Our family, friends, and neighbors have died here in Charleston, and in other places across the country. My prayers – indeed, the prayers of all West Virginians – go out to the victims of this and the other terrorist attacks, and to all of their family members, their friends, and their co-workers, along with all of the people in law enforcement, fire, rescue and medical helping others. We must stand united to protect our nation, and to answer these acts of war. This is not about political differences. It's about Americans coming together. These disgusting acts of terrorism directed against Christians worshipping on a Sunday morning are abhorrent. The United States of America will mourn, will bury our dead, and we will rain righteous vengeance down on those responsible for these atrocities."

Hamilton did not take any questions. As he and his team moved to the SUV, the campaign's director of communications said in a low voice, "That was excellent, Governor. But was 'righteous vengeance' the right phrase? Some people could..."

Hamilton interrupted him, and said, "Yes, 'righteous vengeance' was exactly right."

Chapter 14

Gus Weeghan's daughter and son-in-law – Rhonda and Carl – jumped in their SUV immediately upon hearing the news about the devastation in Big Timber.

While driving west along US 90, they prayed that her father had decided to sleep in on this particular Sunday morning. Gus failed to answer either his cell phone or the home land line.

Rhonda said, "Maybe he's sleeping through all of this."

Carl managed to quietly say, "Maybe, honey."

FBI special agents from Helena, Bozeman and Billings had descended on Big Timber, along with the local police.

The couple had to park about a half-mile from the small Methodist church in the tiny town. They walked slowly through the downtown area, past the brick buildings and shops, with the snow-filled Crazy Mountains looming to the north.

When getting a clear look at the scene, Rhonda gasped. She grew up in the church, but now there was nothing left of it. It was a pile of wreckage. Then she saw the vehicle. It was her father's old, battered station wagon with fake wood paneling on the side. She pointed, and said, "Oh, Carl, it's his car."

Rhonda broke down sobbing. Carl hugged her, with tears in his own eyes. They held on to each other in the middle of the street. And they were not the only people doing so.

A hand intruded on their grief, coming to rest on Carl's shoulder. He turned, and saw a man in his early thirties with a sympathetic face and wearing a clergy collar.

The priest said, "I'm Father Will. I'm so sorry. Can I help?"

Rhonda and Carl simply looked at him without saying anything.

Father Will continued, "Would you like to come to our church? Many have. The FBI, police and fire personnel have suggested that people do so. They'll come there with more information on ... well, you know ... when they have started identifying the victims."

An hour later, while Carl and Rhonda sipped coffee in silence at the Catholic church, they were approached by an old friend. Ben Starr owned the ranch where Gus had worked. They hugged and consoled one another.

Carl eventually asked, "What the hell happened, Ben? Do you have any details?"

"According to the news, it's a string of terrorist attacks in various places across the country."

"What?"

"Islamic shits." In the mix of grief and anger, it appeared that anger was now winning out with Ben. "I've been talking to Sheriff Pound. It seems that there were three terrorists that did this to us here, and they're speculating that they were homegrown."

Carl shook his head, and whispered, "God help us."

Chapter 15

Nico Costello was not one of the many family members, friends, and neighbors who streamed to St. Francis Catholic Church in East Meadow upon hearing the news about the terrorist bombing.

The call had woken him. Nico listened as a friend of his wife wept and struggled to tell him that Tina was dead.

He replied, "What the hell are you talking about?"

Tears filled his eyes as he listened once more.

Nico said, "How? No, it's not true."

The woman calmed her own crying, and said, "Nico, I'm sorry, but it's true. I was sitting next to her. Somehow, I got out, survived. But she didn't. God, I'm so sorry."

Nico began breathing heavily. "No, no, no! God, please no."

The caller said, "Nico?"

He said, "I should have been there. I should have gone. I could have protected her, and ... oh, God ... and our son."

The caller repeated, "Nico?"

He screamed, "No!" and then hurled the cell phone at the wall. It shattered, and Nico fell to the floor. He pounded his fist on the tiles over and over.

But Nico stopped suddenly, and looked at the television. "I know it's not true." He stumbled back to the bed, looking for the remote. He turned on the television, and went to the local news channel. It showed an aerial view from a helicopter flying above St. Francis Church.

Nico wasn't listening to the reporter. Instead, he stared at the pictures, and the words across the bottom of the screen declaring that more than 180 people were killed in a "presumed" terrorist attack.

Ever since his teen years, Nico Costello was high strung, erratic, and in and out of trouble, particularly initiating fist fights for the slightest of slights. Tina came into his life, and brought some stability. He told her time and again, "You make me a better man." And when she said he was going to be a father, the looming responsibility didn't scare him. He welcomed it. Nico decided that he would work to be a good father and a better husband. His family became his foundation.

But now that foundation was destroyed. The scenes passed and voices continued talking on the television, but Nico paid no attention.

He was rocking back and forth on the bed; his hands pulling hard at his hair. Nico repeated over and over, "My fault. I should have been there. My fault. I should have been there."

Nico continued to do this for nearly an hour. Along the way, he actually managed to rip clumps of hair out of his scalp. But he simply discarded the hair, and grabbed more.

His eyes began to glaze over. He finally rose from the bed. As he walked to the kitchen, he whispered, "Tina and my boy." He now began repeating that phrase.

Nico pulled open a drawer, and picked up a steak knife.

The "Tina and my boy" mantra continued, as he now quickly walked to the bathroom.

Nico turned the water on in the tub. He just stood in the middle of the room, staring at the water filling up the tub while continuing the chant.

He finally stepped into the water with the knife in hand, and began sobbing. Nico's "Tina and my boy" chant grew louder, as he lowered himself, still dressed in pajama pants and a t-shirt. His right hand shook as he moved the knife toward his left wrist. Nico screamed out, "I'm so sorry!" He plunged the blade into his skin, pushed it in deeper, and then pulled it across the wrist.

He screamed out in pain, and tried to do the same to the other wrist, though less effectively given the pain and blood streaming from the left wrist. But he still managed to do sufficient damage.

Nico dropped his head back on the edge of the tub, lost the knife over the side, and closed his eyes. He mumbled, "Tina, Tina, my boy, my son, Tina," and wept.

He continued crying and whispering the name of his wife until he passed out, and then death finally arrived.

Nico Costello became the 191st person who died thanks to the terrorist attack on St. Francis of Assisi Catholic Church in East Meadow, New York.

Chapter 16

For three years now, Andrew Russell served as gatekeeper and the closest advisor to the most powerful person on the planet. Yet, Russell did not exactly look the part. His pudgy, youthful face, large glasses and nasally voice made him seem more like an intern, as opposed to the chief of staff of the president of the United States. His appearance also led most people – in the administration and among the media – to reflexively call him "Andy."

At the same time, people quickly learned that Andy Russell was not to be underestimated. He was ruthless in protecting and advancing the presidency of Elizabeth Sanderski. For good measure, it was clear that Russell had the complete trust of Sanderski, which warranted a certain amount of respect.

Russell sat in the Oval Office with Sanderski, who was tapping a pen on a legal pad. They were alone. The president asked, "Who the hell is 'Jihad in America'?"

Russell answered, "No one seems to know, at least not yet."

"That's just wonderful." She shook her head, and leaned back in the large chair. "Building on the speech earlier, let's set some ground rules. If this turns out to be a homegrown challenge, as that pig indicated on the video, then these are criminal acts, not acts of war. Yes, it's terrorism, but if this is homegrown, and not the work of a foreign power, then it's not war. We don't wage war against our own citizens. It must be handled as a legal issue."

Russell replied, "Your opponents won't like that, and they'll push this as part of the larger war on terrorism. That's already started after the speech you gave."

"Yes, I know, but we're not playing their game. This is our game."

"I understand, Madam President. As you also know, Vice President Links will not like this. Can you count on him to go along, or at least, not publicly contradict you?"

She sighed. "I think so. He sees himself as this great patriot. I have no doubt Links will disagree, but I don't think he'll contradict his own president, his own commander-in-chief."

"I hope you're right."

"We're stuck with each other. He's done all I could ask during this first term, that is, keep his views to himself with the media, the public, and Members of Congress. As for him, I'm sure he's biding his time, looking for his own shot at the presidency four years from now. Of course, there's no way I'd endorse him. But that's his problem down the road."

"I agree."

"Back to the challenge at hand. This will not be about Islam. My administration will not partake in condemning a religion. Some of those social media people are right in declaring that terrorism has no religion. We will reinforce that idea, not undermine it."

"Of course," replied Andy, "but how do we do that, and at the same time make clear that we support Christian churches? There's no getting around the fact that this will be presented by many as a case of Islamic terrorism targeted against Christian churches in our own country. After all, that's what it is. Again, the critics already have hit on this in the immediate reaction to the speech."

Whenever Russell presented Sanderski with bits of reality she did not like, the president would go silent for several seconds. It was unclear whether she was weighing the issue, or simply working to control her temper in response. She finally said, "I understand that, Andy. But for the most part, the critics are the usual suspects. It's the Right. They sure aren't our people."

Russell nodded in response.

The president continued, "Besides, as things proceed in the coming days, make sure that it is arranged that I visit each of the terrorist targets, and get an event together here at the White House with the ministers and congregations that support my current campaign."

"Makes sense."

"Also, make sure that the FBI, state police, and local law enforcement across the country, and anyone else that I might be forgetting, understand that I have made tracking down and arresting these criminals to be a national mission, and that we cannot fail and will not fail. That's the message we need to communicate to the public at every opportunity."

"It's already happening, but I'll make sure it's reinforced with everyone in the clearest of terms. What about NSA, CIA, and the Pentagon?"

"No. Not yet. Unless we get solid information that this is an international effort, this is not their fight." She offhandedly added, "I still don't trust any of them." Sanderski turned her chair to look out the windows at the cold winter day. "I think Links is basically wrong."

"What do you mean?" asked Russell.

"It's clear that he thinks this was a well-planned, professional attack. I don't buy it. It looks to me like somebody picked easy targets, and recruited vulnerable, angry individuals willing to die for a perverted cause. I don't necessarily see the evidence of great planning and well-oiled execution. We track down this nutcase on the video, and we'll have this wrapped up."

Russell shifted in his chair.

Sanderski said, "What is it, Andy? You know I expect you to speak up."

"Madam President, if you're right, that this wasn't that hard to put together, and that it was pulled off by some nutcase, is that supposed to make the nation feel safer, or less safe?"

On occasion, Russell pushed the trust that Sanderski had in him to the edge. She was silent a bit longer than usual. Russell once again shifted in his chair.

Sanderski finally said, "That will be all, Andy. Get back to work."

Russell stood up, and said, "Yes, Madam President. Thank you." He turned, walked across the room, and exited the Oval Office.

When visiting the White House for the first time, most people are struck by the West Wing's rather close quarters. The White House is not a spacious work environment. Indeed, it's just the opposite. It has tight spaces, hallways and offices. The Oval Office, however, makes for an impressive space – running nearly 36 feet long and 29 feet at its widest point. Beyond actual measurements, the size of the room seems to vary according to the occupant. Some presidents exhibit strong leadership skills. They radiate a larger-than-life presence. These presidents make the Oval Office seem larger, yet they naturally fill the room. In a very different way, other presidents also create the impression that the Oval Office is larger than it actually is. But they do so because the duties of the presidency are too big for them. They look small in the Oval Office.

On this day, the Oval Office appeared dauntingly large when Elizabeth Sanderski sat at the Resolute desk.

Chapter 17

After Mass, Jerry and Randall Robinson were tossing the football around with a few friends diagonally across from the Basilica of the Sacred Heart and under the Main Building's Golden Dome at the University of Notre Dame.

Randall's roommate approached the group. He had no coat on in the cold. He called out, "Randy, come here, man."

Randy looked over, and immediately started trotting toward his friend. "What is it?"

"Um, I'm not sure. Didn't you say your mom was speaking today at a St. Anthony's in Chicago?"

Seeing the look on his roommate's face, Randy stopped, and replied, "Yeah, why?"

While handing over his phone, the roommate said, "Crap, Randy, I hope it's not this St. Anthony's."

As he read the article and viewed a video, Randy staggered over to a bench, and sat down. His younger brother, Jerry, approached, and asked, "What's up?"

Randy looked up at his brother with tears in his eyes. "It's Mom." He handed the phone to Jerry.

Jerry looked at the screen for less than a minute. "No way." He handed the phone to Randy's roommate, pulled out his own phone, and called his mother. Jerry closed his eyes and stood immobile waiting for his mother to answer. The call went to voicemail. He hung up, and looked at his brother. "Call her."

Randy pulled out his phone, and made the call. The result was the same. Randy stood up, and said to his brother, "Come on. We're driving home."

After getting in their small car, Jerry started calling friends and family in Chicago while Randy drove. Over the hour-and-forty-minute drive, as the two brothers gathered more information, what little hope existed slowly evaporated.

As the miles and minutes passed, the two sons' reactions gradually reflected their respective relationships with their mother. Randall, the older son, had tried to protect his mother since their father had died. As he drove, while his sadness was evident, Randall's anger grew and became more dominant.

In the seat next to him, Jerry, though only two years younger than his brother, was his mother's "baby." During the drive, Jerry was more reluctant to give up hope. But when a call with their aunt confirmed the loss of their mother, he crumbled into sobs and shakes. Jerry's crying became worse when Randy reached out and placed his right hand on his brother's shoulder.

Randy drove on with anger etched on his face, while Jerry curled his body up in the passenger seat.

Chapter 18

Local police and FBI personnel were doing the work for which they had been trained. But even as they swarmed over the shooting scene at the Baptist Church in Brenham, Texas, nearly each one, to a man and woman, managed to find Annie and Bobby Barnes to shake their hands, and either thank or compliment them.

Beyond what amounted to the crime scene, Annie and Bobby shared hugs, tears and prayers with fellow church members.

Inside the church building, the bodies, clothing and weapons of the terrorists were being inspected in painstaking detail, along with their SUV outside the front doors.

After having reviewed the other three dead terrorists, FBI Special Agent Lois Dillon was examining the fourth. In a crouch next to the body, she asked her partner, "Are you surprised by who these guys are?"

Winston Jones replied, "We don't know who exactly they are yet, so you'll have to be more specific."

"Well, quite frankly, a Latino, a black guy and two Caucasians."

Jones nodded. "Yeah, I get it. None of them look like they're from the Middle East."

"They don't."

"That lines up with what the hooded terrorist just spit up in the video."

Dillon sighed, and said, "Unfortunately."

Jones added, "We'll know who these guys are shortly, and start to get a better idea of what we're up against."

Chapter 19

It wasn't until a bit after 7:00 in the evening when things finally quieted down at St. Mark's Lutheran Church on Staten Island.

The latest knock at the door of the parsonage came from a member of the congregation who owned a nearby pizzeria. The man stood in the doorway with two large pizzas in his arms, and tears forming in his eyes. When Pastor Richard Leonard urged the man to come in and sit down, he refused. "I got to get back to the restaurant. I just wanted to drop these off, so you didn't have to make nothing for dinner." He essentially shoved the pizzas into Leonard's hands.

Leonard said, "Thanks, Anthony. I appreciate it."

"It's nothing. I got some more meals to drop off during the week."

"That's not necessary. I'll be..."

"No, no. Hey, we'll do it." He looked down at his shoes, and a tear touched his rough cheek. "Thanks for what you did today, Pastor. The comin' days are gonna be tough, but I know you'll help everyone get through as best you can."

The pizzeria owner turned, moved quickly down the front steps, and climbed into the driver's seat of his van.

Stephen Grant had watched from just a few feet away. He could see that Richard was taken somewhat off guard.

Leonard stared as the van sped off, and then looked at the patrol car in front of the parsonage and the other one down the street by the church. He closed the front door.

Grant said, "From what I've seen, you have a good group of people here, Richard."

Leonard nodded, and said, "Do you have a few minutes for pizza?"

Grant said, "I just spoke with people on the home front. Jennifer's doing okay with friends, and Zack has St. Mary's covered, for now. It's quiet there. I also have a trusted friend keeping an eye on things overall. So, yes, I've got a little time for pizza, and to finally talk with you."

"Good. Come into the kitchen." Leonard led the way.

Grant asked, "Can I help?"

"No. Grab a seat."

Grant did so. As he watched Richard assemble plates, napkins, two glasses, and two bottles of soda from the refrigerator, Grant reflected on knowing both Richard, and his father, Mike, as friends.

No one could mistake Richard for the son of anyone else. The son was the spitting image of the father. While Mike had kept his hair short and was clean shaven, unlike Richard's current longer hair with full beard and mustache, they were both tall and well built. It sometimes took Stephen off guard when Richard spoke, as his voice had the same tone and inflections as his father's.

And while their respective expertise came in different arenas, father and son both had keen analytical minds. Mike could expertly lay out a mission plan for his SEAL team, while also possessing the ability to anticipate and execute a shift in strategies when needed. Meanwhile, Richard's mind could cut through diversions and falsehoods to arrive at the truth both as a historian and a theologian. He also communicated and taught with clarity, authority, and persuasiveness.

Each man also stayed true to his principles, and stood willing to take on opponents with a certain ferocity. Mike revealed this ferocity on the field of battle, while Richard's battlefield, if you will, was mainly in the realm of academia. Indeed, given the state of the world in recent times, his expertise as a history professor in the areas of the Church, the Reformation, Islam and the Crusades often meant that he engaged in a kind of intellectual warfare. And Richard was not shy about engaging. As a result, Grant knew that Leonard's St. Mark's was not chosen randomly by these terrorists. Instead, it was targeted for a very specific reason.

As Leonard cut pieces of pizza for each of them, Grant poured soda into glasses. They each took a bite in silence.

Leonard said, "They came here because of what I've written and said about the conflicts between Islam and Christianity, not just the history, but in today's world as well."

Stephen said, "That's right."

"You sound pretty confident."

"Richard, there's more to today that hasn't hit the news yet, and I don't think anyone passed it on to you." Grant relayed that Fred Pederson, the onetime Navy SEAL who served with Grant and Mike Leonard, had burst into St. Mary's that morning. Grant noted that Freddie was bloodied, offered a too-late warning about the attacks, urged Grant to help Richard, and then died.

Leonard dropped the pizza onto the plate. "God." He got up, and started pacing around the kitchen. "How did this happen? What was Pederson doing?"

"I don't have too much. But from what a friend at the FBI told me, Freddie was undercover, among suspected Islamic terrorists in the U.S. And apparently, he wasn't working far from me on the island."

Leonard sat back down, shaking his head. The two men ate in silence for another couple of minutes.

"I'm so pissed off," declared Leonard.

"Yeah, so am I."

"It's mostly about these terrorists, and everything that stands behind them. But I'm angry at myself, too. Did my speaking out really bring all of this down on the St. Mark's family? What could I have done differently?"

"There are no easy answers. I've wrestled with what my past life might mean for Jennifer and for St. Mary's ever since the shooting at the church a few years ago. And today, a bloody, beaten and stabbed Freddie Pederson came through the doors into the nave. Here, terrorists used St. Mark's as a battlefield, murdering innocents. It also sounds like there's more coming from this Jihad in America. We're engaged as Christian pastors on a very real level, even if many other pastors and priests might want to deny it. But they deny that role at their own peril and at the peril of their flocks. You're engaged beyond that, given your vocation as a historian and, yes, as a public voice. Do we retreat in the proclamation of the Gospel, or face the challenges no matter how severe?"

"You know the answer. I know the answer. But what about the potential danger to St. Mark's parishioners?"

Grant nodded. "That's the part that cannot be answered without talking with your people honestly. And it's not a conversation for now. You've got to focus on getting everyone, including yourself, through the coming days, the funerals. It's going to be brutal."

They finished eating largely in silence.

Grant said, "I'm not really sure this pertains, but when my parents died, your father helped me wrestle with the loss. He told me something simple that helped at the time, and I sometimes think about it when trouble or tragedy arrives at the doorstep. At the time, we were being transported into a dangerous situation, but he was worried about how I was handling my parents' deaths." Grant smiled with a hint of sadness and nostalgia. "He told me that his philosophy on life had seven points. Shit happens. Have faith. Stay strong..."

Richard interrupted to finish, "Love and take care of your family. Pursue excellence. Help others. Enjoy the gifts. Yeah, I know. I've thought about that a lot, basically ever since he died. It certainly came to mind today."

Grant leaned back in the chair. "There's something in that. It's pretty grounded."

Richard smiled. "I remember my dad always being grounded. Maybe he was a Navy SEAL *and* a theologian. Oh, wait, you've got that ground already covered."

Grant looked at the clock on the wall, and said, "Hey, before I head out, how about a prayer for courage and wisdom?"

Leonard added, "And for faith and strength."

The two pastors bowed their heads.

After they prayed, Grant went to leave. As he walked to the front door, Grant said, "Richard, I'm glad you're alright."

"Thanks for being here, Stephen, and for all you've done for me since Dad died."

The two men hugged, and Grant added, "Try to get some rest tonight. You're going to need it."

"You, too."

"And I'll touch base. I'm guessing we're going to have more to talk about."

"Right."

Grant walked to his SUV, started the vehicle, and weaved his way to the Verrazano Bridge. The subsequent hour-plus drive went by quickly in Stephen's mind. He drove by instinct, as his mind worked on everything that happened on this grim day, and what it might mean going forward. He wrestled with questions that weren't all that different from what Richard had raised. What did all of this mean for the people around him, for Jennifer and his friends, for the people at St. Mary's?

But his mind also went to questions raised from his old life as a SEAL and CIA operative. What did today mean for the nation? What would come next from this Jihad in America? He reflected on where his other SEAL brothers were currently. And what about his former CIA colleagues? How would they be engaged in this expanded war with terrorists on the home front, and would he be tapped to play a role in some way? That had happened before in recent times, of course.

Chapter 20

Early Monday morning, the day after the terrorist attacks on the six churches across the nation, the head of the Central Intelligence Agency's Special Activities Division took off his dark gray suit jacket and tossed it onto a couch upon entering his office. The frustration etched on the face of Edward "Tank" Hoard was as evident as his body-builder muscles under a tight-fitting, button-down shirt.

Since day one in his long tenure at the Agency, the nickname "Tank" had stuck. It clearly was earned. He had maintained a Schwarzenegger-like body throughout, and his close-cut light brown hair, now with some gray on the sides, accentuated the square shape of his head.

Hoard sat down, and slammed a fist down on his desk.

With a knock on the office door, he quickly looked up. Hoard returned to his feet, and said, "Aaron. Come on in." The tone in his voice conveyed a mix of frustration, respect and familiarity.

Hoard had just left a meeting led by Aaron Rixey. As director of the National Clandestine Service, Rixey was Hoard's boss. They also were longtime colleagues and friends. Still, it was unusual for Rixey to come to Hoard's office. It was even rarer for Rixey to close the door behind him.

Rixey said, "Sit down, Tank." The director took the seat across the desk from Hoard. "So, what do you think?"

"I think it's stupid bullshit."

Rixey smiled sadly. "Yeah, well, I've come to expect stupid bullshit from our commander-in-chief over the last few years."

Hoard continued, "We've suffered this unimaginable attack. Americans are dead. And rather than having everyone on deck, the president basically is keeping us, the NSA and the Pentagon on the sidelines until there's clear evidence that some other nation or international group is involved? Does she have a clue?"

Rixey shrugged.

Tank persisted, "Wouldn't you expect the president to recognize that this should be a top priority for the CIA, NSA and Pentagon? Aren't we the ones who are going to figure out any international connections?"

Rixey said, "You're right."

"Doesn't she listen to Links at all?"

"No. Nonetheless, we're going to proceed as we should."

"Aaron?"

"We're going to do our job, Tank. And we're not going to conflict with any orders from the White House or from McMahon." Patrick McMahon was the CIA director, who previously had served in the U.S. House of Representatives and was appointed CIA director by President Sanderski. Few career CIA had anything nice to say about McMahon when he tossed about the buzzword of "transparency" while in the House, apparently without any understanding of the need for clandestine activity, and even fewer nice things to say about his clear interest in making social statements since heading up the Agency.

Hoard paused for a moment, and then said, "Okay. What's next?"

Rixey simply said, "Do what you do. We need to know the full story of who's behind this, and we need to know where these shits are."

Hoard replied, "Yes, sir."

After Rixey left the office, at the top of the list of people Tank Hoard needed to contact was Paige Caldwell.

Chapter 21

The bitter cold air of the early morning would not concern Todd Johnson. The political consultant, a partner in Hackling-Johnson Advisors, entered the garage of his large, brick home in Chevy Chase, Maryland, directly from a small hallway leading away from the kitchen.

The five-foot-four-inch Johnson opened the driver's door of his silver Mercedes-Maybach S550 sedan, lowered himself into the hand-stitched nappa leather, and placed his briefcase on the passenger seat. As he did each day for the past month or so since acquiring the car for himself as a Christmas gift, Johnson took a moment apparently to soak in everything about his luxury vehicle. He then eyed himself in the rearview mirror, brushing his gray hair ever-so-slightly with his right hand.

Johnson started the engine, pushed the control to open the garage door, and looked down to check the temperature read out.

As the door rose, Johnson's gaze moved up to see two dark figures standing in the driveway. The Mercedes' headlights revealed a woman and a man.

The woman said, "Mr. Johnson, might we have a bit of your time for a few questions?"

Johnson simply stared ahead, frozen behind the wheel. Sitting inside the very expensive gift to himself, he actually could not hear the request that had been made.

After all, the design was meant to keep out most of the noise that might swirl around the car.

The two figures moved forward. The woman approached on the driver's side, and the man on the other. Upon seeing that each held a handgun, Johnson sucked in air and held it.

The woman used her gun to tap on the window.

Johnson continued to stare straight ahead.

The woman tapped on the window again, but this time a bit harder. She raised her voice, "Mr. Johnson, please."

Johnson allowed his eyes to drift down, focusing on the lit up "D" on the shift lever. He started to move his right hand off the steering wheel.

That bit of movement led the man on the passenger side to swing his hand holding the gun. The butt of the weapon smashed into the window.

Johnson jerked away from the spraying, falling pieces of glass.

After shattering the window, the man, Charlie Driessen, pointed his Glock 21 casually at Johnson. "Sorry about the window, Todd, but the lady asked nice, and you were going to just drive off. Now, let's shut the car off, and go inside and talk."

Johnson's voice shook. "Wh-who the hell are you people? What do you want?"

"We just want some information, Todd. Like I said, it's time to shut off the car, and go inside."

Johnson turned off the vehicle, and the woman standing outside the driver's door stepped back so he could get out. Johnson only looked briefly into the steely blue eyes of Paige Caldwell.

Driessen and Caldwell followed Johnson back toward his kitchen. They made for an unusual team – at least at first glance.

Driessen wore a rumpled trench coat over a slightly-less-wrinkled tan button-down shirt, brown slacks, and brown loafers. The state of his full mustache and thin traces of hair also made clear that fine grooming did not rank high among Driessen's concerns. Meanwhile, Caldwell was polished, utilizing a keen fashion sense to accentuate her beauty. Her long black hair was pulled up in a bun, which managed to magnify the blue eyes, her generous number of freckles and full pink lips. And even under a red peacoat, a light gray, loose turtleneck and dark gray pants, Caldwell's athleticism and strength were unmistakable.

For good measure, Driessen's style was gruff and short, while Caldwell's was smooth and unflinchingly direct.

At the same time, though, the two had worked together for years at the CIA, and more recently, as partners in a private firm called CDM International Strategies and Security. CDM worked for clients across the country and around the world. It also periodically met the needs of their former colleague, Tank Hoard, at the CIA, as well as the FBI. And while the "C" in CDM stood for Caldwell and the "D" for Driessen, the "M" represented their other partner, Sean McEnany. After Caldwell was forced to leave the CIA, Hoard was key in getting Driessen to retire and join her, as well as bringing them together with McEnany.

As different as they were outwardly and in terms of personalities, Caldwell and Driessen were old friends, and worked together like a well-oiled machine.

Driessen directed Johnson to a seat at the kitchen table. Caldwell placed her Glock 20 in the holster attached to the back of her pants, and took a chair across from Johnson. Driessen, though, kept his weapon out as he sat next to the shaken political consultant.

Driessen asked, "Is there anyone else in the house, Todd?"

"No, no, I live here alone. I'm divorced."

"Yeah? Go figure."

Caldwell said, "We won't hold you up, Todd. Like my partner said, we just need some information."

"What the hell about?"

"Well, you obviously know about yesterday's terrorist attacks."

The significant level of fear expressed on Johnson's face actually managed to ratchet higher. His eyes moved back and forth between Caldwell and Driessen.

Caldwell continued, "Your firm raises dollars and lobbies for a group called the Middle East Fund for Medical and Education Support. You know, MEFMES."

Johnson's voice shook ever so slightly. "So, what? MEFMES provides medical care, and builds and repairs schools in war-torn areas of the Middle East. What's wrong with that?"

"Nothing, of course." She looked at Driessen, and added, "Except that one little thing, right, Charlie?"

"Not so little," Driessen replied.

"Very true. Poor choice of words on my part." She leaned forward, and looked Johnson in the eyes. "It seems that MEFMES also funnels some of the money that you're helping it collect in the United States to support the families of dead or jailed terrorists."

Johnson leaned back in his chair, and said, "That is totally ridiculous. Hackling-Johnson would never be mixed up in something like that. We completely checked out MEFMES, and they are clean."

Caldwell sighed, and said, "Really? Like you checked out that group involved in having the pope murdered?"

A few years earlier, the FBI had tied Hackling-Johnson Advisors with a front group that was involved in funding a plot to have Pope Augustine I killed.

Johnson jumped to his feet, and proclaimed, "That's total bullshit. The government never proved its case."

Driessen rose slowly, with the gun still in one hand, and placed his empty hand on Johnson's shoulder. "Sit down, Todd."

Johnson returned his focus to the gun, and thereby regained his fear.

Caldwell continued, "Actually, the money link was clear, but the government, for some reason, apparently decided that it couldn't prove that you or your partner, Arnie Hackling, knew how the money was being used."

"Damn right, we didn't know, and the link didn't exist," said Johnson.

"Whatever you need to tell yourself," said Caldwell. "But now we're back, once again, with your firm having blood on its hands."

"That's absurd," Johnson weakly countered.

"I can't decide if you and Hackling are greedy, stupid or just incredibly arrogant."

Driessen chimed in, "They're all of the above."

"Apparently," said Caldwell. "Allow me to let you in on something, Todd. Our partner, who has intimate knowledge about such things, seems to think that the feds are completely ignorant about the unsavory doings of MEFMES. I'm not sure how that could have happened, but let's chalk it up to good old bureaucratic incompetence."

Johnson remained silent.

Caldwell continued, "Anyway, just last night, our partner not only discovered the ugly work of MEFMES, but also that your buddy, Youseff Sarwar, the head of MEFMES, hasn't been seen since Friday afternoon. Any idea why that might be the case?"

"Of course not."

"So, you don't know where he is?"

"No."

"Here's another question: Who works with Mr. Sarwar?"

Johnson replied, "What do you mean?"

"Again, our partner is a bit frustrated. It seems that the only person working at MEFMES is Youseff Sarwar."

"And?"

"Either the man is fantastically multi-skilled and productive, or he has help. We thought you might be able to let us in on who some of Sarwar's colleagues might be."

Johnson said, "I have no idea." After hearing that the feds were not interested, he apparently regained some self-control. In fact, he even smiled slightly.

Caldwell bolted up from the chair, placed two hands as an anchor on the table, and swung both legs up and around in the air. Driessen leaned back, as Caldwell's boots crashed against the chest of Todd Johnson. He fell backwards, and slid across the tiled floor.

Caldwell pulled her Glock out once again, and walked over to Johnson. She jammed her right knee into his stomach, and pointed the gun a few inches from his forehead.

Johnson screamed and cried, as his eyes were rolling.

Caldwell announced, "Listen you little shit. I'm done fucking around. Do you hear me?"

Johnson managed to nod.

"You have two choices. One, you tell me what I want to know, and we leave and you have time to cover your tracks with the feds. Or two, you offer me nothing, and I put a bullet in your head. Which is it? And trust me, whatever you say better be good. You playing fucking games after these terrorist attacks has me really itching to pull this trigger."

Johnson quickly offered two names that he had heard linked to working with Sarwar – Terif Pasha and Waqqad Rais. Johnson added that he wasn't sure what each person's role was.

Caldwell pressed further, but Johnson served up no one else. She seemed satisfied, stood up, put her gun away, and headed toward the home's front door.

Before following Caldwell, Driessen paused, looked down at Johnson sprawled out on the kitchen floor, and said, "Bet you thought I was the bad cop."

Driessen followed Caldwell out the front door. As he caught up, Paige's phone rumbled. She answered, "Yes."

"Paige, it's Tank."

"What took you so long to call?"

"We're navigating things here, but I just got the green light, and I need you guys on this."

"Yeah, I know. We already started working. We just got a group and some names to start with."

"Good. I want to hear all about it. But just so you know, we're going to have to be especially careful with your payment on this."

"Forget the money on this one, Tank. The way these shits hit us, we want them bad."

Caldwell got into the passenger seat of Driessen's Range Rover, with Charlie slipping behind the wheel.

Hoard responded, "I got it. We'll at least cover any major expenses then. But what do you have so far?"

"We just had a visit with Todd Johnson, a D.C. political consultant, and ..."

Hoard interrupted, "Wait, Johnson of Hackling-Johnson, the guys tied in to funding Pope Augustine's murder?"

"The same. And by the way, at the end of this call, make sure you get the FBI to their offices."

Driessen laughed as he pulled the vehicle away from the curb.

Chapter 22

Stephen Grant brought three Blue Point Winter Ale drafts to a small table. There were only nine customers in the small pub since it was a Monday night without Monday Night Football. Of course, it also was the night after one of the deadliest terrorist attacks in the U.S., and two of the attacks were local for these New Yorkers.

Grant sat down, and distributed one mug to Father Ron McDermott and another to Father Tom Stone.

McDermott took a swig, and asked, "How did you do it, Stephen?"

Grant answered, "Do what?"

"The SEALs. The CIA. You had to deal directly with evil, not as something distant or amorphous. But you've been face to face with evil like we saw yesterday. And even as a pastor, you've wrestled with evil personified."

Grant simply replied, "Yes." He took a deep drink from the glass.

Stephen couldn't talk about any of his missions as a SEAL or when he was with the CIA. While there were some regrets, as always in life, he was proud of how he had served the nation. Grant also had come to terms with that old life recently showing up on his doorstep, and asking for help. But there was one act – no, it was an impulse or intention – that Stephen wrestled with from time to time. In anger, he had pointed a gun, ready to pull the trigger, to murder the man who had kidnapped and brutally beaten his wife. The only reason he didn't was because someone else did, on his behalf. Since then, Stephen had spent an assortment of nights, as well as moments in the Divine Service, confessing, praying and asking for forgiveness. But his guilt persisted, even though he understood, and taught, that a sin confessed was forgiven, and need not weigh on the person's conscience any longer. Yet, this continued to bother him. Why? Grant admitted that if placed in the same situation, his intention would not change. At the most exposed and honest in his reflections, Grant acknowledged actual regret at not being the one to pull that trigger. After wrestling with this inner conflict, eventually, he would push such thoughts and his guilt back into the recesses of his mind – as he was doing now.

Getting together at a bar relatively late on a weeknight was not typical for these three. Rather, they tried to meet early on three mornings each week at a local diner – when schedules allowed – for devotions, wide-ranging conversation, and breakfast. During warm weather, they occasionally switched to a round of golf and lunch.

The trio's friendship grew out of a local group of pastors and priests that had met to discuss articles and ideas offered in *Touchstone*, a magazine focused on Christian orthodoxy. That cluster of clergy didn't last, but the friendship between Grant, Stone and McDermott only grew stronger.

After a bit of silence, Grant purposely shifted the topic, and added, "Zack passed on his apologies for not stopping by." Since his relatively recent arrival at St. Mary's, Pastor Zack Charmichael had become part of the group as well. "But after the prayer service tonight, he wanted to get home to Cara."

"Understandable." Ron added, "That's where you guys should be – home, with your wives. What the heck are we doing here?" He looked back and forth at the other two men with disapproval on his face.

Ron was the youngest of the three, ten years behind Stephen, and served at St. Luke's Catholic Church and School. Those who judged by first impressions likely found Ron a bit standoffish, tough, or even cold. There was a certain formality to Father McDermott – never Father Ron – reinforced for some by his muscular, stocky, five-foot-six-inch frame and close-cut blond hair, along with the fact that he was only very rarely in anything else but clergy attire. But it didn't take very long to realize that Ron cared deeply and would sacrifice for his parishioners and friends, and for St. Luke's school and students.

Tom replied, "Forgive us for caring, and making sure a friend is okay after he just lost someone. And our wives, by the way and as I think you know, would be pretty pissed off if we weren't here for you."

Tom Stone was the oldest of the three, having eight years on Stephen. Leader of the flock at St. Bartholomew's Anglican Church, he possessed a robust sense of humor and an easygoing manner. Stephen appreciated that Tom had never lost his southern California roots, where he grew up and surfed. That background found manifestation whenever the temperature on Long Island topped 60 degrees, as Stone, if off duty from his priestly endeavors, could be found in a Hawaiian shirt and shorts. Indeed, his white hair served as a stark contrast to a rather youthful outlook. Tom also clearly found joy in his wife, Maggie, and their six children, who now ranged in ages from mid-teens to late twenties, with Cara being the oldest.

A slightly chastised Ron replied, "Yeah, I know. Thanks."

For a minute or so, all was quiet. Then Ron added, "Joe was a good guy." Father Joe Schmidt was one of the priests who died at St. Francis on Sunday, and had been a friend of Ron's since their seminary days. "He had a wide range of interests. You could talk to him about a lot of different topics. Plus, he had a good sense of humor. He could laugh at himself. That was kind of lacking at the seminary."

Both Stephen and Tom nodded in response.

That kind of talk – therapeutic after the death of a friend – continued through another ale each.

"I could count on Joe to be, well, normal. Don't take that the wrong way. But he was a regular guy who enjoyed sports, movies, books, some politics, and a beer. And he could be counted on as a friend. I hope he thought the same about me."

Stephen said, "I have no doubt he did."

Ron then redirected the conversation, asking Stephen about how things were with him and St. Mary's. On the phone with each earlier, Grant had briefly explained what had occurred with Freddie Pederson and his warning before dying, that the two had served as Navy SEALs together, and Grant's friendship with Pastor Leonard at St. Mark's. He decided to fill in a few more details on the relationship he had had with the father, Mike Leonard, and the son, Richard.

Tom shook his head. "Man, you two are in this up to your chins. I'm so sorry. Let me know what I can do to help out."

He received nods in response.

Ron said, "Stan already has volunteered to pick up anything needed at St. Luke's given whatever happens with St. Francis." Father Stanley Burns retired not too long ago from active ministry. He had been the senior priest at St. Luke's before choosing retirement. He now lived in a small condominium on Long Island's North Fork. Burns had been an excellent mentor to Ron, and always was ready to help out at his old parish.

Tom looked at Stephen, and said, "Zack mentioned you might be helping out with St. Mark's."

Grant took another sip of ale. "I'm not completely sure yet. As I said, Richard is a good friend, as was his father. And he's going to need help in the coming days." Grant decided not to get into the possibility that Leonard might continue as a target for the terrorists, and how that also played into Stephen's thinking on helping at St. Mark's, given his own skill sets acquired via the SEALs and CIA.

Tom added, "Zack seemed pretty sure that you were going to do that."

Grant didn't reply.

"Stephen, if you're worried on this end, as we were talking, it became clear that Zack's fine in handling things at St. Mary's. And before either of you offer a snide remark, I'm not just saying that because he's my son-in-law."

Stephen and Ron smiled in response.

Grant said, "I have no doubts, believe me, about Zack. But I'm a pastor – yes, the senior pastor – at St. Mary's. How do I go off to help out somewhere else during all of this?"

Ron replied, "You know the answer, certainly more so than the two of us, and even we get it." He glanced at Tom and then turned back to Stephen. "It's not an easy choice, and it's not just about your friendship with Pastor Leonard and his father."

Ron left the rest unsaid, but Stephen understood. His friends knew his background, and even witnessed some of his non-pastor abilities.

Stephen merely replied, "Yeah, believe me, I get it."

The three were nearly at the bottom of their glasses.

Ron said, "I appreciate you guys getting me out of the rectory, but when this glass is empty, it's time to go home."

Tom said, "Fair enough."

Ron stared at the amber liquid in the mug, and observed, "You know, there are times when I envy the two of you."

Tom interrupted, "Well, I can understand that in my case, but why with Stephen?"

In addition to assorted insights, Father Tom Stone could be counted on for bringing humor to the table when these friends gathered. There wasn't much of an opportunity for that this particular night, but he took advantage of this one. His friends smiled with some relief and appreciation.

Ron continued, "I know. It's hard for you to believe, Tom." He drained the last of the brew from the mug. "Many people would probably be surprised, but loneliness does not constantly plague your average Catholic priest. However, any of my brethren who claim that loneliness never comes for a visit are simply lying. In fact, there are times when that loneliness casts a very dark shadow. Prayer, of course, helps. But, quite frankly, there's nothing like the human relationship between man and wife, the intimacy that, in the best marriages, allows a sharing of thoughts and feelings, especially during times like this."

Silence followed.

Stephen finally said, "You're right, Ron. Until I got married, I experienced that same thing over the years."

More silence was broken by Ron declaring, "Well, enough of that. I'm flirting with self-pity, and I don't go for that bullshit. Let's get out of here."

Chapter 23

Stephen Grant, largely due to years of training, was an early riser.

After the terrorist attacks on Sunday, the only things that Grant could be sure about over the coming days, and perhaps weeks, would be increased stress and activity. That being the case, his mind and body would not allow sleep after 4:30 on Monday morning. And even after being out with Tom and Ron on Monday night, that once again was the case on this Tuesday.

He rose from bed, making sure not to wake Jennifer, in order to get a few things done before the rest of the world stirred. Along with countless others, he returned to wrestling with the assaults on churches across the nation.

In the dark, Stephen donned a pair of sweat pants, and layered a t-shirt, a long sleeve shirt and a pullover sweatshirt with a hood and a large Cincinnati Reds logo on the chest. He slipped on and tied his sneakers, left the bedroom, descended the stairs, and pulled gloves and a knit hat from a hallway closet.

Grant entered the large kitchen, and quickly downed a glass of water. He then went through a set of stretching exercises. That effort needed more time as each year passed. It also took him a bit longer to clear out the cobwebs and get his thinking sharp. But once he went out into the cold morning air, Grant's energy, focus and clarity would kick in.

Grant opened the weathered wooden front door, stepped out, and breathed the crisp air in deeply. His run this morning would not be very long, but he'd push the speed. Grant moved onto the circular driveway that separated the tan, 4,200-square-foot, terracotta-roofed, Tuscany-style home, from a three-car garage with stairs on the side leading up to a second floor. The two Grant vehicles – Stephen's red Chevy Tahoe and Jennifer's Mojave Sand-colored, four-door Jeep Wrangler – were sheltered from the cold in the garage.

As Grant's strides took him down the driveway, he moved away from a dock that ran along the west side of the two-acre property and an inlet that emptied into Moriches Bay to the south. The other three sides of the property were guarded by hedgerows. Grant ran past an L-shaped, built-in pool and attached Jacuzzi, a poolside bungalow, an artificial surface putting green and sand trap, and a tennis court – all protected for the winter. At the end of the driveway, the wrought iron gate attached to two light stone columns offered an opening in the hedges.

Grant sped forward onto the quiet suburban road. The Grants' home, which had been in Jennifer's family for decades, ranked as something of an upscale compound carved into the middle-income suburb of Center Moriches on Long Island's South Shore.

Grant appreciated that the morning run he took four or five days a week provided time to reflect. To say the least, Grant had thinking to do.

Lord, 393 murdered. Christians in the U.S. now officially being targeted by Islamic terrorists, just like Christians in the Middle East. What's the U.S. response? Never thought Sanderski was right for the White House, and now this. Maybe she'll rise to the challenge. And how does the Church react to radical Islam launching such broad attacks on Christians?

Grant reflected that this was another morning of many questions, but few answers. He hit the top of his street, and turned right, heading south toward the bay.

Richard has to deal with 11 dead at St. Mark's. He's going to need help with viewings and funerals, while keeping the rest of the congregation together. Is he really prepared for that? Is anyone prepared for it? And there's also the fact that Richard and St. Mark's were targeted for a reason, and that they could still be on the target list.

Headlights approached slowly, and the car moved by.

Can I help? Zack certainly is more than capable of taking charge at St. Mary's if need be. Not sure how pleased some in the parish would be with one of their pastors in effect working elsewhere in the midst of this crisis. Although, with a few exceptions here and there, they've never really fallen short when challenges have emerged. Mutual trust.

Would Sean have time to continue to keep an eye on St. Mary's from a protection standpoint? That's a big "if" given that he and the rest of CDM no doubt have been drafted into the effort of tracking down these assholes. And what about Jennifer?

Stephen reached the dock at the end of the road, and paused for a brief moment to look out at the water and the still dark sky.

Dawn will come no matter what atrocities have occurred.

He turned away from the water, and resumed his run.

I'm the only one who makes sense to help Richard. I know the cops at St. Mark's will make sure that a patrol car is around. But not only can I help with what he faces as a pastor, I can provide up-close protection.

Grant was merely re-confirming what he had already decided after talking with Zack yesterday, with Ron and

Tom last night, and then with Jennifer when arriving
home from the pub.

Thirty minutes later, Stephen had showered, gotten
dressed, and was preparing breakfast.

Jennifer came into the kitchen wrapped in her favorite
light blue, plush robe. "You're up early, again." She came
over to the stove and kissed Stephen on the cheek.

"I hope I didn't wake you."

"No, not until the aroma of whatever you're making
made its way up to the bedroom."

She grabbed a mug, and moved to the Keurig for her
morning beverage. Both were morning tea drinkers, for the
most part. Jennifer chose hot tea, often English Breakfast,
sweet with a touch of milk, while Stephen almost always
drank iced tea.

Jennifer sat at one of the stools at the island bar in the
middle of the kitchen. "And what are you making?"

Stephen turned from the stove and counter with two
plates in hand. "French toast and bacon." He put one plate
in front of his wife, and the other in front of another stool.
He then retrieved utensils, napkins and syrup.

Jennifer smiled, and said, "Wow, thanks. This is more a
weekend breakfast, rather than one for a Tuesday."

"Well, I'm not sure how the rest of the week is going to
play out, so my thought was to at least have a quiet
breakfast together before whatever happens actually
happens."

She nodded in response while chewing a bit of French
toast. She swallowed, and said, "That's good."

The eating continued until Jennifer said, "You're going
to help Richard." It was more an observation than a
question.

Stephen went on to relay everything he thought about
while on his run, pausing along the way to eat. But it was
simply a rehash from the night before.

Jennifer replied, "It makes sense, Stephen. Really, given the situation, it's the only thing that does."

Stephen added, "It might mean staying a few of the coming nights at Richard's."

She nodded again, as they each finished eating.

He asked, "Are you sure you're okay with this?"

Jennifer looked at him, and said, "Of course, I am. I said so last night." She smiled, and rose from the chair to take away both their plates. "In fact, without you hanging around bugging me for a few days, maybe I'll finally finish my book." Jennifer had been writing a history of economic policymaking in the United States.

None of this felt right to Stephen. He never liked decisions that left discomfort or doubt. Jennifer recognized the look of concern on his face.

She deposited dishes and utensils in the sink, and came back to the kitchen island. She pulled her stool close to her husband's, sat down, took his hand, and said, "Stephen, you're not the one who is supposed to be worried. These terrorist attacks..." She paused and drew in a breath. "Once I heard that Richard's church had been attacked, I knew that you'd have to be involved. I'll be fine. You need to help him. He needs your experience, your wisdom, and yes, your protection. And I'm guessing, before this is all over, you might be needed beyond Staten Island as well. Do what needs to be done, and get back to me and to St. Mary's."

"Count on it."

She leaned over and gave him a lingering kiss.

Stephen asked, "What have I done to deserve such a beautiful and understanding wife?"

She smiled, and replied, "You did nothing to earn it, only by grace."

Stephen chuckled, "Nice, a little Lutheran humor."

"I try."

"But you did say that Richard needed my 'wisdom.'"

Jennifer laughed. "Maybe I was overstating that a bit."

As she moved toward the sink, Stephen said, "Leave that alone. Go and get ready for work. I'll clean up."

"Okay, I'll take that."

Just as Stephen finished cleaning up and was wiping down the countertop, his iPhone rang. He looked at the screen and saw that it was Dr. Brett Matthews. Pastor Matthews was the president of the Lutheran Church-Missouri Synod's Atlantic District, and in essence, Grant's pastor and ecclesiastical supervisor.

"Brett, how are things?"

"Continued frantic, as you might think. Dr. Piepkorn is on the call with us from St. Louis."

Dr. Harrison Piepkorn was the president of the national Lutheran Church-Missouri Synod. Stephen knew both men well. In fact, Piepkorn had presided when Jennifer and Stephen were married at St. Mary's. In an ever-so-slight drawl acquired while growing up in South Carolina, Piepkorn said, "How are you, Stephen?"

"As well as can be expected."

"I understand," replied Piepkorn. "And I know it's early, but, as Chaucer noted, time and tide wait for no man. I asked Brett if I could be in on this call to see where you were on what the two of you discussed."

On Monday morning, Matthews had called Grant to thank him for helping Leonard at St. Mark's on Sunday. As that conversation proceeded, it was Stephen who brought up the question, given his experience with the SEALs and CIA, of possibly helping Leonard as part pastor and part bodyguard. Matthews clearly liked the idea but suggested that Grant think it over.

"I've thought about it, prayed about it, and talked with Jennifer. We can't ignore that Richard, and by extension St. Mark's, could very well be targeted, again. Given that reality, that risk, it makes sense for me to be the one who steps up to help. Two birds with one stone."

Brett said, "We were thinking the same thing. But what about Jennifer, Zack and St. Mary's?"

"I only fully came to the conclusion this morning. Jennifer is on board. Zack seems to be as well, but I have to double-check with him. And if he's still okay with this, then I'll check with our church president and some others on council." Before either Matthews or Piepkorn could ask the uncomfortable question of how long that would all take, Stephen continued, "My plan is to have all the ducks in line by early this afternoon. If it all works, I can get to Richard's tomorrow morning."

Piepkorn said, "Thank you, Stephen."

Matthews added, "Yes, thanks, Stephen. I'll be spending some time at St. Mark's as well, but please let Zack know that whatever he needs on my end, don't hesitate to ask."

"I will. Thanks."

Piepkorn said, "I know it's sometimes a little awkward over the phone, but before we go, I'd like to lead us in a prayer."

Matthews said, "Of course."

Grant added, "Please, do."

Piepkorn said, "Since the Church and our nation have been attacked, I'm going to bring together a prayer for persecuted Christians and for times of war from the *Lutheran Service Book*. Let us pray: 'Lord Jesus Christ, before whom all in heaven and earth shall bow, grant courage that Your children may confess Your saving name in the face of any opposition from a world hostile to the Gospel. Help them to remember Your faithful people who sacrificed much and even faced death rather than dishonor You when called upon to deny the faith. By Your Spirit, strengthen them to be faithful and to confess You boldly, knowing that You will confess Your own before the Father in heaven, with whom You and the Holy Spirit live and reign, one God, now and forever.'

"And 'Almighty God, You alone can establish lasting peace. Forgive our sins, we implore you, and deliver us from the hands of our enemies that we, being strengthened by Your defense, may be preserved from all danger and glorify You for the restoration of tranquility in our land; through the merits of Your Son, Jesus Christ, our Savior.'

"Finally, dear Lord, watch over and be with Brett, Stephen, Richard, Zack, the faith families at St. Mark's and St. Mary's, and all of those who serve at and are members of the churches attacked on Sunday. Please provide them with faith, strength, healing, comfort and compassion. We pray all of this in the name of Jesus Christ."

The three men – one in Center Moriches on Long Island, another in his home office in Westchester County just north of New York City, and the third in the church's headquarter building in St. Louis – held phones to their ears, had their heads bowed and eyes closed, and said together, "Amen."

Chapter 24

Pastor Richard Leonard had met with grieving family members starting from sun up and running late into Monday night. The next morning was filled with a struggle to somehow set up and get control of multiple viewings and funerals over the rest of the week, and a bit beyond.

Leonard leaned back in the squeaky chair in his small, cramped office in St. Mark's Lutheran Church, and scratched his beard. He looked up at the cross hanging on the wall, and said, "Dear Lord, I need strength. Am I up to this?"

His cell phone rang. Leonard looked at the screen, and with a tired voice, said "Hi, Brett."

"How are you holding up, Richard?" asked Pastor Brett Matthews.

"Prayer and coffee."

"Additional help is on the way. Not only can I help out, but Stephen has worked it out as well."

Early Monday, Leonard and Matthews had briefly discussed the possibility of Stephen Grant helping with the St. Mark's family and funerals. At that time, Leonard protested, saying that he was sure Stephen was needed at his own church. But now hope could be detected in Leonard's reply. "Are you sure? Is he sure?"

Matthews persuaded Leonard that this made the most sense. Grant had spoken to Zack Charmichael and members of the church council. St. Mary's would be alright while Stephen helped at St. Mark's over the coming days. Leonard made clear his appreciation and relief.

"Plus, Richard, we can't ignore the possibility of a continuing threat."

"Yeah, I get it. Stephen is better equipped than the rest of us if anything happens ... again."

Matthews asked, "Why don't you give me a rundown on what's scheduled at this point?"

The two men went over the grim reality of what would be happening in and around St. Mark's over the coming days.

Matthews recapped, "Okay, so the first two viewings start tonight at the same funeral parlor?"

"Yes, that's right," replied Leonard.

"I'll be at your place then around six."

"Thanks. I have a refrigerator full of Italian meals from a parishioner, so I'll heat something up for us to quickly eat."

"Good. Stephen said he'll be available starting tomorrow morning."

Leonard added that he would touch base with Grant to make sure they were all on the same page.

After finishing his calls with Matthews and Grant, Leonard glanced at the time on his phone. He pushed another name on his contact list. This call went to the president of the Lutheran University of New York, right across the street. Classes had been cancelled for the entire week, given the attack on St. Mark's.

The secretary put Leonard's call through to the Rev. Dr. Carl Pelikan, president of the small university.

Leonard said, "Carl, I know you wanted to talk about what's happened, and what you and the university might be able to do."

"Yes, Richard. Do you have a few minutes?"

"I'm not sure when I'll have free time after this afternoon, but I can come over to your office right now, if that works?"

"Of course, I appreciate it."

When Leonard stepped out the door of St. Mark's, he was greeted by a television reporter, accompanied by her cameraman.

The woman asked, "I'm very sorry to bother you, Pastor Leonard, but do you have a moment to answer a few questions?"

Leonard hesitated.

She said her name was Madison Tanquerey, and that she was a reporter with a national cable news network. She tried to reassure, "It should only take a few minutes of your time. We're doing a special report on what's happened, and trying to make sure to include priests or pastors from the targeted churches." She paused uncomfortably, adding, "Well, you know, if that's possible. And other experts."

Leonard looked around. "Here? Now?"

"If that's okay? Or, we could sit down in your office. Whatever works for you. I obviously understand if you need to do this at some other point during the day. This isn't some kind of media ambush. But I am on a deadline, as the plan is for this special report to be broadcast tomorrow night."

He sighed, and said, "Let's talk here and now. What would you like to ask?"

"Thank you so much." The television reporter slipped into business mode, quickly positioning herself and Leonard so that the doors of St. Mark's served as a backdrop. As the cameraman finished setting up, Tanquerey performed minor adjustments to her dark blue coat's collar and brushed back her long brown hair with blond highlights. She moved next to Leonard. The cameraman said, "We're good."

Holding a microphone, the reporter looked into the lens, the camera's red light came on, and she said, "This is Madison Tanquerey, and I'm with Pastor Richard Leonard of St. Mark's Lutheran Church, the Staten Island church that suffered one of the deadly terrorist attacks on Sunday."

The reporter began by asking general questions about the details of what happened on Sunday, and how members of the church reacted and were holding up. The two quickly became engaged in a conversation in which Leonard was able to talk about the importance of faith during such calamities, and to thank New Yorkers and others from across the nation and around the world for their support and prayers.

Then Tanquerey asked, "Pastor Leonard, I know that you're also an accomplished historian and professor who has written and taught about Christianity, Islam and the Crusades. I realize how close you are to this, how raw it is, but what did you think about the claims made by this Jihad in America spokesman?"

"What did I think? The atrocities committed here and against other churches across the nation were pure evil. What that terrorist said in that video was evil. There is no other word for it."

"I understand. But what did you think of claims like 'American crusaders' being 'hostile to Allah and Muhammad'? For example, he also said," she looked down at writing in a reporter's notebook, "'Jihad in America is carrying out his will against infidels, just as the prophet did. Through your imperialistic ways, and your embrace of Christians and Jews, you have made clear that you reject Islam. That is unacceptable to Allah.'"

Leonard paused, and then said, "I'm not sure exactly what your question is."

"Given your scholarship and study, how does Islam get twisted in such ways by these and other terrorists, and what can be done to correct this?"

Leonard hesitated, and then said, "Unfortunately, your question is based on a dubious premise, Ms. Tanquerey."

"Please explain that."

"The overwhelming majority of Muslims around the world are peaceful and embrace the aspects of their religion that emphasize peace. And I think that is especially the case here in the United States. That, of course, is a positive thing, as we all need to work together to stop terrorists." Leonard paused, and allowed his eyes to glance briefly away from the reporter and to the camera. Uncertainty seemed to cross his expression, but then it was gone and replaced by a look of resolve. His eyes returned to Madison Tanquerey. "The problem is that the essential writings of Islam, if you will, are contradictory, as they also provide ample material to justify these kinds of attacks, and the other atrocities that have come to the forefront of America's consciousness since 9-11. This, again unfortunately, is not foreign to the history of Islam."

"What do you mean?"

"Consider that while Muhammad early on basically taught ambivalence toward other faiths, that fundamentally gave way to him instructing followers that Islam must prevail, saying that Allah told him to fight against all people until they testify to Allah as the one god and himself, Muhammad, as Allah's messenger." Leonard plowed ahead. "And following Muhammad's death, his instructions were followed. Most people have been taught that the Crusades, for example, were offensive actions undertaken by popes and knights seeking treasure, power, to convert Muslims at the points of swords, or other nefarious reasons."

Tanquerey nodded, and interrupted, "That's what I was taught. After all, isn't much of what these radicals, these terrorists, are doing today – a kind of reaction to the Crusades? Many people claim that the Crusades really are to blame."

Leonard was in full professor mode. "In reality, the Crusades were a defensive undertaking. And by the way, they weren't called the Crusades at the time. They basically were pilgrimages. Yes, they were military exercises, but they were undertaken as acts of mercy. They were devotional and penitential in nature. Crusaders responded by noting what Jesus said, according to John 15:13: 'Greater love has no one than this, that someone lay down his life for his friends.'"

As he tended to do during classroom lectures, Leonard started to use his fingers and hands to help emphasize points. "Specifically, the Crusades were a defensive act against several centuries of vast Muslim expansion. Think about this for a moment: By the year 1000, Muslims had conquered some two-thirds of the old Christian world, namely, Syria, Palestine, Egypt and all of North Africa, as well as Sicily and much of Spain. Remember, this is the birthplace of Christianity, and it had been overwhelmingly Christian. Later, in 1071, the Christian Byzantine Empire fell. Again, Asia Minor had been Christian since the time of St. Paul. And Jerusalem was conquered in 1073. In desperation, these conquered and persecuted Christians in the East called out to the Christian West for help. So, Pope Urban II called the First Crusade in 1095 to essentially defend Christianity from succumbing to Islam."

Tanquerey seemed completely immersed in the conversation, and asked, "Is this when the Christian Crusaders came to victory over the Muslims, when Christianity ascended and Islam declined?"

"Well, no, not exactly. The First Crusade was an against-all-odds success, stopping the military advance of Islam and actually regaining the city of Jerusalem in 1099. But after that, Islam resumed its role as the expanding power of the Middle Ages, and actually into the sixteenth century. There was King Richard the Lionheart of England and his successes in the Third Crusade. He took back the coast in a string of victories, and secured a peace that gave access to Jerusalem for unarmed pilgrims. But he was unable to take back Jerusalem. For other reasons, he gave up and left, though promising to return. But that never happened."

"So, what did happen?"

"The Muslim advance proceeded. By the fifteenth century, Christianity was fighting for its very survival. And by 1529, the Ottoman Turks, who had conquered other Muslims and unified Islam, besieged Vienna. In fact, in one of those strange, fascinating moments in history, rainstorms hampered their effort; otherwise, some say, Vienna would have fallen, perhaps followed by Germany and the rest of Europe. The threat of Christianity in Europe falling to Islam was real and clear at the time."

When Leonard stopped talking, Tanquerey didn't let the pause last. She had been staring into Leonard's eyes, and continued to do so. She pressed ahead. "And, what next?" There was an earnestness in her voice. She also leaned forward like a reader fully engaged in a page-turner, or an enthralled viewer unwilling to turn away from a movie or television show.

Leonard smiled – for the first time since before Sunday's terrorist attacks – and returned the look offered by Tanquerey. He cleared his throat, and continued, "There's much more to this history, obviously. My own dissertation, for example, focused on Europe in the early sixteenth century, and the interplay between the Lutheran Reformation, the emergence of other forms of Protestantism, the Catholic Church, and the economics and politics of the era, including the looming external threat from, as they were called at the time, the Turks."

The cameraman held up his watch to get Tanquerey's attention.

She glanced toward her co-worker, and then said, "Pastor Leonard, thank you for your insights, and for your time under these terribly difficult circumstances. I'm sure that I speak for people across the country and around the globe in saying that you and St. Mark's are in our thoughts and prayers."

"Thank you, and God bless you, Ms. Tanquerey."

The cameraman stopped recording, and checked his equipment.

Tanquerey said, "Pastor Leonard, thanks for that interview. The information you provided was fascinating. And I apologize for taking longer than I promised."

"I think that was my fault. I tend to get longwinded on such topics, and with what's happened, well, bad history causes considerable misunderstanding of what's behind these terrorist attacks."

"Yes, I'm beginning to see that. Would you mind if I touch base again if I have any further questions? In fact, as I'm standing here, I've already thought of more questions. It seems to me that people really need to hear more. Again, of course, understanding all that's going on."

"As a professor and a pastor, I completely agree."

"I think the same way as a news reporter. I did some checking, and I have to ask: You're a pastor, have a doctorate in history and have earned quite the reputation in certain circles, and not yet thirty? How did you do it?"

Leonard smiled again, and shrugged. "I guess I could ask the same of you, Ms. Tanquerey, being an accomplished television reporter."

"Please call me Madison."

"Alright, and it's Richard. And I really have to go. Feel free to call, and I'll get back as soon as possible. Take care."

As Leonard turned to cross the street, Tanquerey said, "You, too." She turned back to her co-worker.

The cameraman said, "What was that all about?"

"What do you mean, Sam?"

"First, that may have been the longest, most substantive, yet obscure man-on-the-street interview in the history of television. And second, what was going on between you and the pastor?"

"What!?"

Sam smirked, and said, "Yeah, whatever. So, what are we doing with this lengthy interview?"

"I think the first part will work well for tomorrow night's special. As for the rest, I've got an idea for a follow-up, after a bit of time passes, in which we can dive deeper on the roots of acts like this. Maybe some debate and discussion, who knows where it might go?"

"Right, who knows?"

Tanquerey said, "Like always, Sam, your input is invaluable."

He smiled, and said, "Hey, kid, you know I'm there for you."

Chapter 25

Stephen Grant was at his desk later than normal for a Tuesday night without any church meetings. Having no idea how the coming days would play out, especially regarding the amount of time he'd be able to actually spend at St. Mary's, he utilized a good chunk of the day trying to get ahead on certain aspects of his work.

It was nearly seven in the evening when Zack Charmichael tapped on the door, and walked into Stephen's office. He stopped and leaned on the chair across the desk from Stephen. "Go home. These coming days are going to be tough. I've got everything covered here."

Stephen said, "Thanks. Sit down."

"No. I will not. If I do that we'll only wind up talking about what's going on more than we already have, and you'll spend even more time here tonight, and not get home to Jennifer. Not to mention that I won't get home to Cara."

Stephen smiled, and said, "Smart man. Actually, I just finished up all that I can at this point." He closed a folder on his desk. "I'll leave this for Barb for the morning." Barb was Barbara Tunney, the church secretary who was the model of organization and kept many things running smoothly at St. Mary's.

Zack said, "I'll make sure she knows it's on her desk." He turned back toward the office door just as Sean McEnany entered.

Sean said, "Pastors, how are you?"

Stephen replied, "Hanging in there."

Zack added, "Yeah, that's about it. You?"

Sean answered, "Busy. But so are you guys, obviously. Have we worked out the St. Mark's-St. Mary's challenge?"

Zack immediately said, "Yes." A few seconds of silence led him to add, "Okay, I'm out of here."

Stephen and Sean remained silent while Zack went to his office, dropped things on his desk and grabbed his coat. He waved on the way out.

Even though Zack had exited the building, Sean still closed the office door. He then sat in the chair across the desk from Stephen. His usual deep, raspy voice dropped a hair deeper. "Are you sure you don't need anything more at St. Mark's?"

"Sure?" Stephen replied. "Let's just say, I'm comfortable that I'll be there helping out, and obviously, the police presence is important."

Sean nodded.

Stephen said, "I assume CDM has been engaged."

"Definitely. Paige and Charlie had us get started even before we heard from Hoard."

It was Stephen's turn to nod. "Good for them."

Sean continued, "At this point, I'm digging up information. That, as you know, can change very quickly. But until it does, I can do much of that mobile. And that being the case, I can keep an eye on St. Mary's."

"Sean, that would be a great relief. But how? There's no way you can work your magic via St. Mary's Wi-Fi and phone systems."

"Certainly not. In addition to my home office...," started Sean. His "home office" was unlike any other – a hidden, security-protected operations room in the basement of his large Long Island suburban home with substantial computer power and a global telecommunications reach, all heavily encrypted, along with a mini-armory. The set-up would make many involved in national security jealous, and since he often outdid U.S. intelligence services in terms of contacts, information acquired and overall results, a kind of bewilderment often was evident. "...I insisted on a mobile version. I designed it, and it just arrived last week. On the outside, it's a rather unassuming silver van. Inside, I can do anything in that van that I can in the home office. Actually, a bit more given that the equipment and tech in the van are more up to date than what's in the office. I can park the van in the lot here, keep an eye on things, and not lose anything in terms of what's needed for CDM."

McEnany's voice remained steady, and to some, he might even sound a bit bored, just reporting on work. Grant knew better. *Sean McEnany going on about his new high-tech van. This might be as excited as I've ever seen him.*

"If you're sure?"

"I'm sure, and I am comfortable with it."

"Thanks, Sean."

Chapter 26

A secluded horse farm in northern New Jersey had gained something of a reputation over the past decade for producing thoroughbred winners. But there was more than horse breeding to the place operated by James and Kathleen Kelly – Jim and Kay to their friends – who had retired after doing well in the international business arena.

While traveling during their respective careers, Jim and Kay periodically assisted the CIA. Retirement led to a new relationship with federal law enforcement. While the horse farm was fully operational, it also served as a cover for what lay underneath an indoor riding ring. The subterranean multi-room, high-tech complex served as a location where terrorists and other national security risks captured in the New York City area could be brought for information collection purposes.

One wall and the door of a small conference room were made of clear Plexiglas, with the other three walls covered in a light gray, cushioned fabric. At the black lacquered table sat Special Agents Rich Noack and Trent Nguyen, with FBI Assistant Director Mort Steinberg.

Steinberg clearly was a guy who did not like change, at least in terms of his appearance. He apparently found both a pair of glasses – thick, horn-rimmed – and a hair style – parted down the middle with hair partially covering his ears – in the 1980s, and that was good enough for him. It was the glaring exception over the past three decades, as a New York district attorney or with the Bureau, to see him in anything other than a dark blue or dark gray pinstriped suit. Today, it was gray.

Steinberg pushed back in his chair, away from the paper and laptops spread across the table. He took off the now-vintage glasses and rubbed his eyes. "So, we've got 23 dead terrorists, and one still unconscious in the next room. We know who they all are, or were, but nothing about radical links. Nobody was on anyone's watch list. Seven came into the country via student visas or supposedly for business purposes, and 16 were born and raised here."

"Yes," replied Nguyen.

Steinberg continued, "Plus, we haven't gotten shit from these guys off of their computers or devices."

"Not yet," observed Noack.

"I don't like any of this. The targets, the execution. These assholes operated in our country, but have left nothing behind in terms of telling us about their links and how these attacks happened. This reeks of something much more organized and strategic than anything we've dealt with before on our own soil."

Noack and Nguyen did not respond to that last remark.

A man in a red jumpsuit quickly approached the conference room. He knocked on the transparent door and then pushed it open. "Assistant Director Steinberg, he's coming around, waking up."

Steinberg nodded, and then said to Noack and Nguyen, "Our 'guest' is Janan Nuristani, global traveler supposedly for business?"

Nguyen replied, "Right. He actually does work for an Afghani exporter."

Steinberg asked, "What the hell do they export?"

"Dried fruits and nuts."

Steinberg, Noack and Nguyen walked down a short hallway, and entered a hospital-like room with a single bed. Nuristani was lying on a gurney, wearing a gown, and smiling ruefully as the three men entered. A woman in a lab coat stood to the side. In addition, two large men in red jumpsuits, each equipped with a holstered Glock 22 and a sheathed tactical knife, were erect against a wall.

Steinberg's look made clear his utter disgust. "I'm not going to waste time, Nuristani. You're a coward and a piece of shit. The doctor here saved your life" – he pointed to the woman in the lab coat – "by pulling three slugs out and sewing you up. Nonetheless, I'm pretty damn sure that every person in this facility, including myself, would like to put a bullet in your head. The death penalty is in your future. Your only chance of staying alive rides on what you tell us about the attacks on Sunday, and who was ultimately behind them."

Nuristani's smile widened, and he simply laughed.

Steinberg continued, "Let me make this clear, Janan. Only a tiny number of people on the face of this planet know where you are right now. And while you were patched up in this room, there's a larger room here that is dedicated to tearing you down physically, psychologically and emotionally in order to gain information. If you do not cooperate here, then in that other room, you will give us what we need, eventually."

Nuristani said, "I can tell you something. This was but a first strike, and I only wish that I could be part of all that is forthcoming and new in our Jihad in America."

Noack and Nguyen glanced at each other.

Steinberg said, "What does that mean?"

Nuristani smiled once again, and said, "The ghazis will fight to expand the house of Islam. And Allah cannot be defeated." He then closed his eyes, took a deep breath, quickly raised his left hand to his mouth, and bit down on the nail of his pinky finger. Nuristani ripped off the fake nail, and began chewing on it.

Nguyen had moved first toward the terrorist. By the time he grabbed Nuristani's face, however, the nail was in pieces inside the terrorist's mouth. That meant the poison already was released, and being absorbed into his body.

The doctor, pulling on surgical gloves, screamed, "Get his mouth open!"

Steinberg watched as Nguyen, Noack, and the two in red jumpsuits desperately tried to pry open Nuristani's mouth.

Noack turned to one of the guards, "Give me your knife." The guard obliged, and Noack then plunged the blade into Nuristani's thigh.

That caused the terrorist to scream, and hands moved to hold open his mouth.

The doctor had pulled over the suction hose. She commanded, "Let me in there."

But foam then began to emerge from Nuristani's mouth, and his body started convulsing.

The doctor stopped. "That's it. There's nothing we can do."

The five stood helplessly around Janan Nuristani. His body shook for another 15 seconds, and then his heart and lungs ceased functioning.

Noack whispered, "Shit."

Steinberg said, "You can say that again."

Chapter 27

If you were going to be involved in national security work with the federal government, then Crystal City in northern Virginia, right across the Potomac River from the District of Columbia and just south of the Pentagon, wouldn't be a bad place to set up shop. That's where CDM International Strategies and Security had recently moved, taking the top floor of a shiny glass and silver building.

The landlord was more than pleased to allow CDM to substantially upgrade the security protections – both physical and technological. Once finished, what Sean McEnany, along with two CDM employees, Lis Dicce and Chase Axelrod, had accomplished rivaled the systems in one of the world's largest buildings sitting just across I-395 housing the U.S. Department of Defense.

Not only was the CDM floor secure, but it was rather spacious and stylish, with ten offices and a conference room running around an outer horseshoe ring of the space. Each room had large windows. They were separated by clear, bullet and explosive resistant walls. The large inner bullpen area featured assorted workstations, along with a couple of couches and chairs for more comfortable interactions. Other rooms included a kitchen, small men's and women's locker rooms, and weapons storage.

Paige Caldwell made clear through word and action that she approved of the new – as she called it – "base of operations." What was there not to enjoy? The view spanned from the Pentagon to the Washington Monument and Capitol Dome in the distance. And then there was Caldwell's short drive to work from her townhouse in Old Town Alexandria.

In just a few short years, Caldwell had become passionate about running CDM. While she, Charlie Driessen and Sean McEnany were, on paper, equal partners, it was Paige who truly led the firm. That was openly recognized and agreed upon by the three partners. Charlie and Sean certainly played their important roles. Driessen was the generalist who could perform almost any role in the business well, while being able to tap into his own network of contacts at various places around the globe who were willing to get dirty. He also offered sage, balanced insights and advice from the longest and most diverse career in the group. Meanwhile, Sean brought a cold, dispassionate calculation to their work, an assortment of lethal skills, and most impressively, an unparalleled, secretive ability to acquire information from seemingly anywhere on the planet. Some viewed McEnany's abilities regarding technology and information gathering as bordering on mystic.

Caldwell already had formidable skills learned and honed at the CIA, such as mastering assorted weapons, excelling at hand-to-hand combat and threat assessment, and understanding the need for deception and loyalty. She quickly went on to master leadership abilities that brought all of the strengths and talent at CDM together into a cohesive, productive team. In conversations that she could only have with Charlie, Paige admitted to, at first, being surprised at how much she relished leading CDM.

On the day that CDM officially moved into its new base of operations, Caldwell and Driessen had lingered late into the night, talking over a couple of beers.

That night, Paige leaned back in her office chair, and said with satisfaction in her voice, "Not bad, Charlie. We've created something here."

"We have. But you're the one who led the way, Paige, and really made it happen."

"We've all done our parts. But I really do love this." She took a sip from the bottle. "You know, when the shit hit the fan with the Agency, and I was pushed out the door, I wouldn't have survived without this. The CIA was my life. I had to make this work."

Charlie replied, "You would survive no matter what, Paige. That's who you are."

She smiled slightly. "Maybe. When Tank pitched the idea to me, I jumped at it, but not just as an opportunity. At the time, it was more of a lifeline."

"Yeah, you served up the typical Paige Caldwell confidence, but I suspected that there was more driving you."

"Once we got up and running, I discovered that this was what I was meant to do. My CIA years were great, but they also were preparation for this. And the ability to call our own shots, making things happen without being hampered by a government bureaucracy, and still have the purpose of our work, what could be better?"

Previously when Paige would sing the praises of such work independence, Charlie usually added that while being free from bureaucracy, they also were flying without a net. The CIA wasn't going to catch them. But he refrained from making the point at that moment. Instead, Driessen said, "Careful, Paige, you look content."

She smiled and shrugged her shoulders, adding, "Let's not get crazy."

On this Wednesday morning, Caldwell had gotten into the office by five. Over four hours later, she was drinking her third vanilla biscotti coffee, while taking a moment to look out at the Pentagon.

Her desk phone rang, and she could see on the screen that it was a secure call from Sean McEnany.

"Sean, what's up?"

"Paige, I've got something." McEnany wasn't much for small talk, to say the least, and that was especially the case when deep in his work.

"Let's hear it."

"Quick background: Once you gave me the names from Todd Johnson, I began digging around and staying in contact with Tank's people on this MEFMES trio. Beyond what we already knew about the group funneling dollars to terrorists' families, it's become pretty clear that Terif Pasha is the big funder of the group. He's an Egyptian, an international investor, and handles the portfolios of assorted Middle East leaders. As for Waqqad Rais, the other name Johnson coughed up, he's a case of hiding in plain sight. He quietly travels around the U.S., and now that Johnson linked him to MEFMES, his travels line up with meetings with potential and actual MEFMES donors."

"Okay, so we know what these guys want us to know, or don't care that we know. I know you have more."

"Right. I managed to get an intel friend across the pond to do some monitoring of calls and email of these MEFMES guys, including, when possible, listening in on calls."

"Nice, Sean. And?"

"I just got off the phone with my friend. Khalil Bari is a radical imam located in Camden, New Jersey, and he called Terif Pasha in Egypt a few hours ago. Bari was bragging about what had been done on Sunday, praising Allah, blah, blah, and thanking Pasha for making him a part of this, as his, as I was told he put it, 'honored guests' had arrived. Pasha quickly chastised him – basically calling him an ignorant little shit – told him to be quiet as previously instructed, and ended the call."

"Holy crap, this could be it, Sean."

"Agreed."

"You call Tank, and I'll let Noack know. He'll have the FBI and local LEOs all over Bari, his home and mosque within the hour."

Chapter 28

After the call from Khalil Bari, Terif Pasha was distracted from his work, pacing around his office in Cairo, not taking calls he normally would.

Finally, after a few hours, he reached into his briefcase, and pulled out a specially encrypted phone used to call only one person.

Far off in Philadelphia, Pennsylvania, the man answered, "Yes?"

"It's about Bari. It's probably nothing, but I thought you should know."

"What is it?"

The man listened to Pasha, and declared, "You were correct to call. Thank you. And you should not take any chances."

Their call about Bari ended at the same time Sean McEnany was being filled in by his European contact about the contents of the Bari-Pasha call.

*   *   *

Outside St. Mark's Lutheran Church on Staten Island, a significant number of people had assembled in the morning cold. It was the first funeral at the church after Sunday's terrorist attack.

The street running in front of the building, along with immediately connected arteries, were kept clear of both pedestrians and general vehicles. Only the funeral hearse, limousine and law enforcement automobiles were allowed. Mourners, along with some curiosity seekers, however, filled the sidewalks and university grounds. No doubt, most did not know the deceased, Alice Law, who ran St. Mark's food pantry. Nonetheless, while the church was filled with her family members, friends, fellow church members and co-workers, outside were a few thousand people. Most stood in relative silence, while others assembled in small circles to pray. The requisite number of media lurked about as well.

Inside the church doors, standing in front of the coffin, the pall bearers, and Alice's husband, children and grandchildren, Pastor Richard Leonard had just finished reading part of Psalm 122, and he then proclaimed: "In Holy Baptism, Alice was clothed with the robe of Christ's righteousness that covered all her sin. St. Paul says: 'Do you not know that all of us who have been baptized into Christ Jesus were baptized into his death? We were buried therefore with him by baptism into death, in order that, just as Christ was raised from the dead by the glory of the Father, we too might walk in newness of life. For if we have been united with him in a death like his, we shall certainly be united with him in a resurrection like his.'"

*   *   *

Imad ad-Din Zengli pocketed the phone, and walked over to a wooden table where his three ghazi leaders were seated. He announced, "Khalil Bari has spoken foolishly, making a call he should not have. While it's unlikely that it was detected, we can't take any chances. Contact each of your teams. As a precaution, we'll separate according to our emergency plan, and reassemble tomorrow at the safe house in Youngstown."

One of the men asked, "What are we going to do about Bari?"

Zengli replied, "I will take care of it. He will have to pay the price and sacrifice so that discipline is maintained. We will not fail."

The three men nodded in agreement.

Zengli then smiled at his handpicked warriors, and proclaimed, "As the Quran tells us, 'Those who believe, and have left their homes and striven with their wealth and their lives in Allah's way are of much greater worth in Allah's sight. These are they who are triumphant.'" He vigorously slapped each man on the back. They stood and hugged.

Two of the men said their good-byes and left. Zengli looked at the third, and said, "Get the car ready. This should not take long."

*   *   *

A pall was spread out to cover the casket. Pastor Leonard said, "Lord God, maker of heaven and earth and giver of life, we give thanks for all the mercies You granted Alice during her earthly life, especially for calling her to faith in Jesus Christ through Holy Baptism. Comfort all who mourn her death with the hope of the glorious resurrection of the body and a happy reunion in heaven. Remind us that we, too, are mortal, and prepare us to fall asleep in faith and on the Last Day receive the glory promised to all who trust in Your beloved Son, Jesus Christ, our Lord, who lives and reigns with You and the Holy Spirit, one God, now and forever."

After the response of "Amen," Leonard added, "Peace be with you."

He then turned, and led the casket and its accompanying group into the nave, and up the center aisle toward the altar. Waiting to the side of the altar stood Pastors Brett Matthews and Stephen Grant, ready to assist in all that would come.

*   *   *

Zengli reached the top of the stairs, walked down a short hallway, and knocked on the door of Imam Khalil Bari's office. Zengli didn't wait for an answer, and turned the door knob.

Bari jumped up from his desk, and said, "Please, please, Imad, come in. How can I be of assistance?"

"We need to talk."

"Yes, of course." Bari looked at his two security men, and sternly ordered, "Leave."

Zengli stood in their way. He looked at Bari, and asked, "Is there anyone else in the building?"

Bari smiled, and said, "No, no need to worry. No one else is here at this time."

Zengli reached inside his coat, pulled out a hand gun with a suppressor attached, and fired a bullet into the head of one guard, and another into the other guard's forehead. They each fell and struck the floor with a thud.

Bari shouted, "No, what are you doing?"

Zengli turned the gun on Bari, who immediately went silent.

The two men stared at each other. The physical difference was striking. Zengli stood still pointing the gun, with Bari nervously shifting. Zengli was nearly six feet tall, and had fair skin, brown eyes and hair, and an average build. He wore dark brown boots, tan pants and a button-down shirt. His appearance seemed to more aptly fit his former name – Barry Hill – as opposed to his adopted Imad ad-Din Zengli. He stared down at Bari, who

Lionhearts

was five inches shorter. Bari carried a protruding stomach, and had thick black hair, along with a long beard, dark, olive skin and large brown eyes. He also wore a shiny, gray suit, white shirt and black tie.

Bari said, "Why, Imad? What is this about?"

Zengli replied, "You did something very foolish, Khalil."

Bari's nervousness managed to grow. "What do you mean?"

"You called Terif Pasha. Why would you do that?"

Bari glanced down at the dead men. "Terif is a great supporter of this mosque."

"You called to thank him for making you a part of this jihad, for his recommending you to me."

Bari admitted, "Yes, yes, I did. Of course, I wanted to thank him. We are fighting in the cause of Allah. I was humbled to be part of the Jihad in America. As commanded, you were bringing terrible agony as punishment on the unbelievers, and the goal was to bring this nation, finally, to Allah. But now...?" He trailed off.

* * *

Pastor Grant moved to the lectern to read 1 Thessalonians 4:13-18: "But we do not want you to be uninformed, brothers, about those who are asleep, that you may not grieve as others do who have no hope. For since we believe that Jesus died and rose again, even so, through Jesus, God will bring with him those who have fallen asleep. For this we declare to you by a word from the Lord, that we who are alive, who are left until the coming of the Lord, will not precede those who have fallen asleep. For the Lord himself will descend from heaven with a cry of command, with the voice of an archangel, and with the sound of the trumpet of God. And the dead in Christ will rise first. Then we who are alive, who are left, will be caught up together with them in the clouds to meet the

Lord in the air, and so we will always be with the Lord. Therefore encourage one another with these words."

* * *

Zengli walked around the desk separating him from Bari. The two stood only inches apart, with Bari looking up at Zengli. Zengli said, "Khalil, it is Allah who fights and will accomplish what you say. We are but his instruments. And you have proven a faulty instrument."

Bari stood a little taller, and locked his eyes onto Zengli's. "How dare you? What do you mean?"

"I told you to do nothing that might expose that we were here. And yet, you called Pasha on an unprotected telephone. I explicitly told you not to do that, among a list of other measures. You assured me that you understood. Didn't you understand, Khalil?"

"This is why you have killed these men?" Outrage found its way into his voice. "My call to Terif was fine. It was not a risk."

* * *

After the Alleluia, Leonard approached the lectern.

Leonard read the Gospel from John 14:1-6: "[Jesus said:] 'Let not your hearts be troubled. Believe in God; believe also in me. In my Father's house are many rooms. If it were not so, would I have told you that I go to prepare a place for you? And if I go and prepare a place for you, I will come again and will take you to myself, that where I am you may be also. And you know the way to where I am going.' Thomas said to him, 'Lord, we do not know where you are going. How can we know the way?' Jesus said to him, 'I am the way, and the truth, and the life. No one comes to the Father except through me.'"

*   *   *

Zengli stared down at Bari, and declared, "Of course, it was a risk, you idiot."

Bari's anger erupted to the surface. "Idiot? I have been fighting the infidels and their ways long before you took up the fight. Indeed, long before you even knew of Allah and his blessed prophet."

"Yes, Bari, you have fought long and hard." He slipped the gun back into the holster inside his coat.

Bari visibly relaxed.

Zengli then moved quickly. While grabbing Bari's hair with his left hand, he slipped a knife out of the holder on his belt with his right. He plunged the blade into the imam's chest.

As he gently lowered the bleeding Bari into a chair, Zengli whispered, "Discipline is vital in this war, Khalil. But you'll be rewarded. As it is written, 'Whoso fighteth in the way of Allah, be he slain or be he victorious, on him We shall bestow a vast reward.'"

Zengli pulled the knife from Bari's chest, and wiped it clean on the imam's jacket. He turned, and left the room.

As life slipped away, the look of shock remained on Khalil Bari's face.

*   *   *

Before the final hymn and the recession, Pastor Leonard proclaimed, "The Lord bless you and keep you. The Lord make His face shine on you and be gracious to you. The Lord lift up His countenance upon you and" – he raised his right hand in the air and made the sign of the cross – "give you peace."

*   *   *

Twenty-five minutes later, FBI and Camden, New Jersey, police vehicles descended on the mosque previously led by Imam Khalil Bari. They found Bari and the two dead security men.

Chapter 29

Just after the murder of Khalil Bari and the funeral at St. Mark's, a meeting got under way in the private quarters of West Virginia Governor Wyatt Hamilton.

The invitation to Alexandria Rappe had been extended well before the terrorist attack on churches across the nation, including the one in Charleston. Nonetheless, the appointment proceeded.

The typical niceties expected during a face-to-face gathering between Hamilton and Rappe, a former undersecretary of state, were eliminated. There was no tour of the Georgian Colonial executive mansion, including the checkered black Belgian and white Tennessee marble floor upon entering the building, the dual staircases on each side of the space, and the main floor's ballroom, state dining room and library. Instead, it would be a quick, down-to-business meeting in the private quarters on the second floor.

Ryan Thornton, Hamilton's chief of staff, led Rappe into a dining room that clearly had been overtaken by Hamilton's presidential campaign.

Thornton announced in a pronounced drawl, "G'vner, Secretary Rappe is here."

Greetings were exchanged, and the three sat down at what had been the dining table, but now was covered with three laptops, and assorted piles of paper. Thornton seemed to be glad to sit down, with a look of relief passing across his face as he pushed strands of brown and gray hairs back on a scalp where hair had been in retreat for a couple of decades.

Hamilton said, "Secretary Rappe, thank you, again, for coming, even though we're going to have to make this short, given, well, what's happened, and with the arrival shortly of President Sanderski."

Rappe smiled politely, and said, "I completely understand, Governor." She was in her mid-forties, and had been immersed in foreign policy and national security issues, both inside and outside government, since finishing graduate school. Rappe ranked as a favorite of politicians favoring a strong U.S. role in the world and various members of the media seeking a no-nonsense quote or interview on the latest developments in foreign affairs. It also didn't hurt that Rappe was attractive, with red hair, blue eyes, and a wide smile, along with an easygoing self-assuredness and a sense of humor far too rare in Washington political circles these days.

She continued, "And I'm so sorry about your losses here in Charleston."

"Thank you. That's appreciated. It's been brutal on so many people, and these coming days will be as well."

"They will."

Hamilton asked, "What's your assessment on this, if I may ask?"

"I did an interview yesterday with Madison Tanquerey, and that's what she asked. Given what we don't know at this point, some of this is speculation. I have a similar feeling with these attacks as I did with 9-11. But given the targets selected this time, and the message delivered afterwards, I don't think the hooded figure in that video was simply spouting off after getting lucky with these attacks. At the very least, we cannot afford to assume that they just got lucky. This person spoke of Jihad in America, and that this, to a significant degree, is now a homegrown threat. That was born out, according to my contacts in the government, with the majority of these terrorists."

Thornton interjected, "Since we're not fighting them over there, we're now fighting here?"

Rappe nodded. "Yes, there's something to that. Under President Sanderski, we've retreated from the world to a dangerous degree, and if this plays out under a worst-case scenario, that's what we could be facing."

Hamilton merely commented, "I agree."

Rappe added, "Governor, I do not think of myself as an alarmist. Nor do I in any way believe that we should be bashing Muslims. I've learned via my global travels and meetings that most Muslims basically are like most everyone else, simply seeking a better life. And in the war against terrorists, we want them on our side. After all, they arguably have suffered most at the hands of these radical terrorists. At the same time, it's obvious that Islam has enormous challenges in terms of getting its house in order, and I'll leave that to the theologians to sort out. My concern is the national security of the United States. That being the case, I cannot afford to think well of everyone, to indulge in the illusion that conflict is just the result of misunderstandings, and to ignore real threats. I think, unfortunately, that's exactly what President Sanderski has done. Given all of this, and the targets mentioned in the video, my concern is growing that terrorism in the U.S. will move beyond suicide bombers to a more sustained effort."

Hamilton leaned forward in his chair. "What does that mean?"

"Shifting from finding people willing to blow themselves up to creating soldiers that strike and live to fight again. After all, what's more appealing to the radicalized terrorist – a onetime, suicide mission or becoming a soldier for Allah, carrying on a sustained fight against infidels?

There's a term – ghazis – for Islamic warriors that blend in, strike, disappear and come back to strike again."

Thornton chipped in, "Lord, help us."

Hamilton said, "Have you put this theory out into the public, Secretary Rappe?"

"It's been in the back of my mind for some time. But the Sunday attacks brought it to the fore. I did touch on it with Ms. Tanquerey in my interview. Afterwards, I realized that probably wasn't the right venue for taking it public, given the whims of television editing. The interview is supposed to run tonight, so, fortunately, I was able to spell it out in an op-ed that was published on the *Journal's* website this morning. It'll run in the actual paper tomorrow."

Hamilton nodded in response, and then glanced at Thornton. He turned back to Rappe, "Well, Secretary Rappe, as discussed when we set this up, our meeting would be to discuss the campaign, and the role you might play. I've long been impressed with your career, and can't really think of an issue I heard you speak or write on where we had any substantive disagreement. This conversation, even though it's cut short, has fully convinced me that I would love to have you on board as the campaign's national security and foreign policy advisor. Interested?"

"Governor Hamilton, I would be honored."

All three stood up from the table, and Hamilton said, "Excellent. And I like to keep it more informal and friendly with my key team members behind closed doors, so call me Wyatt."

Rappe smiled. "And please, call me Alex."

"We'll work out the details on your..."

Thornton had glanced at his phone, and now interrupted, "Shit."

Hamilton asked, "What is it?"

Thornton digested the news on the screen and spoke at the same time. "Apparently, G'vner, some imam and two other men were murdered this mornin' in Camden, New Jersey." He paused as his eyes remained fixated on the small screen. "No arrests."

"Independent incident? Some kind of revenge or retaliation?"

Thornton answered, "Nothing on motive, and so on..." His voice trailed off as he continued reading.

Hamilton turned to Rappe. "Your first assignment, Alex?"

"I'm on it."

Chapter 30

Madison Tanquerey and her cameraman parked their network van across the narrow street from a mosque wedged into a tight neighborhood in Bridgeport, Connecticut.

Tanquerey glanced at her watch, and then said, "We're a little early, but Imam Abdullah told me that would be fine. Final interview, and we can put the show together for tonight."

Sam said, "Cutting it close."

Tanquerey smiled and replied, "You know the biz, Sam."

"Yeah, kid, I'm well aware."

Five minutes later, Tanquerey, Sam and a camera faced a seated Imam Anwar Abdullah. The tall, thin man dressed in a dark suit had black hair, dark brown eyes, a thin beard and mustache, and broad smile. His slight Iraqi accent was barely detectable.

After the camera light came on, the conversation began with a focus on the atrocities of the terror attacks. After expressing his own horror at the entire situation, Abdullah explained, "I offer no excuses for these people and their actions." He went on to share stories about a family member and two friends of his who had been killed at the hands of terrorists back in Iraq. "I know what it is to lose loved ones, murdered by such madmen." He paused, shook his head, and added, "This, in part, is what Islam is, and it is what Islam most certainly is not."

Tanquerey replied, "Imam Abdullah, what does that mean? Is this why you are calling for a Reformation in Islam? You have done that, correct, called for such a Reformation?"

He nodded. "I have said that Islam needs our own Martin Luther. Luther led a Reformation in Christianity, and that is what Islam needs."

"Again, what exactly does that mean?"

"Islam must become compatible with modernity, we must accept, for example, freedom of worship, and we must accept that government needs to be a secular institution. Trust me, Ms. Tanquerey, these are not easy things for many Muslims to hear, but they must. About the Quran, we must contextualize the violence, and embrace the message of peace. I believe we can do this. Judaism and Christianity have done it. The Crusades and the Inquisition were terrible things that have been left behind, for example. Belief does not come at the point of a sword. We must come to understand that parts of the Quran simply reflect seventh century views, and do not hold for today."

"I get the impression that you might be putting yourself in danger for talking this way. Is that right?"

Abdullah smiled sadly. "Here we are, you and I, Ms. Tanquerey, two people, I assume, of differing beliefs, having a civilized conversation. Americans take this for granted. But in many parts of the world, this right or privilege does not exist. Yes, unfortunately, there are many people who want to silence me on this. But I am a faithful Muslim, and I must speak out to play some role in saving Islam."

A few seconds of silence followed, until Tanquerey took a deep breath and said, "Thank you, Imam Abdullah for your time. Is there anything else that you would like to add?"

Abdullah's wide smile returned. He laughed and said, "No, I think I've probably said quite enough for today."

As Sam was packing up the equipment, Tanquerey and Abdullah casually talked. She then asked, "You heard about the imam and two others murdered earlier today in New Jersey?"

Abdullah simply nodded in response.

"Did you happen to know him at all? Was he along your line of thinking on Islam?"

Abdullah stared at Tanquerey for a moment, and then responded, "I did not know Khalil Bari. But I knew of him. Let's just say that he and I had very different views on Islam and how it should interact with the world."

Chapter 31

President Elizabeth Sanderski emerged from Air Force One and began descending the stairs. At the bottom were Governor Wyatt Hamilton and his wife, West Virginia First Lady Vanessa Hamilton, waiting on the tarmac of Yeager Airport. The air was cold, but unusually still for such a flat, open area.

Sanderski extended her hand to Governor Hamilton, and said, "I'm so deeply sorry, Wyatt."

"Thank you, Madam President. How are you holding up?"

She shrugged in response, exchanged condolences with Vanessa, and the three made their way to the waiting presidential limousine. Key White House and a few gubernatorial staff followed in the accompanying, large SUVs.

Inside the tank-like limousine, the drive began in a cool silence. Sanderski and Hamilton were rivals for the most powerful position in the world. Sanderski desired four more years, with Hamilton currently ranking as the leading Republican candidate looking to deny her a second term.

It was Governor Hamilton who broke the silence. "Thank you for coming, Madam President. I know the people of West Virginia appreciate it, and I certainly do."

"It's my responsibility to be there for the nation through terrible times like this."

He nodded in response. "And rest assured that I view this as a time when our nation must come together. It's not a time for politics. There will be plenty of other opportunities for us to hash out differences. Now, we must stand in unity against those who have committed these heinous acts."

Sanderski paused briefly, and said, "Yes, thank you. I wholeheartedly agree."

President Sanderski was scheduled for two stops. The first came at a high school not far from the Community Christian Church in Charleston. Sanderski, with Chief of Staff Andy Russell walking closely behind, followed by the Governor and Mrs. Hamilton, moved around the school's large gymnasium. They greeted family members of the 123 people who perished at the church.

The differing interactions were striking. Sanderski, in a dark brown pantsuit, was alone, never having married, and she moved stiffly among the raw, stricken individuals. Her instincts led her to shake hands and talk at a bit of a distance. When a family member moved in to hug her, Sanderski clearly was working not to show her discomfort.

In contrast, Wyatt and Vanessa Hamilton began to fall behind Sanderski as they lingered with various mourners. The individuals in the gym apparently felt something genuine in the embraces, condolences and tears offered by the state's governor and first lady.

Reaching the end of the assembly, Sanderski and Russell stood awkwardly waiting for the Hamiltons to catch up.

Last in line was an elderly couple – Mr. and Mrs. Morris. Just a few moments earlier, the two had appeared embarrassed at shedding tears as they told President Sanderski that they had lost their only son. But as they did the same with Wyatt and Vanessa Hamilton, nothing was held back.

Mrs. Morris said, "Our son, Kevin, was lost to the streets for ... for so very long. He hated us, blamed us."

Her husband added, "He blamed everyone."

His wife nodded, and continued, "But then... That church saved him. Jesus saved him. We got him back. And now this..." She broke into deep sobs.

As Vanessa's round blue eyes shed tears, she opened her arms to the older, frailer woman. Their bodies came together in an embrace and shook in grief. The woman's taller husband simply covered his face as he wept. Wyatt steadied the man, preventing him from falling, while patting his back.

After a few minutes, the state's governor and first lady led the couple back to a set of chairs. Wyatt and Vanessa then crouched down in front of them. Before departing, the small woman said, "God bless both of you."

Vanessa whispered, "Thank you, and never doubt that Jesus was and is with your son, and He is with both of you."

The governor and his wife walked next to President Sanderski as they made their way to the limousine. The three sat in silence during the short ride to the partially destroyed Community Christian Church building. Sanderski looked out the window. Wyatt and Vanessa did the same, while they held hands.

No one said or did anything about the stains of other people's tears on the shoulders and around the collar of Vanessa Hamilton's gray dress.

After taking in the site of the terrorist attack, the media stood waiting. Sanderski offered comments that largely reflected those made in her speech to the nation three days earlier, and what she had said on the previous day visiting Montana and Texas. She spoke sympathetically toward the victims and their families, expressed outrage at the attacks, and declared that no one involved would evade justice.

The initial questions focused on what the administration was doing about finding the leader, or leaders, and about plans for retaliation. She was asked about the murders in Camden as well. Sanderski's somewhat vague responses seemed to agitate a press corps that was normally quick to give her the benefit of the doubt.

In the midst of questions, one stood out from a Charleston reporter: "Madam President, do you agree with Governor Hamilton when he declared that the United States would – and I quote him here – 'rain righteous vengeance down on those responsible for these atrocities'"?

Without expression, Wyatt Hamilton watched just a few feet away.

Sanderski responded, "That is a sentiment that many Americans, I think, have felt and expressed since the attacks on Sunday. And I completely understand it. I sympathize with it, and I pledge to each and every one of them, right here and right now, that I will not rest and my administration will not rest until those responsible get their just desserts." She paused, and then added, "So help me God."

Sanderski ended the meeting with the press at that point. Within an hour, Wyatt and Vanessa Hamilton were thanking Elizabeth Sanderski for her visit, and sending her off as she ascended the stairs of Air Force One.

Sanderski's supporters spoke about the strength of her comments in Charleston. Across much of the media spectrum, there was near-ubiquitous praise of President Sanderski and her leading political opponent, Governor Hamilton, putting aside politics for the sake of the nation.

Chapter 32

After the long, purposefully circuitous westward drive across nearly the whole of Pennsylvania, Zengli and one of his key team members, Dale Shore, checked into separate rooms in a small hotel in Ellwood City.

Shore was the only person that Zengli still had any contact with from his life growing up as Barry Hill. The two came from upper middle income families in Massachusetts, but each seemed to work to make himself an outcast in high school. It was Hill who first bought into the conspiracy theories about 9-11 that he discovered online, including that it was all an Israeli plot. He consumed them unquestioningly. It didn't take much to drag Shore along with him. Eventually, each convinced their respective parents that going to college in England would be a new opportunity, offering the promise to get their acts together. Family money was quickly forthcoming, and once the two arrived in London, it wasn't difficult for Hill to find a radical mosque. University was left behind, and they made their way to Egypt for discreet training. While Shore kept his name, he welcomed radicalization and the training, as did Hill, who adopted the name Imad ad-Din Zengli.

While proficient in much, Zengli proved particularly adept at envisioning and executing operations and grander strategic plans, while Shore, long a basement computer nerd, discovered an unexpected appreciation for outdoor survival.

Zengli soon began making his argument to go beyond only suicide bombs in the West, and instead, train ghazis to carry out raids against soft targets, particularly ones that would work to undermine the will of the West. Of course, when the opportunities were presented, it would pay to target those holding political power. He made the case that while it would be difficult to make this happen in Europe, given each nation's relatively small size and challenges for evasion, the wide open United States, expansive Russia, and parts of Latin America would be ideal. Zengli assembled a plan to start in the United States. His Jihad in America was welcomed by key players.

Like tens of millions of people across the U.S., Zengli sat up in bed, clicking through television channels with a remote. At 11:00 PM, however, he clicked over to watch the replay of the hour-long report – missed earlier while driving – on the fallout of Sunday's attacks.

As the program began, Zengli jumped out of bed and began pacing the room. For the following 60 minutes, his anger grew watching interviews with people such as Pastor Richard Leonard and Alexandria Rappe. An obvious tipping point, though, registered with the interview in which Imam Anwar Abdullah called for a Reformation in Islam. When Abdullah's face faded from the widescreen television and Madison Tanquerey began her wrap up of the program, Zengli picked up the television, ripping the electrical cord out of the wall socket and tearing free the cable connection. He then smashed it on the floor.

Less than thirty seconds later, a knock came at the door. Zengli opened it, and Shore was standing there. The thinner, shorter man went from wiping his brown eyes to scratching his close-cut light brown hair. Shore tentatively asked, "Everything okay?"

Zengli nodded. He took a couple of deep breaths, and said, "Don't worry about it, Dale. Sorry about the noise. Go and get some sleep. I've got some additional planning to do."

Chapter 33

"How are you holding up, Ron?" asked Father Stanley Burns.

"Reasonably well, Stan," responded Father Ron McDermott.

Burns had just arrived at St. Luke's large, white Victorian rectory, and the two men were making their way back to the kitchen, where the housekeeper and cook, Mrs. Kennedy, was preparing breakfast.

"I learned that when you use any qualifying language, like 'reasonably,' things are not well with you."

For several years, both Stanley Burns and Ron McDermott served the parishioners and school families at St. Luke's Catholic Church and School. The age disparity between the two was significant, though most people who knew him over a long period of time had a difficult time figuring exactly how old Burns was. His saggy face, thin black hair, slow movements, deliberate speech, and large, black horn-rimmed glasses had changed very little over time. But Father Burns eventually did retire. By staying on Long Island, however, it allowed him to occasionally come back and help out at St. Luke's when necessary. His appearance this week, of course, was the most extreme of cases where Burns was needed, as Ron was assisting with the grim results of the terrorist attack on St. Francis of Assisi's.

The two men had shared many meals over the years, and had developed something of a father-son relationship.

Upon entering the kitchen, Mrs. Kennedy, a short, wide woman, wiped her hands on an apron and waddled over to give Father Burns a hug. She smiled, and proclaimed, "Jesus, Mary and St. Joseph, it's so good to see you, Father Burns." When Father McDermott had told her the day before that Father Burns would be arriving early the next morning, Mrs. Kennedy insisted that she would come in early on Thursday morning to make them "a proper breakfast."

Burns returned the hug and smile, saying, "And it's good to see you, too." They quickly caught up with each other on some of the basics of life, and then Mrs. Kennedy declared, "Now, you two sit down or breakfast will get cold. I'll leave you to talk about your business" – she blessed herself – "with these attacks and so many gone. I have other work to do around the house."

After a prayer, the two men dug into a hearty meal of eggs, bacon, hash browns, toast, juice and coffee.

Ron said, "Thanks again, Stan, for coming to help."

Burns waved his hand in response. "Of course. But I'm going to nag a bit, and get back to my question: How are you really holding up? I know Joe Schmidt was a friend."

Ron did not respond at first. They chewed in silence. And then he said, "You're missed here, Stan."

"Well, thanks. And...?"

"I miss opportunities like this, you know, to just talk over a meal."

Burns nodded, and took another forkful of scrambled eggs.

Ron continued, "You were the lone priest here at St. Luke's for a long time. How did you handle ... being alone?"

Burns put his fork down. "Right. Well, first, the further you go back in my career as a priest, the more involved parishioners were with their priests. What I mean by that is that it seemed like you were going to someone's house for dinner or some event nearly every day. But that changed. When loneliness hit – and by the way, it still does – I remind myself about what I tell parishioners. We're never alone, as Christ is always with us, guiding us, comforting us. And with that, I make a more distinct effort to prioritize my prayer life. Of course, there also are our own family members and friends. I learned early on that friendship, especially with fellow priests, is vital – and it takes work to maintain those friendships over the years. Although, I have to admit that the Internet has made that easier." He paused to take a sip of coffee. Burns then smiled, and added, "If all else fails, my advice to you is to start drinking heavily."

Ron laughed, and said, "Did you just quote *Animal House?*"

"Yes. I was doing that 35 years ago, and people thought it was cool to hear a priest quote that movie. Now, it just confirms how old I am." He chewed, swallowed, and then returned to his unanswered question, "Again, how are you doing with the loss of Joe?"

Ron replied, "As good as can be expected, I guess. He's been a good friend since seminary. We both grew up around here as well; we shared that New York sensibility."

Burns smiled. "Sensibility? Is that what you call it?"

Ron laughed, and then simply said, "Joe was a good guy."

They finished up the early morning breakfast.

Burns added, "Ron, in terms of the loneliness, it obviously hits hard right now with what's happened. In many ways, these are the most difficult times when we don't have our own families. But this also is a time when we have a freedom, if that's the right word, to work for Christ and His Church wherever and whenever we are needed. And while there are always costs involved, this is a great gift that you and I have been given."

"Amen to that, Stan."

Within a few minutes, Father Ron McDermott was in his car, heading in to Nassau County to assist in a funeral for a family lost in the attack on St. Francis. Meanwhile, Father Stanley Burns was looking at the schedule left for him by McDermott regarding the day's events at St. Luke's.

Chapter 34

It was only 7:00 AM on Thursday morning, but Paige Caldwell already had been in the Crystal City offices of CDM International Strategies and Security for nearly an hour.

The phone on her desk rang. "Yes."

Noack announced, "We've got a break."

"What is it?"

"We just got video sent over from our Newark office, thanks to legwork by the Camden police. It gives a clear look at the driver and passenger of the car that left the Camden mosque."

"I thought there weren't any traffic cams."

"There aren't. But we did get an ID from a witness who saw a car pull out of an alley next to the building at about the time of the murders. The witness couldn't identify who was in the vehicle – just a nondescript driver and a passenger. But a few blocks away, there's a shop owner sick of getting ripped off, having his neighbors ripped off, and a bunch of other shit in the area. He went and set up a rather comprehensive security system. That cameras that not only covered each entrance to his store and inside the store, but he also offered coverage up and down the street."

"Nice."

"Sure is. One of the Camden cops knew about the guy's system. Suddenly, we have a clear shot of the car that drove away from the mosque. Some techie magic cleans up the video, and we have who these two guys are."

"And?"

"Barry Hill and Dale Shore. They grew up and knocked around Massachusetts together. Then they went off to study in England, and basically disappeared. Parents made inquiries. It looks like they left the U.K., possibly for Egypt. Trail ends there. We've got agents bringing in both sets of parents right now in Boston."

"Egypt, also where our Mr. Terif Pasha is."

"Right. We've gotten this out to the entire team, including Hoard over at CIA."

"Send me everything, and I'll get Sean up to speed and working his angles."

"Perfect. Thanks."

Chapter 35

Barry Hill's parents divorced after he left for England. They now sat as far away from each other as possible at a table on the fourth floor of the FBI's building in Chelsea, Massachusetts.

Attempts by two FBI special agents to gain something worthwhile was proving challenging. The lone area of agreement seemed to be mild surprise at Barry adopting the name Imad ad-Din Zengli. Otherwise, the interview regularly degraded into Rick and Sally blaming each other for what their son had done. Rather than sadness or regret, the former spouses seemed to focus on anger, pointing fingers at each other, and avoiding any personal blame.

After trying for nearly an hour, an exasperated agent pushed back his chair, and asked, "Is there anything that either one of you can actually tell us about your son that might help?"

The question was met with silence for several seconds. Rick Hill glanced at his ex-wife, and said, "Barry was always very good at organizing things that teachers and his schools didn't like."

"Rick!"

"Oh, shut up, Sally. People's lives are at stake because of our son."

The second FBI agent asked, "Give us specifics."

Rick Hill said, "He'd get into trouble. We just thought it was him acting out because he was bored. But about a year after graduating from high school, we stumbled on a plan that Barry had put together to..." He hesitated, but then continued, "... kill his former principal, a few teachers, and the priest at our old church."

Both agents leaned forward, with the first asking, "And what did you do?"

"Well, I spoke with him, of course. Told him this was crazy. I made it quite clear."

The agents glanced at each other. The second asked, "And?"

"Well, well, we destroyed all of the material, and kept an eye on him. You know, as best we could."

Sally nodded. "We did. We did. And then we saw something different. He calmed down, and talked with us more. And then he came to us with this idea of studying in England. Barry said he wanted a fresh start."

The first agent shook his head, while jotting down some notes. The second looked back and forth at the parents, and said nothing more.

Sally stared at the top of the table. She said, "I wanted him to get a fresh start. I believed him." She looked up. "I so wanted it to be, you know, true."

*   *   *

In a similar room one floor up, two other special agents – a man and a woman – were interviewing Dale Shore's parents, Duncan and Ella.

The Shores' chairs touched, and Ella leaned against her husband, who had an arm around her shoulder. Both sets of eyes were red and tear-filled. They were bewildered at everything going on, and seemed to have more questions for the FBI than the agents had for them.

Finally, Duncan Shore slammed his fist down on the table. "It's that fucking Barry Hill. It's his fault."

The female agent asked, "How so, Mr. Shore?"

"I never liked that little son of a bitch. He was always getting into trouble in high school, and dragging Dale into it with him." He shook his head.

Ella added, "I questioned Dale about hanging out with Barry. But he'd tell me that Barry was fine. How do you control who your kid hangs out with? It's so hard. We really didn't get too worried. But after high school, the two of them weren't doing much of anything. And then Dale started making some weird comments about 9-11."

The male agent asked, "Like what, Mrs. Shore?"

"That the government was lying, and Bush and the Israelis were behind it all."

Duncan added, "Yeah, it was stupid. And I'd tell him so."

Ella said, "When he first told us about going to school in England, I got excited. I mean, it would be real tough financially, but I thought it'd be good for him to get away. But then he told me that it was Barry's idea and they'd go together."

"Yeah, that didn't sit well with me," interjected Duncan. "But I figured, okay, sometimes kids need a change to get on track."

Duncan and Ella looked at each other, and tears resumed.

"Anything else?" asked the female agent.

"I just keep thinking of when he was leaving the house." Her eyes suddenly had a distant look. "I remember exactly what he said, 'Mom, everything's going to be different from now on. Barry is a leader, and I'm going to help him change the world.'"

Chapter 36

It was early Thursday night, and Imad ad-Din Zengli and his leadership team were going over plans for the coming days.

The house, just on the outskirts of Youngstown, Ohio, had been rented from a landlord anxious for cash and uninterested in his tenants' business.

Seated around a kitchen table for several hours, the group of six had been going over the plans in detail, asking and answering questions, offering contingencies for when things didn't go exactly as planned, and so on. But for the last hour or so, it was Zengli repeating and drilling point after point into his men. He said, "Again, it is likely that the authorities have identified some of us. I don't know this for sure, but that is the assumption that we now must operate under. That means stealth and disguise are even more important. Slip-ups, errors and sloppiness cannot happen."

There were affirmations around the table.

Four parts of the overarching plan were under review.

Youseff Sarwar and Waqqad Rais, the two who used MEFMES as a cover for financing, recruiting and organizing purposes, had emerged from hiding for this meeting. They would be splitting up with new identifications, going to separate airports, and flying to different points in South America. Each would then board flights to points in Africa, and make their ways to Egypt, where they would resume the work they performed under MEFMES. The escape plans for Sarwar and Rais were the easy part.

Next came the attacks, with teams led by Dale Shore, Mikel Rostoff, and Osbert Kusuma. The assaults would come in different parts of the country, but unlike the suicide attacks on the churches, the teams would now be targeting individuals and Zengli's ghazis would live to continue the fight.

Zengli hammered away on every point for taking down each target. Shore, Rostoff, and Kusuma made clear that they knew what had to be done, how it would be accomplished, and that their respective teams – each with four members including the cell leader – were ready for the challenges. The assignments ranged from the seemingly impossible to the relatively simple. But Zengli communicated the importance of each, all fitting into the larger Jihad in America agenda.

Zengli concluded: "Understand that our successes will lay the foundation for more to come. You are not alone. There are other cells that have been formed, and they are training. And after Youseff and Waqqad leave, they will be working in places like Europe, Russia, and Mexico to add to the camps we have here in the U.S., and in Canada, Venezuela and Afghanistan to gain more such warriors for Allah. But we must succeed over the coming three days, and then with our next set of targets. It is my mission to make the West, the crusaders, the Americans, the Jews, all those against Allah, fear not just suicide bombers, as they call those who have made the great sacrifice, but to fear warriors, ghazis, who will show the ability to strike, over and over and over."

Chapter 37

Most of Chicago loved President Elizabeth Sanderski, or at least that's what the election results said nearly four years earlier. The latest polls were no different. Sanderski met with city officials and victims' families at the City Hall and Cook County Building. Afterward, as the presidential motorcade made its way to St. Anthony's Catholic Church on the South Side, crowds lined South Michigan Avenue to show appreciation for her coming to the city after the terrorist attack.

As she watched waving, but subdued people out the window of the limousine, Sanderski said, "Andy, we've got the right spot set up to speak to the press?"

He said, "Yes, Madam President."

She reached her hand out, and said, "Give me the talking points. I want to give them one last read through."

Chief of Staff Andy Russell pulled a sheet of paper out of his portfolio, and handed it to the president.

While reading, Sanderski nodded. "This is the right tone with that background. I'm going to put to rest this idea that I'm not tough enough." She would be speaking on the front steps of St. Anthony's on West 31st Street.

Several blocks away from the church, four vans were strategically parked in different directions. In one van, Dale Shore was in the front passenger seat next to Imad ad-Din Zengli, who was behind the wheel. Two more in

Shore's unit were in another vehicle, and the last two vans were manned by Mikel Rostoff's men. Each man wore a coat with a hood.

The fourth person in Shore's unit stood in the large crowd outside St. Anthony's, waiting for the arrival of President Sanderski.

In the back of each van, under a tarp, rested an advanced drone, equipped with the latest high-powered, low-sound technology, a high-def camera, and the ability to deliver a package of significant weight. The controller resting at the feet of the person in the passenger seat of each van was accompanied by a set of FPV goggles displaying the feed from the drone's camera. The aerial machines could be guided up to seven miles away.

After arriving at St. Anthony's, President Sanderski was escorted through parts of the bombed-out building with the mayor and the cardinal of the Chicago Archdiocese. Twenty minutes later, the group began to emerge from the building through the space once filled by a church door.

Shore's man in the crowd sent a text message: "Now."

The driver of each van sent back the appropriate response, while those in passenger seats reached back to pull off the tarps covering the drones.

The man in the crowd began moving away from the scene.

Sanderski shook hands with more people on the steps of the church, including the two sons – Randall and Jerry – of Jean Robinson, who had lost her life inside the church.

Each drone was started, and readied for launch. The drivers of the four vans hopped out of the vehicles, and swung open the back doors.

With goggles on, the operators flew the drones out of the back of each van and up into the air. The ascent of each drone was unaffected by the identical packages being carried, consisting of C4 explosives and a detonator.

The back doors of the vans were slammed shut, and as people on the sidewalks stopped to watch the drones rise into the air, the drivers were back behind their respective steering wheels. They slipped the vans into gear, and began to drive away – in the opposite direction from St. Anthony's.

President Sanderski stepped up to the microphones on the sidewalk in front of the church. Behind her was a blown out stained glass window, a cracked wall, and the arched entrance without a door.

Each drone operator flew his machine above the streets on the South Side, parallel to the top floors of many of the buildings along the way.

Before a large number of reporters, and the crowd that stretched across and down the street, Sanderski began, "My fellow Americans, coming here to Chicago, seeing this first hand and meeting with the victims' families, it all breaks my heart, but it also hardens my resolve..."

Flying over West 31st Street, one drone approached from the west and a second from the east. Secret Service members spotted the approaching vehicles, and shouted and radioed warnings.

Other Secret Service moved in to cover the president, and get her moving to the armored limousine.

Screams, and people pushing and trampling each other trying to escape, spread like waves across the crowd.

Bullets from Secret Service weapons flew into the air and the two approaching drones were hit, and began to falter. As part of Zengli's plan, if the drones were going to fall short of the president, then the operators should steer the machines into the crowd and detonate the C4.

One could imagine that after hitting the two incoming targets, a small measure of relief might have been given birth among the Secret Service. If so, it was cut short.

From the north, on the side street running along the west side of the church, and from the south, on the road running just to the east of St. Anthony's, emerged two more drones.

Bullets again ascended. Meanwhile, the original two damaged drones crashed into fleeing innocents, with the explosions killing dozens. The four Secret Service agents moving and partially carrying President Sanderski were within five yards of the limousine.

But the drones acted like the keenest of hunters, as if they were alive and completely focused on acquiring their prey. The machines descended toward the group of five people. A Secret Service agent's hand reached out for the limousine door. Another agent fired into the air, trying to fend off the death looming from above. The aerial hunters would not be denied. The two packages nearly detonated at the same moment.

The ring of Secret Service agents was annihilated – as was President Elizabeth Sanderski. Chief of Staff Andy Russell just a few yards behind was blown to pieces.

Dale Shore controlled one of the drones that had successfully reached the president. With eyes covered by the bulky set of goggles, he pumped his fist forward, as if he were merely playing a video game. The results were immediately shared among the four vans and the spotter. Communications, as planned, then promptly went dark.

The spotter stayed quiet riding on a public bus. The vans sped out of and away from Chicago – two going in opposite directions on I-90, another on I-290, and the third on I-55 – each pair of drivers and drone operators celebrated.

Zengli had not smiled and laughed like this in years. He said, "Dale, we did it! We have done what others could only dream of accomplishing. The Americans and all of the West will have no idea what to do. They will be lost in their sorrow, and we will not stop."

Shore replied, "Allah be praised!"

Each van moved along at the general pace of traffic on the interstates, and eventually exited the highways to take advantage of moving on local roads.

Meanwhile, with significant alterations to their respective appearances, Youseff Sarwar and Waqqad Rais had managed to slip through the U.S. security nets at two separate Midwest airports, and were now safely on their way to different locales in South America.

The day went exactly according to Zengli's plan.

Chapter 38

Pastors Richard Leonard and Stephen Grant left the cemetery after committing to the earth the body of a St. Mark's parishioner killed on the previous Sunday. With Leonard driving, the two men sat in silence. Neither turned his phone back on, and the radio was left off. Grant was trying to calm his mind and emotions. He assumed that his friend was doing the same.

Leonard turned his car into the small driveway of St. Mark's parsonage. As they got out, Grant turned on his phone. The plan was to eat lunch, return any phone calls, and perhaps even get a little rest before the two men split up, each heading to different viewings for other victims.

As Leonard unlocked the front door, Grant stopped at the bottom of the stairs. It seemed that every alert tied to his phone was buzzing, clicking or rumbling. Within the last 15 minutes, there were several news alerts, three phone messages, and six texts. He assumed the news drove the communications, so he went to the headlines first.

"Dear God..."

Leonard had the door open, and turned to look at Grant. "What is it?"

Grant looked up. "The president has been assassinated."

Leonard didn't respond with words. Instead, his face and entire body sagged.

As Grant climbed the front steps, he began to read details from the small screen. They moved into the living room. Grant continued reading, until Leonard turned on the television.

Grant lowered himself onto the edge of a chair. Leonard remained standing. Each stared at the screen, and listened to what was being reported. After the attacks just five days earlier, Grant was struggling to absorb this additional evil. Harried television reporters offered ugly details.

"President Sanderski and several Secret Service agents have been killed in the massive explosions..."

"Chicago's Mayor Woodbury also lost his life, as did Cardinal Williams."

"There's no way of knowing at this point, but it appears that dozens or perhaps hundreds of people have been murdered."

"The White House chief of staff also has perished."

"We do not have any reports on who was behind this, but early witnesses have said that this appeared to be some kind of aerial attack. Several have mentioned seeing drones..."

Grant called Jennifer.
"Stephen. It's just awful."
"I know. Richard and I got back from the cemetery a few minutes ago. We just heard coming in the door. Where are you?"
"I'm home. I have the television on in the office."
Stephen suddenly felt even more uncomfortable not being home, or at least nearby at St. Mary's. "I'm

processing all of this. We're each scheduled to get to funeral homes by mid-afternoon."

He got up and walked into another room for privacy. "Jen, this is crazy. I should be with you and St. Mary's."

"That would be ideal, of course. But this is anything but ideal. You know that better than the rest of us."

Stephen understood. While assuming that amidst the wakes and funerals he would stay one or two nights at the St. Mark's parsonage with Leonard, he wound up finding excuses to make the long drive back home to Jennifer late on the previous two nights. In order to get some extra rest, Stephen and Jennifer agreed earlier this morning that he would remain at St. Mark's tonight, while she stayed at the home of Joan and George Kraus. Though also members of St. Mary's, Joan and George were more than friends of the Grants. Jennifer and Joan were as close as the closest sisters. Stephen was planning to drive down to southern New Jersey on Saturday for the funeral of Freddie Pederson. He now decided, once again, to head home for the night.

As their conversation was about to end, Stephen said, "I'm coming home tonight."

Jennifer offered no protest. "I'm glad. I love you."

"Love you, too."

Grant came back in the living room after the call, and Leonard was now sitting on the couch. Grant reclaimed his chair.

They listened as more bits of information emerged about what happened and the damage wrought.

Grant finally said, "This is war. No one should think otherwise."

"Agreed."

"The question is: How deep does this run and how far does it reach? This clearly is not about some lucky terrorists getting all the breaks. This all ranks as a substantial planning effort, and incredible execution. First, they took out soft targets, and made a statement about Christians in America being vulnerable. Now, it's an attack at the other end of the spectrum. They have taken out the most powerful person on the planet, and from what we're hearing, this attack doesn't appear to be about suicide bombers. And have they escaped? Have these bastards really killed the president, and gotten away?"

Leonard was silent for several seconds, and then said, "This is a new stage of Islamic terrorism for us. But it's not new in terms of history and other parts of the world."

Grant knew this quite well, and nodded in response. "And remember what was said on the Jihad in America video that took credit for the church attacks. That person made specific threats, against political leaders, places of worship, the media, referencing Jewish people in the media, what he sees as apostate Muslims, and – it almost snuck by me – even homes. What if this wasn't a haphazard list of enemies, but something along the lines of a checklist?"

Leonard replied, "Would they actually provide a specific target list?"

"Arrogance. People like that are prone to it. Doesn't history teach that?"

"True."

"They provide enough information to taunt their opponents, but not enough so that anyone can stop them. Or at least, that's what they believe. And in this case, if this is a checklist, it just might be vague enough to offer no real help in stopping them."

The final tally of the dead in the Chicago terrorist drone attack eventually would be President Elizabeth Sanderski, Andy Russell, seven Secret Service agents, four White House staff, the Chicago mayor and two aides, the cardinal of the Chicago Archdiocese, and another 82 people on hand – 99 souls in all.

Chapter 39

At his desk in the vice president's West Wing office, Adam Links had his dark blue suit jacket off and draped over the back of his chair. Links was combing through reports from the FBI and CIA regarding the terror attacks early in the week.

After a sharp knock on the door at the other end of the room, no one waited for a reply. Three Secret Service agents and Links' chief of staff burst through the door, and moved toward his desk.

Links stood up. "What is it?"

His chief of staff answered, "Mr. Vice President, it's ... I..."

"Out with it."

"The president. She's been killed, assassinated."

Links took a step back, and then moved forward, placing his right hand on the desk in front of him.

The lead agent declared, "Mr. Vice President, we need to get you into the emergency bunker, sir."

Links did not seem to hear the agent. "I need to know what exactly has happened." He turned to his top aide, who quickly filled his boss in on everything known to that point.

Links whispered, "Son of a bitch," and shook his head.

The Secret Service agent interrupted, "Sir, you need to come with us."

Links looked at the man, and said, "Not going to happen. And I don't want to hear anything else about it."

His aide interjected, "Okay, sir, I'll get the Attorney General and the others in here."

Links nodded, then moved across the room, and stepped outside his office. He moved among weeping and shocked White House staff. Links looked at each person that he passed, extending a hand of support on an arm, shoulder or back.

As he proceeded, two Secret Service agents were glued to him.

As the chief of staff returned, Links asked, "What's next?"

"They're waiting back in your office."

Links was met by the Attorney General of the United States, along with other key administration officials who happened to be in the White House on this Friday. A White House photographer was in the mix as well. The AG wore a distraught look, and held a Bible in her hands. She said, "Dear God, Adam, can you believe this?"

"No, Julie, I can't." His narrow eyes appeared much wider than normal, and his thick eyebrows also were more active than was typical.

She glanced down at the Bible, and then asked, "Are you, well, ready?"

His chief of staff grabbed Links' jacket off the chair, and handed it to him. Links thanked him, and slipped it on his wiry, five-foot-ten-inch frame. His light brown hair was touched with a few gray streaks, and he ran a hand through it while taking a deep breath. Links looked the AG directly in her eyes, and said, "Yes, I am." He then added, "But first, we need to remember our fallen leader, President Elizabeth Sanderski, and the others who have died today. We will never forget that they have made the ultimate sacrifice for this nation, for the people of our country, and we must pledge that we will not falter in our own efforts to protect, to serve, and to dispense justice." His voice broke, but then he recovered. "Let's bow our heads in a moment of silence."

The room fell quiet.

After nearly a minute, Links said, "Thank you, and God bless each of you as we face this challenge and whatever might follow." He looked deeper into the room, and his eyes stopped on the Secretary of State. Throughout the Sanderski administration, the two had disagreed on most foreign policy issues. Links said, "Mr. Secretary, would you mind holding the Bible?"

The Secretary of State clearly was surprised at first, but then gave an appreciative look, and replied, "Of course, sir, I would be honored."

After Links was sworn in, he somberly shook the hand of the Attorney General and then the Secretary of State, who said, "I'm not sure exactly what to say under the circumstances, but you have our support, Mr. President."

"Thank you. I'm counting on each one of you, to say the least."

President Adam Links then said, "Okay, where do we stand on all fronts?"

His chief of staff said, "I think we do need to get to the Situation Room now, sir, so we can stay on top of the latest information."

Links said, "Fine." He led the way, followed by a string of cabinet members.

Upon entering the main conference room, Links hesitated, but then took the chair at the head of the long table. "Please, sit down." Everyone else took a seat.

Links listened to the latest details coming in from the scene of the attack, and the report on the transportation system, namely, that, as protocol called for, airports and trains were being shut down, and that state and local police, along with the FBI, had closed off most of the highway system radiating out from Chicago. The CIA and NSA were searching for international ties.

Links eventually concluded the meeting by declaring, "Make no mistake, people, we're at war, and we will wage it in full, wherever it may lead. We will make the resolve, strength and force of the United States of America very clear to all responsible for these heinous acts. And I plan to communicate this forthrightly to the American people when I address them."

Chapter 40

According to plan, each van was abandoned at remote locations well off the interstates, with other cars waiting. The vans eventually might have been identified by cameras in Chicago, but there were no cameras to capture the switching of vehicles.

With two of the terrorists in each, the four cars would journey through the afternoon and into the night primarily on back roads, eventually arriving at safe houses. One was an apartment in Grand Rapids, Michigan; the second, a small house outside Madison, Wisconsin; the third, another small home just south of Springfield, Illinois; and the last was a farm outside of Fort Wayne, Indiana.

The farm would host Dale Shore and Imad ad-Din Zengli.

Shore was behind the wheel of the silver midsize sedan. Next to him, Zengli glanced at his watch. "Just about time."

He withdrew a smart phone from his jacket pocket, and powered up the device. He would be looking for text messages from six sources – the other three pairings involved with the killing of President Sanderski, the spotter, and the two other teams with different assignments.

If things basically were going as planned, each message would say, "All is well," and Zengli's response would be

"Good." If anything had gone astray, specific messages were assigned to signal how far off target matters had gotten, and Zengli would respond to each accordingly.

As he waited, Zengli stared out the passenger window at the flat terrain populated by patches of white snow, dirt, dead crops, farmhouses, barns and silos.

The phone pinged, but he continued to just look out the window.

Another ping, and Shore glanced over. Zengli continued to stare.

In quick succession came four more pings.

Zengli smiled, and looked over at Shore. "I believe we have pleased Allah, my friend." He looked at the texts, and his smile grew wider. "Indeed, we have."

Chapter 41

With her back to an expansive view of Washington, D.C., Paige Caldwell stood facing the long table in the firm's conference room. Charlie Driessen was the last person to enter the room. He sat and leaned back in a chair at one end of the table. Seated across from Caldwell were CDM's four employees – Jessica West, Phil Lucena, Chase Axelrod and Lis Dicce. A speaker in the middle of the table brought the voice of Sean McEnany from Long Island.

Caldwell said, "Okay, we just went from the highest alert level to something I, quite frankly, don't really know how to describe." She paused for a couple of seconds, took a deep breath, and continued, "I'm not sure what each of you is thinking. But my guess is that, like me, you're pissed and frustrated, with other emotions rolling in and out like the tide."

Dicce and Lucena responded with nods. The always cool Axelrod offered no visible reaction.

Caldwell looked at West, whose response was silent but clear. Clenched teeth combined with a tight fist turning her right-hand knuckles white. For West, taking on Islamic terrorists was deeply personal. It verged on a self-imposed calling. In fact, this striking woman – slim, six-feet tall, blue eyes and long blond hair – left a promising career at the FBI because Caldwell said she'd have greater likelihood and freedom to directly engage Islamic terrorists with CDM. West had suffered deep losses at the hands of such extremists. Her father was killed in Afghanistan, and a few years later, her brother perished in Iraq. Both were Marines. But there was more. Her fiancé, a fellow FBI special agent, died in a terrorist attack in New York during the pope's visit. She once explained to the FBI's Trent Nguyen why she left the Bureau by declaring, "It's simple, Trent. I want to kill Islamic terrorists, as many as I possibly can, before they murder more innocents. That wasn't going to happen with the FBI."

Caldwell continued, "The anger and emotion is expected. But I also know that we can count on each other to get the job done."

West leaned forward, and asked, "And what is that job?"

Caldwell said, "Sean, tell everyone what you found."

McEnany began, "We all know the link Terif Pasha has to this mess, and his role as a funder. The CIA's trail on him has gone cold, and the regime in Egypt is not playing nice. The current Egyptian president had no use for Sanderski, and from what I've heard, is keeping his powder dry on Links. In recent years, trust has been hard to come by given the U.S. stepping back from the region. But there's a group that I have worked with in the past that is traditionally pro-Western and quietly works behind the scenes. It's rather formidable. They've managed to get their own people inserted in a variety of groups, including with Islamists, the military, key businesses, and even the Christian minority. They keep eyes on all of the big players, and fortunately, that includes Pasha. So, yes, we know where he is."

Axelrod said, "Good, so what's the plan?" McEnany had brought Axelrod into CDM from CorpSecQuest, the private security firm with CIA roots. The two men had similar personalities, namely, quiet and no-nonsense. Caldwell and Driessen had been immediately impressed with Axelrod, a six-foot-three-inch black man who grew up in a tough area of Detroit. He went on to become a star tight end with a 4.0 grade point average in college, and then earned a master's degree in foreign languages from N.C. State. He mastered seven languages. In addition to English, Axelrod spoke Mandarin, German, French, Russian, Spanish and Japanese.

Caldwell answered, "Sean and I just spoke with Aaron Rixey and Tank Hoard at the Agency. They understand that there's no time for diplomatic bullshit. But they don't want any official U.S. personnel on the ground in Egypt without permission. So, they want us to grab Pasha."

"It's not like we haven't done this type of thing before. I like it," inserted West.

"Yes, well, I told them we would do it, and we hammered out some of the very basics of a plan with them over the phone."

"Great. When do we leave?" asked West.

"Not so fast. They have to get the okay from our new president."

Driessen declared, "Links was one of us, and he's not a pussy like Sanderski was." All heads turned in his direction. He stopped and added, "Oh, sorry. God rest her soul."

Caldwell ignored Driessen's comment, and said, "So, while we await the green light, Sean and I will explain what was outlined with Rixey and Hoard. Then we'll detail what's needed in terms of equipment and so on, beef up the plan, and lay out assorted scenarios. And at some point soon, we'll need Charlie and Lis to get to the airport early to get the Gulfstream ready."

Lis Dicce normally stood out in the group. She not only had a unique look, featuring large, penetrating brown eyes, a small nose, and thin lips, along with blond streaks in short brown hair, but she also was unwilling or unable to remain silent for very long. She had worked with Caldwell at the CIA, and it had taken Paige a long time to adjust to Lis's near-constant talking. But Caldwell learned that Dicce knew her stuff, including on national security matters as well as weapon systems. Since joining CDM, she'd also earned her pilot's license, and mastered all aspects of CDM's Gulfstream G650. However, she was unusually silent so far on this day.

Caldwell said, "Lis, anything to add?"

Dicce merely shook her head.

Caldwell's gaze remained on Dicce. "We'll need your insights on Egypt."

Dicce seemed to get more focused. She responded, "Right, yes, of course, Paige."

Caldwell looked around the table, and said, "Okay, we'll obviously have plenty of time on the plane to review everything. As we all know, it'll be a long flight."

Illustrating his unflagging politeness, Phil Lucena raised his hand into the air slightly, signaling that he wanted to say something. His courteousness and appearance – a stocky five feet six inches, neatly cut brown hair and a face that looked very young, especially since losing a beard – belied a skill set honed while at the CIA that included expertise and ruthlessness in close combat. "Once we get the details on this plan, I'll make sure we're equipped appropriately. If that makes sense?"

Caldwell said, "Thanks, Phil, I'm counting on that."

As Driessen took over the discussion, Caldwell's smart phone buzzed, signaling the arrival of a text message. She pulled it up. It was from Stephen Grant: "The Jihad in America crackpot in the video made threats against political leaders, places of worship, the media, in particular Jews in the media, apostate Muslims, and homes. Haphazard list of their enemies, or an actual checklist? Just a thought."

She texted back: "See your point. Sanderski and churches would check two items off this list. Will mention this thought to my group. Thanks."

Chapter 42

Nearly two hours later, the CDM team dispersed to take care of various tasks and ready themselves personally for the mission that was still awaiting final approval.

In her office, as Caldwell double checked the contents of her "go" bag, the phone on her desk rang. She answered, "Caldwell."

"Paige." The man on the other end of the call hesitated, and then continued, "Paige, how are you?"

It was rare when Paige Caldwell was caught off guard, but this was clearly the case. She gradually lowered herself into the desk chair. "Adam? ... I mean, um, Mr. President."

"I think we can stick with 'Adam' when it's just us."

"Oh, okay, is it just us? I'm so sorry about President Sanderski. How are you?"

"I'm not really sure. But there's no choice. It's time to step up for the country."

"That's the Adam Links I knew and..." Her voice trailed off. She cleared her throat, and added, "How can I help?"

"Thanks for asking. Well, there are two things, and as you know, I don't like to rush things that shouldn't be rushed, but as you can imagine, things are moving fast."

"Right, I understand."

"First, you have a green light on this mission. And you know the situation if anything gets messy."

"Yes, I know how this works."

"But there's no one else I'd want running this. I know your team will get it done."

"Thanks, Adam."

"As for the second issue, I would really like more time to talk with you on this, but suddenly, I'm president of the United States."

He paused, and Caldwell said, "Yes, I know. The world knows."

He managed a chuckle. "That's the point, and I don't have – to put this in purely clinical terms – any kind of support system."

Caldwell laughed at that. "Only you would put it in those terms."

"See, you understand. Paige, I need someone I can trust – to bounce ideas off, to garner advice, to just talk."

"Adam, I..."

"Wait, please let me finish. Those years we were together at the CIA, I learned that there was no one else I could trust more than you with anything I said or did. You never said anything after I ... well ... moved on into politics. And you never even contacted me when you had to move on from the Agency. By the way, I am sorry about that, and that we never talked about it."

"No need for apologies. It turned out that I was meant for the job I have now."

"That's the impression I've gotten. Listen, I know this is sudden, to say the least. But I'm not asking you to give up anything. There are times, though, when politics can make the world of espionage almost seem tame. I know that you would hold nothing back, and would be completely honest. There is no one else I can trust without hesitation. You're the only person. I just need someone that I can be completely forthright with, knowing that I'll receive the same in exchange."

"Adam, I said I would help however I could, and I meant it."

"Thanks. I appreciate it. But this is more than just 'help.' If you're open at least to some reconnection, we can talk more about this when there's a bit more time?"

Apparently becoming more confident and comfortable during the conversation with a man she'd had a relationship with while at the CIA and had not spoken to in years, and who now, incredibly, had just become leader of the free world, Caldwell smiled. "Is this going to involve any late-night booty calls at the White House? Because I'm not quite sure I'm into that sort of thing. Although, maybe I am."

"Ah, now there's the Paige I know. But to start off on a forthright, honest note, I have never regretted the choice I made to enter politics. But what I have regretted nearly every day for some 15 years is how we ended things."

Her voice once again lost some of its comfortable confidence. "Adam, I don't know what to say." She stood up, and began walking around her desk while rubbing her forehead.

"Nothing needed right now. And on a completely different note, I'm about to call Wyatt Hamilton."

Caldwell said, "What? Oh, Hamilton. Isn't he likely to be your opponent in November, well, if you're running?"

"I want him to be my vice president."

"Really?"

"What do you think?"

She paused, and answered, "I think it would surprise just about everyone, but it could be the kind of step that helps to bring the nation together when needed most. I like it."

"Thanks, Paige. I have to go. Please take care, and may God be with you and your team. Good-bye."

"Good-bye, Adam."

The call ended, and Paige dropped back down into her chair. She stared at the phone, and said out loud to herself, "Holy shit. And thanks for dropping that on me, Mr.

President, as I head off to kidnap a terrorist businessman from Egypt."

Chapter 43

Wyatt Hamilton leaned back in his chair and rubbed his eyes. "My God, Ryan, who could have imagined all of this?"

Sitting across the desk in the governor's office from Hamilton, Ryan Thornton said, "I sure as hell didn't."

There was a knock at the door. Hamilton said, "Come in."

Alexandria Rappe entered and closed the door behind her.

Hamilton said, "Alex, pull up a chair. I was just going to ask Ryan if he wanted a drink. How about you? It's been a long day, to say the least."

She approached, and said, "The longest. Actually, Wyatt, I need to ask you something. My plan had been to go home for the weekend. My daughter was coming home from college for our traditional Super Bowl party."

"Is she still coming?"

"Yes, she doesn't have classes on Friday. She actually arrived home just as the news broke on President Sanderski."

Hamilton nodded. "Alex, head home. People need to be with family after this. All I ask is, if possible, can you be available via phone if I need to tap your expertise?"

"I appreciate that. Of course, you'll be able to reach me whenever you need to do so."

He glanced at his watch. It was almost 10:30 PM. "Are you actually driving back to Waterford now?"

"I am. It's about a five-hour drive. But the weather is okay, and I'm still charged up on the caffeine I've been pumping into me all day."

"Are you sure?"

"Yes. I'm going to get on the road in a few minutes. It will give me time to think about what's going on, and generate some ideas on what might lie ahead and our possible responses."

"Fair enough. No drink for you then."

She smiled. "Thanks again."

"If we don't talk over the weekend – as unlikely as that might seem right now – let's make sure we talk early Monday."

Rappe said her good-byes to Hamilton and Thornton. Wyatt then poured two glasses of bourbon, and handed one to Thornton.

"Thank you, G'vner."

They both took sips of the amber liquid.

Thornton said, "A Super Bowl party? Does she strike you as the Super Bowl party type?"

Hamilton replied, "Actually, yes. She's different from much of D.C., more down to earth."

Thornton nodded, and took another sip. "Think it was the right call to delay the Super Bowl?" The news had just been released that the game was being put off for a week.

"Normally, I'd say no. I hate the idea of these bastards changing what we do. But, given everything that's happened, I reluctantly agree."

The intercom on Hamilton's phone beeped. He hit it, and said, "Yes, Crystal?"

"Governor, the White House is on line one."

Hamilton sat up straighter.

Thornton whispered, "Aw, shit."

Hamilton replied, "Alright, Crystal, I'll obviously take it." He picked up the receiver and hit the "Line 1" button. "Hello, this is Governor Hamilton."

A woman's voice on the other end said, "Thank you, Governor, I have the president of the United States for you."

Thornton quietly left the room. It was Hamilton alone, talking with President Adam Links.

Links said, "Hello, Wyatt, how are things going there?"

Hamilton and Links knew each other from their days in the U.S. Senate, having worked across the aisle on several issues, in particular, on national security and foreign affairs.

Hamilton offered his condolences on the death of President Sanderski and so many others. He added, "I know it must be bizarre, but I have faith that you will lead the nation appropriately in these dire times." Links thanked him, and Hamilton went on to bring Links up to speed on the latest happenings and reactions from West Virginia.

Links said, "Thanks for all you've done throughout this crisis, this mess, and how you have handled matters. I appreciate it, and I think the nation does as well. The last thing we need right now is ugly partisanship."

"I completely agree."

"Along those lines, I'm going to cut to the chase, and ask you something that will seem like it's coming out of nowhere. But I ask it with what's best for the nation in mind."

"Okay, what is it, Mr. President?"

"Wyatt, I would like you to take the job of vice president of the United States."

After a few seconds of silence, Hamilton managed to say, "Mr. President, I'm honored, truly honored. I'm not sure what to say."

Links managed a small chuckle, and said, "Yes, I would not have a clue how to respond either if a Republican president asked me to become his vice president. But let me quickly sum up my thinking in three points. First, this would bring the nation together. We might be able to roll back a bit of the cynicism that has engulfed too much of our politics, and give the people actual hope. Second, you and I view national security matters from a similar perspective, I think. Namely, that the U.S. must fulfill its unique role in the world, operating from a position of unparalleled strength, willing to take on and defeat every threat to our nation, including the current war with these terrorists. We need to be a global leader, and a light for freedom and security. And third, we all have our strengths and weaknesses, and I try to understand my own, as well as assessing those of my friends and opponents. I know that you have strengths on a variety of issues where I do not, such as on certain topics relating to the economy. If you came on board as the VP, it would help move the nation forward on those fronts."

Links stopped talking. Hamilton took a deep breath, and said, "Mr. President, thank you for all of that. And you were right, this certainly did come out of nowhere. I'm incredibly honored and humbled that you would make this offer, and I want to help the nation in whatever way is best. But I hope you're not looking for an answer at this exact moment?"

"No, of course not."

"I definitely have to think about this, talk with my family, and pray on it."

"I understand. Take the weekend, if you need it."

"That's more than generous, and of course, I will keep this quiet, talking with just my family and my top advisor."

"Good. Thank you, Wyatt. I need to go. You, your family and the people of West Virginia are in my thoughts and prayers."

"And you are in ours, Mr. President."

Hamilton hung up the phone, and sat motionless for several seconds before downing the bourbon left in the glass.

Chapter 44

It was just after midnight on Saturday morning when the wheels of the Gulfstream G650 lifted off the runway at Dulles. The full CDM team was on board.

In the cabin, Sean McEnany was prepping for the briefing that would get rolling about two hours into the nine-and-a-half-hour flight. Scattered in various seats were Chase Axelrod, Phil Lucena, Lis Dicce and Jessica West.

Paige Caldwell and Charlie Driessen manned the cockpit.

Caldwell said, "Charlie, I have something to tell you."

"Yeah?"

"Clearance for this mission came directly from the top."

"Meaning?"

"I got a call from our new president."

Driessen grunted. "From Links directly?"

"Yes."

"Interesting. Professional courtesy from a former colleague?"

Silence prevailed for another minute.

Paige said, "Something like that."

Charlie smiled ever so slightly.

Paige looked over at him, and asked, "What the hell are you smiling about?"

"Me? I wasn't smiling."

"You son of a bitch."

"What?"

"You know?"

He turned to his partner, and smiled broadly.

"Shit. You and who else?" asked Caldwell.

"Actually, I'm pretty sure I'm the only one who knew about you two getting horizontal refreshment at the Agency."

"How the hell did you find out? Adam and I didn't work directly together, and we took great pains to make sure no one could find out."

Driessen laughed, and said, "First, I'm not just anybody, and I'll never tell. Second, isn't calling him 'Adam' a little too familiar for the president of the United States?"

Paige shook her head, and said, "You're a pain in the ass."

"Sure I am."

"And you never said anything to me over the years?"

"Neither did you."

More silence was broken by Driessen. "So, what does this history between you two mean, if anything? Any more on the call than giving us a green light?"

Caldwell feigned outrage. "There was, but I'm not sure I'll tell you now."

"Oh, come on, you know I'll find out anyway."

Caldwell shot him a look, and then confessed, "He said that he had no one else to really trust, and wanted to know if I would be willing to act as a kind of sounding board for him, you know, discuss ideas, offer advice, or just talk."

"Hmmm. And?"

Paige shifted uncomfortably in her seat. "He said he wanted to, as he put it, 'reconnect.'"

"And what does that mean exactly?"

"I have no idea." She paused, and then added, "But he did say that he regretted how we ended it years ago."

"Well, holy shit, and all of this before a mission."

"Yeah, that was my reaction."

Driessen asked, "And do you regret how it ended, or that it ended?"

Caldwell didn't answer, and the two flew the plane on in silence.

Chapter 45

Early Saturday afternoon, Freddie Pederson's funeral was scheduled at a church at the southern end of New Jersey, not far off the New Jersey Turnpike and just north of the Delaware Memorial Bridge. Jennifer joined Stephen, and volunteered to drive to give her husband a little rest and down time. Free from traffic snares, the journey in Jennifer's Jeep Wrangler took just over three hours. The time on the road and alone with Jennifer made Stephen feel a bit rejuvenated. Temporarily escaping from the heavy cloud of death and terrorism, they talked about wide-ranging things, from a few upcoming movies they wanted to see to Jennifer's work on her book. Along the way, they were able to laugh, and listen to playlists on Stephen's iPhone – an eclectic mix including Brad Paisley, the Beach Boys, Kenny Chesney, Big Bad Voodoo Daddy, the Beatles, Sinatra, Keith Urban, Glenn Miller Orchestra, The Monkees, Justin Timberlake and Carrie Underwood.

The funeral was at 12:30, but they pulled off the Turnpike before 11:00.

Stephen asked, "How about something to eat?"

"Perfect, and there's a Cracker Barrel."

Since her childhood, Jennifer loved stopping at Cracker Barrel restaurants while on the road. Stephen said, "Well, that's settled."

Jennifer smiled, "Yes, it is."

They made their way through the country store and to the hostess, who showed them to a table under an assortment of old, local advertisements and photos, along with covers of "The Saturday Evening Post."

As they looked at the menu filled with comfort foods and home-style dishes, Jennifer said, "Isn't it amazing what triggers strong memories? Whenever we stop at a Cracker Barrel, I think about the summer drives my mom and I used to take between Las Vegas and St. Louis. Those were such fun, and we always managed to stop at least once each way at a Cracker Barrel."

Stephen smiled at her, and Jennifer asked, "What is it?"

"I love the fact that you tell me that almost every time we stop at a Cracker Barrel."

She returned a sheepish smile, and looked at the menu.

Stephen said, "Talk about memories."

Jennifer looked back up at him. "What?"

"Three of my SEAL brothers just walked into the room."

Jennifer turned to see the hostess seating three men at a table. "Members of your old team?"

Stephen nodded, "I told you that I would see a few today. But, it's been how many years?"

Jennifer said, "Go over, and then you can introduce me."

He smiled in return. "Thanks."

As Grant approached the table, Bobby O'Brien was the first to spot him. O'Brien's hair and mustache were split evenly between red and gray, but his many freckles gave him a youthful look. He said to the other two seated at the table, "Watch your language, guys, there's a priest coming at us. Oh, hell, no, it's just Stephen Grant."

O'Brien stood first, shook hands and then hugged Stephen. "Grant, man, how are you?"

"Good, Bobby, how are you?"

"All in all, not bad."

Miguel Ramos said, "Grant, why are you dressed up as a priest? Is this some weird thing that the Agency has you doing?"

Ramos and Grant also shook hands and hugged. Grant said, "Miguel, it's good to see you. And the hair dye looks completely natural." Ramos' black hair had not a trace of gray.

That generated laughs all around.

"Shit, am I allowed to tell a priest to f' off?"

"Well, you just told a Lutheran pastor to do so."

Finally, Isaiah Green dispensed with the handshake, and went right to a hug. "I like the look, Grant. God bless you, man."

Stephen always remembered Isaiah as being a deeply committed Christian, and that apparently had not changed. The strength and big smile of the tall black man had not changed much either. One difference was that his full head of hair and clean shave of a quarter century earlier had given way to a shaved scalp and a goatee.

"God bless you, too, Isaiah."

O'Brien interjected, "Tough news about Freddie. He came to your church?"

Stephen nodded. "Yes, I was at his side when he died."

Ramos observed, "The official story is crap. I assume his death ties in with the shit-fest of the past week."

Green glanced back at the table from which Grant had come, and asked, "Hey, is that your wife?"

Grant said, "Yes."

Green continued, "Bring her over. This table will work for five."

After a waitress brought over two more chairs and introductions were completed, everyone sat. While reviewing menus, the conversation largely focused on Jennifer – her being an economist, where she was from, and how she and Stephen got together. After the orders arrived – everyone settled on early lunches – the conversation turned to Freddie Pederson and the events of recent days.

Stephen tried to eat his country-fried steak, hash brown casserole, corn and coleslaw, while filling in and answering questions from his old friends. Jennifer listened while partaking in her chicken-fried chicken, dumplings, and country green beans.

Knowing that he could trust these three men with information not known by the public, he explained what he knew about the undercover work that Pederson had been doing, and that he lost his life trying to warn people about the terrorist attacks on the churches.

The three SEALs remained silent as Stephen spoke.

And then Stephen mentioned Richard Leonard.

O'Brien shook his head and said, "Yeah, Mike's kid. What's up with that? Any idea why his church was targeted?"

Stephen explained Richard's prominence as a historian, professor and speaker on matters relating to Islam and Christianity. He also noted his own work in helping and protecting Leonard.

Ramos observed, "The kid's a fighter, just like his old man."

Stephen again nodded in response.

The conversation turned back to what Ramos, O'Brien and Green were up to these days, including their respective families. O'Brien was living his post-Navy dream of operating his own hardware store. Both Ramos and Green retired after two decades in the Navy. Ramos now headed up security at a university, and Green similarly ran security at a private Christian high school.

The waitress came over, and asked, "Will that be all, folks?"

"Yes, thanks" was the general response from around the table.

While waiting for the check, Green asked, "What about your church, Stephen? With you helping out Richard Leonard, is someone keeping an eye on your place? You know, if these terrorists get a whiff of why Pederson went to St. Mary's or of your own background? I know it's an outside shot, but as the SEALs taught each of us, best to be prepared for any scenario."

Stephen glanced at Jennifer, and then he answered, "Believe me, I've been thinking about that. I actually have a member of my congregation who has been keeping an eye on things. And he's well-equipped to do so. But let's just say that he was pulled away to other work after the assassination of President Sanderski yesterday."

Stephen's fellow SEALs looked at each other.

The check arrived, and Stephen proved quickest in grabbing it. After protests, he prevailed, and then looked at his watch. "It's just about time to head over to the church."

Green said, "Right, but before we go, let me toss out an idea."

Chapter 46

On this cold early Saturday afternoon, Anwar Abdullah sat at a desk in his home office just off the kitchen. He was sorting through mail and bills for both the household and the mosque. He lingered over a few letters that had arrived in support and in opposition to what he had said during his televised interview with Madison Tanquerey, along with quotes in a few follow-up newspaper and online articles.

His wife, Daria, remained in bed upstairs, nursing the flu.

Parked in the street in a silver sedan, just a few houses away, were two FBI agents. Anwar Abdullah earned an FBI detail after the Bureau decided he was a potential target given the media interviews. But there was an additional concern. While in Iraq years before, Anwar and Daria helped U.S. troops in tracking down terrorists. The couple eventually left the country with the help of U.S. authorities, and the work they had done in Iraq was known by very few in the U.S. government. As for who might have been aware in Iraq, however, that was an unknown.

In the car, FBI Special Agent John Smith said, "If you told me a week ago that we'd be pulled out of Omaha to wind up watching a house in Bridgeport, Connecticut, I would have said you were nuts."

"We go where needed," replied Special Agent Jane Johnson.

"Yeah, I know. But it's still weird."

Smith started to lift a cup of coffee toward his mouth when a black van turned onto the street, sped at the Abdullah home, and stopped on the sidewalk. Smith's cup stopped halfway to his mouth. "Shit."

Four men jumped out of the van, each with a semiautomatic rifle.

Smith opened his door and dropped the coffee on the ground. He and Johnson drew their weapons, and ran toward the home.

The assailants were led by Osbert Kusuma. Two ran around to the back entrance of the home. The third moved through the front door with Kusuma.

Anwar spotted two heads outside running by the window of his office. He yelled out, "Daria, it's happening!" The couple had prepared for something like this.

Anwar withdrew a handgun from the bottom drawer of his desk. He moved behind the open office door, and held his breath.

The first assailant, holding his rifle high for aiming purposes, turned into the office. When he took his second step, Anwar reached around with his gun and pulled the trigger. The bullet plunged into the terrorist's stomach, and the man staggered backwards against the wall. His rifle fell to the floor. Anwar moved around the door, grabbed the man by his jacket and pulled him forward. The terrorist's face was an inch away as Anwar squeezed off two more shots into the man's chest. Anwar pulled the terrorist even closer, hugging and supporting his body against his own, as the second assailant came forward. The terrorist managed to fire two shots into the body of his dead partner before Anwar took him down, with two of three shots finding their target.

After coming in the front door, Kusuma directed his partner to move forward on the main floor, while he took the stairs. He stopped at the top step, scanned the hallway and then moved forward. As the shooting began downstairs, he turned to look toward the stairs. With that mistake, Daria, dressed in pink cotton pajamas, darted into the hallway, and plunged a knife into the side of Kusuma's neck. She then pulled it around until hitting his spinal cord. Blood splattered in multiple directions, and Kusuma's body fell to the floor.

Agents Smith and Johnson never hesitated at the front door. The fourth assailant was moving toward the shots in the back of the house. Smith led the way, and didn't bother with any warning shouts. Both he and Johnson hit the back of the terrorist with several shots each.

Anwar came down the hallway. His shirt and pants were covered in the terrorist's blood. Smith nodded at him.

Descending the stairs, Daria called out, "Anwar? Anwar?"

Her pink pajamas also were soaked in the blood of one of their attackers. The two hugged.

Chapter 47

Terif Pasha owned six homes – three in Egypt, with the others in Saudi Arabia, Dubai and France. He also very quietly bought three additional homes as "gifts" to three women, none of whom was his wife. As a precaution, after the assassination of President Sanderski, he chose to lay low in the most secretive "gift" in the town of Luxor – on the Nile and more than 300 miles south of Cairo.

It was nearly midnight as Paige Caldwell and her CDM team moved in on the luxurious two-story home from different directions. On the river, Caldwell, Chase Axelrod, Jessica West and Phil Lucena approached in a rubber raiding craft with a specialized, silent-running motor.

Meanwhile, on land, a long, dark van turned onto the street with its lights off. Charlie Driessen stopped the vehicle a few houses from the one where Pasha rested in bed with the woman who had received this particular home as a gift. Sean McEnany and Lis Dicce slipped out and crouched next to the van – McEnany positioned to watch what was ahead, and Dicce what was behind.

Each team member was dressed in black combat attire, equipped with a tactical knife, a Glock with suppressor attached, and night vision goggles, along with an HK MP5 submachine gun and grenades, if things went completely sideways.

The home sat on a three-quarter acre lot. An eight-foot wall ran around three sides, interrupted by an iron gate on the street for the driveway. Security camera coverage also was comprehensive. However, no physical obstruction existed between the home and the Nile's waters. Ornamental foliage, fortunately, provided handy cover as the boat touched the shoreline.

Carrying a black suitcase, Axelrod stepped onto the muddy sand, and moved forward several steps. Caldwell, West and Lucena followed, while pulling the raft forward to hide it among the bushes. Axelrod placed the suitcase on the ground, and clicked it open. Inside was a bulky silver and gray rifle with a coil serving as the barrel. Axelrod quickly checked two read outs, and announced, "Good to go."

With everyone wired for sound, each team member heard the declaration.

Axelrod picked up the weapon, settled the stock into his shoulder, aimed, and pulled the trigger. If you were focused on the directional EMP rifle, it would appear as if nothing happened. But everything electronic in the home – from cell phones and landlines to security system cameras and vehicles parked in the garage – was disabled.

Caldwell announced, "Let's move, people."

She led Lucena, West, and Axelrod – carrying the EMP rifle now returned to its case – toward the back of the home.

At the same time, Driessen drove the van to the front of the house, pulling it inches from the wall. McEnany climbed onto the roof of the vehicle. Lying on his stomach, he had a clear view of the entire front of the home and front yard. He steadied his Glock using the top of the wall. If anyone looked to escape via the front, McEnany would stop their progress. Dicce remained on the ground, scanning for any possible hostiles arriving from outside the small compound.

With her Glock 20 in hand, Caldwell stopped at the sliding glass door on the back patio. She kept watch looking through the glass as West stepped forward, drawing out a glass cutter. West attached the suction cup to the glass door, moved the blade around in a circle, and then pulled back, which left a hole through which she could reach in and unlock the door.

Voices could be heard in the dark as Pasha's small security team tried to figure out what was happening. McEnany had been told not to expect any more than four people guarding Pasha.

Caldwell led the way into the building, followed by Lucena, Axelrod and West.

As she approached a nearby couch, Caldwell stopped as a head suddenly popped up from behind the pillows. She silently slipped the Glock in its holster and drew out her knife. She reached over the back of the couch, placing her gloved left hand over the man's mouth. Caldwell pulled him back, and drew the knife across his neck. She held him as blood and life drained from his body.

To Caldwell's right, Axelrod moved to one hallway, and to her left, Lucena moved ahead with West following.

Lucena and West came to the kitchen, from which the voices had been emanating. One guard was inside a pantry closet. He announced, "The flashlights do not work either."

The second guard replied, "How can that be? I don't like this. I am going to check around outside."

While reaching for a gun on the table, the guard was confronted by the dark figure of Phil Lucena, with his goggles glowing. If he had immediately grabbed the gun, the guard might have had a chance. But he hesitated ever so slightly, and that was more than enough for Lucena. As the guard lunged for the gun, Lucena already had the knife positioned perfectly. The guard's chest seemed to be drawn to the knife's point. Lucena easily guided the blade through clothing and flesh, past ribs and into the heart.

But the silence of the attack was broken by the sound of a gunshot coming from the guard emerging from the pantry. The bullet ripped across the skin encasing Lucena's left shoulder. He growled in pain. Two muffled shots followed from the gun of Jessica West. The projectiles entered the man's chest. He fell back into the pantry closet and to the floor.

Lucena pushed away the dead body of the first man, pulling his knife out as he did.

West flipped up the goggles, and arrived at his side. "Phil, where are you hit?"

Though gritted teeth, Lucena said, "Shit." He slammed his night vision goggles down on the table.

"Are you alright?"

"Fuck that hurts, but it only caught my shoulder." He looked at West, adding, "Sorry about that."

She eyed his shoulder, and asked, "Sorry for what?"

"The cursing."

Jessica West smiled at him, and said, "Phil, you were just shot, and you're apologizing for cursing in front of me?"

"I guess I am."

On the other side of the house, Axelrod reached the stairs to the second floor just as the shot that caught Lucena was heard,

"Lost the surprise." Axelrod sprinted up the stairs.

Caldwell announced into her microphone, "Chase, I'm on your six."

At the top of the stairs, Axelrod went right, so Caldwell turned left.

As Axelrod moved, a large, bearded man holding a handgun came out of the first bedroom door without looking. By the time the guard's eyes found Axelrod, Chase was pointing his Glock. Axelrod pulled the trigger, and the man's forward momentum was terminated. He was dead before hitting the floor.

Caldwell didn't find anything in the first room she came to, but as she approached the second, a woman's crying could be heard. With her Glock held out in front, Caldwell quickly moved into the doorway.

On the bed, Terif Pasha had the woman next to him by the hair with his left hand, and he pointed a gun at her with his right.

Caldwell said, "Terif Pasha."

He said, "I will kill her. You need to get out of here, or I will kill her."

Caldwell took a deep breath, and replied, "I'll save you the trouble." She squeezed off two shots into the woman's chest.

Pasha let go of the woman's hair, dropped the gun, and fell backwards. "What? What have you done? Are you insane?"

He moved a little farther away from his dead lover's body, and then tumbled backwards off the bed and onto the floor.

Caldwell flipped up her night vision goggles, and approached the hairy, fat man who only wore a pair of boxer shorts. "I'm insane, you terrorist piece of shit?" She grabbed pants and a white shirt from a chair, and threw them at Pasha. She ordered, "Get dressed, you fat pig."

Caldwell announced to her team, "I have Pasha. Status?"

The replies confirmed that the house was clear and secure, and that Lucena's injury was a grazing.

Over the next few minutes, the driveway gate was opened so the van could enter the small compound. Driessen pulled a portable generator from the back of the vehicle, and he and Dicce had it hooked up to the home within five minutes.

From the outside, everything appeared normal in the home that had just been seized. Inside, Lucena, with a patched-up shoulder, sat in the kitchen holding a gun on a bound Pasha. Driessen kept an eye on the front of the building from a second story window, while West did the same in the back. The rest of the team pulled the place apart for information.

At this point, the plan called for taking all relevant information and Pasha to the airfield, where their plane awaited the return trip. But that changed.

Axelrod was in the dining room looking through the contents of Pasha's briefcase. He called out, "Paige, can you come in here?"

As Caldwell entered, she asked, "What do you have?"

Axelrod said, "It looks like Mr. Pasha is due to have two new house guests in a few days. Look at his calendar book."

Caldwell glanced, and said, "French? Why is he writing his calendar items in French?"

Axelrod shrugged. "I assume so fewer people around him would be able to make sense of it if they got a look."

"Okay. You know French, not me."

"Well, he actually wrote down the following for Wednesday morning: 'Sarwar and Rais arriving at Taalea's. Discuss next steps on financing front.'"

Caldwell smiled, "Since this was Taalea's home, how nice of Mr. Pasha to let us know that Youseff Sarwar and Waqqad Rais are headed here. I hope the fridge is full. I think we'll likely be waiting for those two to show up."

Chapter 48

After the early Divine Service at St. Mary's Lutheran Church on Sunday morning, Pastor Zack Charmichael was shaking hands and chatting with people as they moved from the nave into the narthex.

Jennifer Grant approached, accompanied by two men, and made introductions. "Pastor Zack Charmichael, this is Miguel Ramos and Isaiah Green."

As they shook hands, Charmichael said, "Good to meet you. Thanks very much for your help."

Ramos said, "Not a problem."

Green added, "We're more than glad to help."

Charmichael asked, "Can we talk quickly in my office?"

Green nodded. "Of course, Pastor."

"Great. Just give me a few minutes."

Five minutes later, the four were seated around Charmichael's desk.

Charmichael said, "I spoke to Stephen last night, and I understand his concerns. It's extremely generous of you to take the time to help out here and at the Grants' home."

Jennifer said, "It's wonderful to have house guests, and with Stephen helping Richard at St. Mark's, I got to hear stories about my husband that he never saw fit to tell." She smiled.

Ramos grinned. "Oh, we've got more."

Charmichael added, "I'll take you guys to breakfast tomorrow to hear some of those stories."

Ramos replied, "Deal."

At the end of their Cracker Barrel meal the day before, Green had volunteered to come to eastern Long Island to keep an eye on Jennifer and St. Mary's. Ramos decided to join him, while Bobby O'Brien regretted that he would not be able to get away from his business, and had to immediately return home.

Green asked about the schedule for the next few days at St. Mary's, so he and Ramos could figure out how they would handle watching the church and making sure Jennifer was safe.

Jennifer said to the two former SEALs, "I can't tell you how much I appreciate what you're doing. At the same time, I have to admit to mixed feelings. I absolutely feel safer, but I also wonder if your taking this time is really necessary. I feel kind of awkward about it, like we're intruding on your lives."

Charmichael said, "I know exactly how you feel, Jennifer. I was thinking the same thing."

Ramos said, "No reason to feel awkward or uncomfortable about any of this. As SEALs, we were trained in a certain mindset. I don't think we ever really turn that off."

He glanced at Green, who shook his head. "No, we don't. In addition, our respective jobs allow for some flexibility in order to help."

Ramos continued, "Our nation is under attack, and if this is how we can help, and we're able to, then that's what we'll do. And then there's the fact that Stephen is a brother."

Green added, "And you're part of his family. Plus, terrorist attacks on churches take me to a whole new level of pissed off."

"Me, too," said Ramos.

Green said, "So, in a sense, I feel blessed to be able to help protect Stephen's church and family. And of course, the best-case scenario would be that our being here turns out to be unnecessary. But that doesn't mean that it wasn't the right course of action. Quite frankly, the news from Connecticut yesterday made clear the benefits of being prepared. Not only was the FBI ready, but the targets themselves were."

Ramos smiled, and said, "That apparently was one bad-ass couple in Iraq, and they obviously still are in Bridgeport, Connecticut."

*   *   *

Stephen Grant helped out as best he could with the Sunday services at St. Mark's exactly one week after terrorism and murder descended upon the church and its members. But realistically, there wasn't much he could do other than play a supporting role. This was Richard Leonard's congregation.

Leonard managed to carry the load. From the pulpit, he hit the right notes of Christ being with each congregant during these hellish times, and the need for the people in the pews, as members of the Church, to be there for each other and for the larger community.

And then there were the longer-than-usual lines of deeply hurting and angry people exiting the nave. Each person thanked Stephen, but the emotions flowed with their own pastor. Stephen was amazed at Richard's strength.

What possibly prepared him to sustain himself and these people? I see the strength of his father, but there's more. The Holy Spirit at work. Dear Lord, thank you for giving Richard the courage and grace to help each person here today, and for what he's done over this past week. Uplift him for the struggles that he yet faces in the days to come.

After the second Divine Service, it took an extra hour for true quiet and a bit of calm to settle on St. Mark's. With everyone else gone, Stephen sat in a creaky chair across Richard's small desk in the tight office. "You did a heck of a job this morning."

Richard merely shook his head. "I don't know about that."

"I do."

"We would have been lost without your help."

The two men laughed, with Stephen saying, "Mutual admiration society."

"Yeah, right, enough of that. And all we need to do is find a way to get through a viewing this afternoon, and then – what? – four more days of funerals, and that includes two-a-days tomorrow and Tuesday."

Oh, that's all!

Stephen said, "Okay, here's the plan. Let's go to the parsonage, and get cleaned up. We'll head over to the funeral parlor. At the latest, we'll be done by 5:30. I'll buy dinner."

Leonard's face brightened some. "Sounds good. Count me in."

Chapter 49

Even during the cold of winter, Alexandria and Blake Rappe were walkers. Unfortunately, they had to work at making time to do so, especially together. While Alex moved in Washington, D.C.'s policy circles, Blake also had carved out a notable career as a lawyer in the District. Such careers too often crowded out family time – unless one made a point of making such time.

While living in Waterford, Virginia, was not convenient relative to their offices in Washington, they long ago decided that a home in the historic village would provide a much-needed retreat from politics and the law. It turned out to be the ideal place to raise their daughter, Lilly.

When not travelling, Sunday truly served as their day of rest. The day usually consisted of early Mass, a big brunch, general laziness during much of the afternoon, an early-evening walk around town, a light dinner, and perhaps a movie on television.

This Sunday evening was supposed to be different with the Super Bowl. But that now changed, with the big game put off for a week while the nation dealt with the assassination of a president and the other terrorist attacks. Alex and Blake decided that a walk was needed. Their daughter had chosen to visit a few friends from high school who still lived nearby.

It was already dark, and Blake and Alex were dressed in layers against the cold wind that swept across the open fields beyond the homes before hitting Main Street. Blake, who stood a half-foot taller than Alex, held his wife's hand. They walked slowly and talked about what might lie ahead.

"So, what do you think?" she asked.

"Of course, I'm behind you 100 percent. Hamilton seems like a good man, and this is what you do. Correction. This is what you're meant to do. You've made a difference, and now, with everything that's happened, you're the right person to help make these decisions."

She stopped and looked up at her husband. "But?"

"But what?"

"For a lawyer, you're not very good at lying."

He grimaced at that.

Alex continued, "Sorry. But what is it?"

"If Hamilton wins, he's obviously going to make you secretary of state. He'd be an idiot if he didn't. That's what we're talking about here. And that makes you a target. That's the part I don't like."

They resumed walking. Alex finally said, "I know what you're saying..."

This time he stopped. "Hey, I'm just being honest about what worries me. That doesn't mean you should back off from this. And it doesn't mean that I don't want you to do this. As we said when we first got married, there's going to be a cost to every decision we make, even the ones that seem like there is no downside. Life will have its worries. But we've been so fortunate. The plusses have far outdistanced the negatives and the worries. I have no doubt that this will be the case when you become Secretary of State Alexandria Rappe."

He smiled, and she returned it.

Alex said, "Thanks."

They turned around, and took a few steps back toward their home.

The SUV turning onto the narrow street was at their backs.

Blake said, "I love you, Madam Secretary."

She laughed. "You, too, but I don't know about that secretary thing. Obviously, everything has changed. But Hamilton would be an excellent president. I believe in him, and want to help."

"I can see that he's a man of integrity."

As the vehicle's engine gunned, the two were slow to turn around. By the time they did, it was impossible to respond quickly enough so that both could avoid the consequences.

Blake pushed his wife away from the speeding SUV. The grill of the vehicle struck him head on, and sent his body flying into a high staircase of a home just a few feet off the street. His head struck the stone.

Alex was lying in the road, trying to regain her bearings.

The SUV stopped, and two men got out of the back seat.

One walked over, pointed a handgun with a suppressor attached, and fired a bullet into Blake Rappe's head, and two into his chest.

The other assailant approached Alexandria as she struggled to get to her knees.

She saw her husband's body in the distance, and her face began to contort. She screamed, "No!"

The second terrorist stopped several feet away from the kneeling Alex. Her tear-filled eyes turned and looked up at the man pointing a gun at her.

The assailant proclaimed, "Allahu Akbar."

Her face was transformed into anger and hatred. "Go to hell, you son of a..."

A shot from a different direction pierced the air, ripping into the skull of the terrorist standing in front of

Alexandria Rappe. Blood, flesh and bone splattered as the terrorist fell sideways to the gravel road.

Standing in front of his home was one of the Rappe's neighbors – Walt Sayers. The onetime Army colonel turned toward the other assailant. As they exchanged gunfire, the terrorist was retreating, walking backwards, getting closer to the SUV. At the same time, Sayers advanced.

A third terrorist opened the front passenger door. Sayers stopped. As two more shots zipped by, narrowly missing him, he further steadied his massive Desert Eagle .50 caliber semiautomatic. He fired two shots into the retreating terrorist, who fell to the ground. Sayers shifted his focus to the man emerging from the vehicle. As the terrorist's foot touched the ground, a bullet to the chest sent part of his body back into the SUV.

The driver was team leader Mikel Rostoff, and he apparently decided on a complete retreat.

As Sayers started running toward the vehicle, he slipped a new magazine into his gun. He was only a few yards from the SUV when it started to accelerate. Sayers whispered, "No way, you bastard. Not when you come into my neighborhood, my home."

Sayers stopped and aimed. The first shot shattered the back window of the SUV. And then he fired off six more.

The SUV swerved hard to the left, and crashed into a home that had been built in 1812. Part of the front wall fell onto the hood of the vehicle.

Sayers moved quickly. With his gun held in front of him, he approached the driver's side door. Sayers looked inside, and saw that two of his shots had found their target. Part of Rostoff's head was missing.

Sayers lowered the gun, and ran back to Alexandria Rappe, who was still kneeling in the same place in the road. He crouched down in front of her. "Alex, are you alright?"

She looked at him. "Walt?"

"Yes, are you okay? Have you been hurt?"

Her blank stare melted into one of pain and grief. "Oh, Walt, what have they done?"

She got up and ran over to her husband's body. She dropped down to her knees once again, next to him. She touched his cheek and his hair. "Oh, God, what did they do?"

Walt Sayers had witnessed the horrors of war during his 20 years in the Army. Nonetheless, his eyes teared up as he watched Alex slowly lower her head onto the bloody chest of her murdered husband.

Chapter 50

The news of what happened in Waterford, Virginia, naturally spread across the news, sweeping the nation and the globe. Imad ad-Din Zengli and Dale Shore watched on an old television set in the farmhouse just outside Fort Wayne, Indiana. Zengli's anger grew as one reporter, Madison Tanquerey, spoke about how eight terrorists were killed over two days now, in Connecticut on Saturday and in Virginia earlier on this Sunday. She asked, "Is this the turnaround that the entire nation longs for, as we still mourn the loss of so many, including, of course, President Elizabeth Sanderski? Let's hope so. But of course, we cannot forget that Blake Rappe lost his life today."

Zengli turned off the sound, and said, "I expect losses as we wage this holy war, but this should not have happened. Mikel and Osbert should have been better prepared, obviously. How could Osbert let that apostate Anwar Abdullah defeat him? Disgusting."

Shore replied, "I understand. But we also have to realize that this is a nationwide manhunt now. We just killed the U.S. president."

Zengli simply stared back at Shore in silence. After more than a minute, he asked, "And what would you suggest, Dale?"

"We just need to lay low for a while. Keep attention off, and then we can get back and execute the next steps in your plans."

"You advise caution?"

"For now."

Zengli got up from his chair, walked into the adjacent kitchen, and picked up his encrypted phone. Over his shoulder, he said, "I don't believe caution is called for."

He punched in a number, and when the expected voice answered, Zengli asked, "How are things there?"

"All goes well. In fact, I am pleased with the progress of several individuals."

"Good. Is the Durham team ready?"

"Absolutely. They've just been waiting for your go-ahead."

"Send them. Also, do you have two more teams that are ready for action?"

"Yes. I am confident in them."

"Excellent. Send one to the safe house in the Bronx, and the other to the one in Elizabeth, New Jersey."

"Tonight?"

"Yes, and take extra precautions."

"Of course."

Zengli ended the call, and turned back to look at Shore. "We must strike, and keep them reeling."

Chapter 51

"I have never been so unsure about a decision in my entire life." Governor Wyatt Hamilton slumped back in his chair in the Governor's Office in the State Capitol Building. "I'm not used to indecision."

Sitting in a chair across the desk, Ryan Thornton replied, "Yeah, I get it. But I still think you're makin' the right call, Wyatt."

"I hope so." He sat up straight, and indicated that Thornton should leave. After the door closed, Hamilton punched in the number for the White House. An operator answered, and Hamilton said, "Yes, this is Governor Hamilton calling for President Links."

Hamilton waited on hold for less than a minute, and then he heard President Links' voice. "Wyatt, how are you?"

"I'm well, Mr. President. And you?"

"Working. And to cut to the chase once more, have you decided to work with me?"

"Mr. President, I certainly look forward to working with you in this time of crisis. But, while I deeply appreciate your offer, what it took for you to make it and why you did so, I'm afraid that I cannot work with you as your vice president."

"Why not?" There was a clear sliver of frustration in Links' voice.

"I think you're right about the need for all of us to come together right now, and that includes Democrats and Republicans working against this common enemy."

"Well then?"

"But I don't think this moment calls for something along the lines of Republican Abraham Lincoln reaching out to Democrat Andrew Johnson to run as his VP in 1864."

"I'll ask again: Why not?"

"Believe me, this is the most difficult decision I've ever had to make. But it came down to two key reasons for me. First, this crisis stands far and above as the most pressing matter right now, and who knows for how long going forward. You and I agree that we are at war. But as history teaches, our nation is so strong that we still have free and competitive presidential elections during wartime. And I know we would still have such an election in November, but I think I have a responsibility, given my frontrunner status among the GOP candidates, at least for now, to continue in such an election. I think the nation would benefit from the two leading candidates on both sides of the political aisle agreeing on the need to wage this war. Second, while you and I probably agree on 95 percent of foreign affairs and national security issues, there are other important areas where we do, in fact, disagree, such as on the economy, budget items, and certain social issues, and those issues still very much matter. The nation deserves a full discussion on those important points as well."

Hamilton stopped talking, and waited for Links to reply.

After a few seconds, Links said, "I understand, Wyatt. And right now, I wish we didn't have those other disagreements. You're a good man, and I thank you for giving this full consideration."

"Rest assured, Mr. President, I have not really slept since you made this offer."

Links chuckled, and said, "Well, I am sorry about that."

Hamilton added, "Mr. President, I also pledge my full support on the matter of taking down these terrorists, and protecting our nation. And I will make that abundantly clear on the campaign trail, whenever we all get back to campaigning."

"Thank you, Wyatt. And perhaps you're right in that we can do more to bring the nation together by showing that we are able to stand together, unequivocally, even during a campaign, when the nation and our people are threatened."

"I hope so."

"Alright, I have to go find another vice president now. We'll keep you up to date as things develop with this manhunt."

Hamilton again thanked Links, and the call ended.

Hamilton placed his elbows on the desk, lowered his head and rubbed his temples. "Dear God, I hope that was the right decision."

Chapter 52

At St. Mark's Lutheran Church on Staten Island, Monday promised more pain and exhaustion. And the next three days would offer more of the same. This day and the next would be particularly challenging, as Pastors Richard Leonard, Stephen Grant and Brett Matthews faced two funerals a day – one each morning and a second each afternoon. The late funerals would be followed by burials. Some kind of reprieve could be seen after the coming Thursday. At least, that was the hope.

As the three men prepared for the first funeral on Monday morning, Leonard said, "Think about what we've been through losing 11 here at St. Mark's. Other than what happened in Texas, we suffered the smallest number of deaths compared to the other four churches."

Matthews replied, "It's all too strange. I spoke with Bishop Carolan in the Rockville Centre Diocese. He said dealing with 190 dead at St. Francis remains unfathomable, even as they are doing it. He has priests who are suffering deeply. They're forging ahead, but there's something other worldly or oddly distant."

Grant shook his head slightly. *I've got to talk to Ron today, and see how he is doing.* He added, "And there's the national mourning over the president. That's going to hit a crescendo with the state funeral on Wednesday."

They finished the preparations in silence, until they finally huddled together for a prayer. The three bowed their heads, and Matthews said, "Dear Lord, we would be unable to survive such trying times alone. We rely completely on You, and that is the only way we are able to carry on. It is only through Your suffering servant, His atoning sacrifice, and His resurrection that we can make sense of any of this. Your gifts of love, faith, redemption and salvation sustain us. We know that You are with us every step of the way, and that provides strength. As written in Psalm 23: 'Even though I walk through the valley of the shadow of death, I will fear no evil, for you are with me; your rod and your staff, they comfort me.' We pray this in the precious name of Jesus."

*   *   *

After the first funeral, the three pastors had about an hour-and-a-half free. They retreated to the St. Mark's parsonage.

Leonard went up the stairs to his bedroom, and sat on the edge of the bed. He pulled out his phone, and saw that Madison Tanquerey had left a message. Her message was simply a request for him to call back.

"Hi, Madison, it's Richard Leonard."

"Thanks so much for calling back. I can't imagine how busy and, well, exhausted you must be."

"Believe me, especially with everything going on, it was a pleasure to hear your voice."

"Well, thanks. It's good to talk with you, too."

A brief awkward silence was broken when Richard asked, "How can I help?"

"Oh, right. I wanted to see if I could pick your brain, again. I interviewed Anwar Abdullah, the imam in Connecticut who wound up taking down that terrorist group."

"Yes, I saw your interview, and what he and his wife did was amazing."

"It certainly was. I wanted to get your thoughts on what he had to say during the interview, specifically about Islam going through its own Reformation like Christianity had. Given your expertise, you were the natural person to go to in a follow-up."

"There's a lot to unpack there. From what I remember, I largely agreed with him when he spoke about the need for Islam to become compatible with modernity and to disavow beliefs that justify violence and forcing people into Islam. I think he's largely correct when he spoke about rejecting Muhammad's declarations and examples regarding warfare, and getting across that Muhammad was not infallible and that large parts of the Quran simply reflect seventh century views."

Tanquerey said, "Anwar said that was analogous to Jews and Christians writing off violent passages of their scriptures to the past, as well as undertakings like the Crusades and the Inquisition. He pushed the idea that Islam needed its own Martin Luther."

"This is where Mr. Abdullah and I would disagree."

Tanquerey smiled on the other end of the call, and said, "I thought so."

"You and I already spoke about the realities of the Crusades."

"Yes."

"So, that analogy does not really work. As for abuses and atrocities carried out by individuals during the Crusades, not to mention the Inquisition, which largely was carried out by the Spanish government, these can't be ignored or downplayed. But they must be understood as sinful acts by sinful human beings. Such actions directly contradicted what Jesus called for and did."

"Okay."

"As for a 'Martin Luther' for Islam, I would counter that, in a very real sense, Islam needs the exact opposite of a Luther."

"What does that mean?"

"Luther's point was to bring the Church back to God's Word. He wanted to correct where the Church had wandered away from, added to, or misinterpreted Holy Scripture. In a bizarre way, it seems to me that Muhammad presented himself as a kind of reformer in this sense. The Quran claims that Muhammad did not start a new religion, but instead, he was sent to reclaim the religion of Moses and Jesus that had been altered and corrupted by Jews and Christians. The Quran asserts that Allah sent Muhammad to tell the truth in the Quran."

"Interesting."

"It also should be understood that Luther, as he acquired more information about Islam, became more critical. He noted, for example, that while Christianity grew via miracles and preaching, Islam did so by the sword and murder. Luther also saw Islam as being invented by Muhammad, while the Gospel has been preached since the beginning of the world."

"So, why are some looking for a Luther for Islam?"

"Unfortunately, many don't really understand what Luther was doing. I would argue that Islam needs an anti-Luther. Martin Luther wanted to bring Christianity fully back to Holy Scripture, if you will. But in order to abide peacefully in the world, Islam needs the exact opposite of what Christianity needed."

"What does that mean?"

"Islam needs a mighty dose of liberal revisionism. It needs religious leaders that will pick and choose from the Quran, keeping what's peaceful and positive, while discarding the war, violence and gross intolerance."

"Are you arguing that Islamic beliefs need to be gutted?"

"That's not how I would put it, exactly."

"Hmmm," said Tanquerey, with a reporter's skepticism apparent.

"Madison, I actually would like to continue this conversation, but I have another funeral this afternoon."

"Of course, I'm sorry. But given this talk, I am the host of a roundtable discussion being taped very late on Tuesday afternoon in our studios in Manhattan. I would love to have you on as one of the panelists. Is that possible? I know what you're dealing with and that this is short notice, so I completely understand if you cannot.

Leonard hesitated briefly, and then said, "Sure, I would be glad to do so. Can you email me the details?"

"I most certainly will. Thanks."

"Okay, well, if we don't talk before then, I'll see you on Tuesday."

"Great, I appreciate this, and am looking forward to it. Good-bye, Richard."

"Take care, Madison."

Leonard ended the call, and offered up another rare smile during these tough days.

Chapter 53

After a day of two funerals and a burial, piled on top of terror attacks, other funerals, wakes, and viewings over the previous week-plus, Stephen Grant was relying on his long-ago training with the Navy SEALs and the Central Intelligence Agency to continue plowing forward.

I've got the background. How Richard has been doing it, I'm still marveling at him. Lord, continue to give him strength, and me as well, please.

After dinner with Richard and a talk with Jennifer on the phone, Stephen was hoping for a long, deep sleep in the guest room of St. Mark's parsonage. But his mind raced. He laid on his back staring up at the ceiling.

I wonder what Paige, Charlie and Sean are up to, given the assassination.

His phone rumbled on the nightstand. It was a blocked number. "Hello."

"Stephen, it's Paige."

After his time with the Navy SEALs, Stephen Grant served with the Central Intelligence Agency as an "analyst." However, he spent far less time at his desk in Langley, Virginia, than did co-workers in neighboring cubicles. Instead, Grant often moved internationally, utilizing skills that he acquired with the SEALs, along with other abilities mastered at the Agency itself.

During part of his CIA time, Grant's partner was Paige Caldwell. Their professional partnership rather quickly expanded into something far more intimate. That intense relationship did not exactly end well when Grant decided to leave the Agency for the seminary. It was a decision beyond Paige's willingness to understand or come to terms with, so they had not spoken for many years. More recently, though, the return of the CIA into Stephen's life had been handled, at least initially, by Paige. Her subsequent exit from the Agency did not put a stop to occasions where the two would be brought back together. That was fine with Stephen, and even his wife, Jennifer, as Stephen and Paige's old relationship evolved into a friendship – of the platonic variety. Indeed, even while moving in very different worlds, Stephen and Paige again came to rely upon each other in numerous ways. In fact, other than Jennifer, there probably was no one else that Stephen trusted more than Paige Caldwell. They had saved each other's lives over the years, and Paige also laid her life on the line for Jennifer and sacrificed for Stephen in ways unimaginable to most people. Stephen also hoped that while he still looked to Paige for occasional advice, he might serve as an example or, if asked, provide guidance for Paige in terms of her faith life. Unfortunately, that last part of their friendship had not yet developed, at least as far as Stephen could detect.

"Paige, I was just lying here in bed thinking about you."

Wow, that came out the wrong way.

"Stephen, I'm flattered and intrigued, but what would Jennifer say?"

Knew she wouldn't let that slide.

Given all that the two had been through, and the change in their relationship, Paige still possessed an ability to tease Stephen, and make him feel just a bit uncomfortable. And she clearly enjoyed doing so.

"That's not what I meant. I was thinking about what you, Charlie and Sean might exactly be doing in all of this."

"Oh, sure."

"Paige."

She laughed. "Well, I can't tell you where I am, or what we're up to, right now."

"Yeah, I get it."

"Where are you?"

"Staten Island."

"Still playing body guard with the pastor there?"

"More or less."

"While I'd love to catch up, unfortunately, I have to make this fast. But I need to give you a heads-up on two things."

"Yes?"

"You're using the encryption software that Sean passed along for your phone, right?"

"Of course."

"Okay, I need to officially but unofficially bring you into our team after the Sanderski assassination. Until these terrorists get cleaned up in the states, I need someone on the ground in the New York metro area in addition to Sean."

"Come on, how can Sean McEnany not be enough?"

"Hard to believe, but he'll tell you the same thing. I know you're going to say you're a pastor and not a gun for hire, or some such bullshit. But you know the realities and implications of the U.S. being under attack. You also know that, if needed, you can help. And that is an 'if.' I understand and will keep your realities in mind. Also, I will..."

Grant interrupted, "Fine."

"What?"

"You don't have to give me the sales pitch – at least not this time. I get it, and I'll help however I can."

"Okay. That was easier than I thought it would be. Now, the second item on my list is to let you in on something that happened years ago but suddenly has new implications."

Caldwell paused.

Grant prompted, "What?"

"A while after you left the Agency, I had a relationship with Adam Links."

Grant sat up in bed. "What? You and the president of the United States?"

Grant heard an unusual defensiveness in Paige's voice. "He wasn't president at the time."

"Wow. So, how long did this go on for?"

"About three years."

Same as us. Paige, you do have a pattern.

"Why are you telling me this now?"

"I have no idea how long this major engagement with terrorists on U.S. soil is going to last, and he has contacted me about giving him some behind-the-scenes advice, and to serve as a kind of sounding board."

"He must have a high level of trust in you, Paige."

"And I in you, Stephen, that you obviously will not say anything to anyone on this."

"You don't even have to ask. Well, except for Jennifer."

"I figured that. Thanks. Anyway, this relationship might bring in certain information, and I wanted you to know how sensitive it is."

"I get it."

"I also wanted you to know because I think I might be needing your advice."

"How so?"

"Let's just say I'm not sure that the relationship I had with Adam has ended completely. There are indications otherwise."

"From you or him?"

"To be honest, both of us."

"Paige, when you need to talk about this or anything, you know you can call me at any time."

"I appreciate it. And now I have to go. I'll be back in touch."

After they ended the call, Grant fell back onto the bed. *Paige Caldwell and President Links. Crazy. Wait until Jen hears about this in the morning.* The call with Paige led to more tossing and turning. About an hour later, the phone rumbled again. Once more, it was a blocked number.

"Hello?"

"Pastor Stephen Grant?"

"Yes, who is this?"

"Pastor Grant, this is Adam Links. I hope I didn't wake you."

Grant moved beyond sitting up in bed. Instead, he jumped to his feet. "Mr. President, sir, I actually was up. I'm having a tough time sleeping."

"I bet."

"To what do I owe this honor, Mr. President? What can I do?"

"I understand that you spoke with Paige Caldwell earlier."

"Yes, sir."

"I know that both of us rely on and care for her. I just wanted to thank you for agreeing to help her out. It must be unusual for a pastor, to say the least?"

"For me, given my background, that's a 'yes' and a 'no' in response."

"Yes, given that both of us spent parts of our careers at the CIA, I completely understand that. Stephen – may I call you 'Stephen'?"

"Of course, Mr. President."

"I obviously spoke with Paige tonight after you did. She made clear how much she trusts you, and since I trust her judgment, my own trust is extended to you. Think of it as the transitive property of trust."

Did he just make an algebra joke?

"Thank you, sir."

"Since my wife died many years ago, before my CIA days, I've been pretty closed off. People probably think that's pretty odd for a politician, but it's not, at least not at the level I'm talking about. I have failed to build up or reach out to a group of people whom I can completely trust. Paige really tops a very short list. I also know that Paige is not the person to turn to on certain matters. If I needed to, might I contact you on occasion, Stephen?"

"Of course, Mr. President. I'd be glad to help in any way."

Is this for real?

"Good. I'm not a Lutheran, by the way. I'm Catholic."

"Well, I won't hold that against you."

That garnered a small chuckle from Links.

Grant added, "I would be remiss in not mentioning that my wife, Jennifer, is an economist, and is periodically active in D.C., testifying and such."

"Jennifer Grant?"

"Yes, that's her."

"That's interesting. I did not know that she's your wife. We've crossed swords a few times on policy matters."

"No doubt."

"But I have enormous respect for her. She is a straight shooter."

"She is, and I know she respects you as well."

"Excuse me for asking, but wasn't she once married to Senator Brees?"

"Yes, she was."

"Between you and me, that guy is an asshole."

"He most certainly is, Mr. President."

"I like you, Stephen. You're my kind of clergy. Thank you, again, and try to get some sleep."

"Thank you, Mr. President."

Grant decided to pace the floor. *And the night just got a whole lot weirder. Okay, I think that call justifies waking up my wife.*

"Stephen, is everything alright?"

He could hear that she had been in a deep sleep. Stephen felt a twinge of guilt, but then realized that she would have been mad if he didn't call. "Sorry to wake you, but wait until you hear this."

.

Chapter 54

After managing to get roughly three hours of sleep, Grant checked the time on his phone. 5:17 AM.

More sleep is unlikely. Time for a morning run.

It was pitch dark outside, and he knew it would be bitter cold. *Just what I need to get charged up.*

After slipping on a pair of dark sweatpants, a t-shirt, a hoodie with a zip front, and a Cincinnati Bengals knit hat, with a rather wild pom-pom sitting atop, he stepped out the front door of St. Mark's parsonage. Fortunately, the crisp air was unusually still for early February. Grant stretched, and in a few minutes, was at full stride.

His plan was to do about three miles, with a path that would take him by the waterfront where the Staten Island Ferry terminal and a minor league ballpark sat.

When he reached the terminal area, Grant actually slowed and stopped. He stared across the waters of New York harbor at the Freedom Tower reaching into the sky, well above the surrounding skyscrapers. Viewing the building from a distance usually generated mixed feelings in Grant. He appreciated that after 9-11, another building eventually rose from the ashes of where the Twin Towers once stood. But that also was the source of lingering anger. There was a small part of him that still saw the Freedom Tower as out of place.

Those Twin Towers should still be there. And now we're under attack, on our own soil, again. On 9-11, the targets carried meaning in part because they were big physically – the World Trade Center, the Pentagon. The attacks now also carry weighty significance, obviously – killing the president of the United States. Duh, Grant. But also churches, the reform-minded imam, and the foreign policy expert outside her home in a small town. These are individualized, and carry meaning for many Americans – faith, the president and our government, and home. Goes back to the list idea from the Jihad in America video. He mentioned political leaders, places of worship, apostate Muslims, homes and the media. Anything else? Crap. Young people seeking safe spaces. Add to the list of meaningful things for Americans? Freedom of the press and – what? – education. I don't like this at all.

Grant's phone rumbled in the pocket of his jacket.

"Hello?"

"Stephen, it's Paige. I hope we didn't wake you."

We?

"No, actually, I'm out for a run."

"Can you stop for a few minutes? I've got Charlie and Sean here with me. Rich Noack and Tank also are on the line. We just wanted to go over a few things quickly now that you're on board."

Grant knew each person on the call well. "Good morning, everyone. Your timing is perfect. I want to talk to all of you about something. I mentioned this, just in passing in a text, to Paige a few days ago. But I increasingly believe that there's something to the idea that this Jihad in America leader has told us who his targets are, at least broadly speaking."

Chapter 55

"Sorry about this, Stephen."

Pastor Richard Leonard was apologizing for the fact that after two funerals and a just-completed burial on this Tuesday afternoon, the two were about to head into Manhattan. Leonard had agreed to be a panelist on a televised roundtable discussion being hosted by Madison Tanquerey. The taping was scheduled for 5:30.

"But you really don't need to come with me."

Grant replied, "Yes, actually I do, Richard."

Grant opened the front door, and stepped onto the porch, followed by Leonard.

In the driveway, two men in rumpled suits and trench coats stood leaning against a dark sedan. They looked like cops. And that's what they were.

Frank Godfrey said, "Detectives Godfrey and Baldwin at your service, pastors."

Leonard replied, "Frank, Mac, what are you doing here?"

"We're giving you a lift to your big TV gig," answered Godfrey.

"That's not necessary."

"Yeah, well, that's not what your buddy there thought." Baldwin nodded toward Grant.

Leonard looked at Grant. Stephen said, "I called Detective Baldwin earlier today, and they volunteered to drive us back and forth to the television studio."

Leonard asked, "Why?"

Grant replied, "Can't be too cautious."

Godfrey smiled, and added, "Besides, you'll never get to the studio on time without our ability to circumvent traffic." He pointed to the siren light sitting on the dashboard inside the car.

Leonard shook his head, and said, "Okay, I'm not going to argue." The two pastors got in the backseat.

In fact, Detective Baldwin made astounding time journeying from Staten Island to Columbus Circle. As the car pulled up in front of a towering glass building, Madison Tanquerey came around the corner of the neighboring building. Across the street, two men sat on benches in the middle of Columbus Circle, with fountains dormant in the February cold and at the base of a 70-foot column atop which stood a statue of Christopher Columbus. The two men rose to their feet.

"And there is the show's host," announced Leonard. He said to the two detectives, "Thanks so much for the lift. I appreciate it."

Godfrey nodded, and Baldwin said, "Hey, break a leg, Pastor."

As Leonard got out of the car, Grant simply said, "I'll let you know when he's finished. Thanks."

Again, Godfrey nodded, and Baldwin answered, "You got it."

Grant shut the door of the car, and followed Leonard, who was walking toward the approaching Tanquerey. That's when he felt the "red alert." Since his days with the SEALs and the CIA, Grant had this knack for knowing when trouble was at hand. He'd feel a tightness in his ears and head. The feeling came upon him now.

He'd failed to mention it to Leonard, but his Glock 20 was nestled in a holster in the small of his back, under both his dark gray overcoat and his black suit jacket.

Grant stepped up the pace to catch up to Leonard. While doing so, he scanned the people around them.

Madison Tanquerey spotted Leonard, and her face broke into a broad smile. Leonard returned the look.

Grant focused on a man behind Tanquerey in a rather nondescript, dark jacket and jeans. He kept his head down, with eyes focused on the ground. Then he looked up at Tanquerey, and back to the ground.

Grant maneuvered ever so slightly to get a better look. And then he saw the man pull something out of a pocket.

What the hell is it?

Grant passed Leonard.

"Stephen?" asked Leonard.

Grant ignored him.

The man was only a few yards from Tanquerey. And then he spotted it. *A syringe. Crap.*

As he bolted forward, Grant calculated that his gun would be a last resort with so many people behind the would-be assassin.

Tanquerey stopped dead in her tracks as she saw a man running at her in a clergy collar, long coat flying in the wind.

The man with the syringe looked up just as Grant shoved Tanquerey to the side. The terrorist froze for a second, looking even more perplexed than Tanquerey at the unique, approaching figure. Grant took advantage of the pause.

*   *   *

Leonard ran to Tanquerey, who was now on the ground.

However, approaching from behind Leonard was another assailant who had not yet removed a syringe from his pocket.

*   *   *

Grant grabbed the assailant's wrist, and as he began to work to point the syringe away from the two of them, Grant drove a fist into the man's side. But layers of clothing softened the blow.

The terrorist recovered his senses, and grabbed Grant's ear with his free hand.

As they struggled, Grant heard a nearby scream, and then Leonard yelling, "No!"

Enough.

Grant moved his right leg, swept it behind his opponent, and used his body and both arms to drive the attacker downward. As they fell, the terrorist lost control of the situation, while Grant expanded his control. He moved his right hand to the assailant's throat. When they crashed to the concrete sidewalk, Grant drove his fist down with full force behind it. And once on the ground, Grant used more of his weight to push further down on the neck.

Suffocation began. The syringe fell onto the sidewalk. Death would come soon, as the man's eyes darted around in panic.

*   *   *

As Leonard leaned down, he said, "Madison, are you...?"

But before the full question was out, the other assailant arrived, and shoved the unprepared Leonard out of the way. The terrorist was then on top of Tanquerey, and he pulled out the syringe.

Tanquerey screamed, and reached for the man's arm. It delayed him for a couple of seconds.

Leonard yelled, "No!" and launched his shoulder into the terrorist's side. The two men tumbled away from Tanquerey. They both quickly stood, and squared off.

Leonard moved first, and the terrorist swung the point of the syringe and barely missed Leonard's left cheek. The pastor tried to drive his body once more into the terrorist, but the man reacted too quickly this time. The terrorist used Leonard's speed and size against him, stepping to one side, and pushing Leonard so that he continued forward, losing control and balance.

As Leonard stumbled and fell, it left more than enough time for the assailant to turn back on Tanquerey, who was still sprawled on the ground.

He took two steps toward her.

Grant, just having finished off the other terrorist, saw that the distance was too far. He pulled out his Glock, aimed, and fired off two shots. Both found their target – one in the terrorist's cheek and the other in the stomach.

The assailant staggered and struggled. He dropped to his knees, let go of the syringe and then fell forward.

Tanquerey watched the man fall, and then turned to look at Grant.

Leonard rose to his feet, and began to return to Tanquerey. But more shots rang out. One hit Leonard, and he fell backwards.

Grant turned to see two men crossing the street. They were firing in his direction, as well as at Tanquerey. He yelled to her, "Stay down."

She didn't seem to be listening, however, as she stared in the direction of the fallen Leonard.

The few who were left in Columbus Circle accelerated the pace of their exit with more bullets flying.

Before the shooting had started, Detective Baldwin had moved the sedan away from the curb. With shots ringing out, he accelerated around Columbus Circle, and had a clear run at one of the shooters.

Godfrey said, "Do it, Mac."

Baldwin accelerated through the assailant, whose body hit the car's grille, then the front windshield, and flew some fifteen feet into the air. Any chance of survival was wiped out by landing on his head, with his neck snapping as a result.

Seeing things disintegrating, the final terrorist yelled, "Allahu Akbar," and ignoring Grant, started running at Tanquerey. He pointed the gun at her and squeezed off one shot. But he was felled by two shots penetrating his arm and the side of his head, and three entering his back from behind. Those five projectiles – two from Grant and three from Godfrey – put an end to this terrorist attack.

Grant sprinted to Leonard. Madison already was at his side. Grant saw where the bullet hit the right side of Leonard's neck, but there was little penetration. *Thank you, Lord. It only grazed.* Grant actually smiled. "If you're going to get shot, that isn't such a bad way to do it."

Leonard looked up, and managed a smile.

Grant spotted a handkerchief hanging out of Tanquerey's blazer. "Excuse me, Ms. Tanquerey, but we need this." He reached inside her overcoat, and pulled out the handkerchief.

Tanquerey largely ignored Grant. But she then asked, "Is he going to be okay?"

Grant nodded, as he pushed the cloth against the wound.

She smiled shakily, and looked back to Leonard. "Was all of this to avoid my television show?"

Leonard managed a laugh. "Beautiful, smart and a sense of humor."

She nodded. "If I were you I'd take me to dinner before you lose the opportunity."

Well, this is interesting. Seeing that Tanquerey wasn't moving, Grant asked, "Can you hold the handkerchief in place?"

She replied, "Of course."

Godfrey and Baldwin came from behind Grant. Baldwin looked at Leonard, and said, "Hey, Pastor, ambulance is on its way. Looks like you'll be alright."

Godfrey turned to Grant, and said, "You did a hell of a job here, Pastor Grant. It's apparently true what I heard about you."

Grant shrugged.

Leonard looked at Grant, and said in a low, slow voice, "Like Dad used to say, Stephen, 'Shit happens.'"

Chapter 56

The New York City Police Department, FBI, and emergency service workers descended on Columbus Circle. Leonard was taken to the hospital, with Madison Tanquerey going with him.

Two FBI special agents swept in, grabbed Grant, and took him downtown to the Javits Federal Building. Sitting in the back seat of the darkened SUV, Grant updated the two agents on everything that occurred.

He knew the answer, but decided to ask anyway. "So, why did you guys pull me out so quickly?"

The two men glanced at each other, and then the one in the front passenger seat said, "Orders from Supervisory Special Agent Rich Noack. For whatever reason, he wanted you out of there as soon as possible." The man turned in his seat to look at Grant. "You have special skills, for a pastor, I mean."

Grant volunteered, "I was a SEAL."

The agent nodded in response, and said, "Damn nice work."

"Thanks. Do you mind if I call my wife?"

"Of course not."

He pulled out his iPhone. One ring and she answered, "Stephen, everything okay?"

"Jen, it is now."

"What does that mean?"

"Are you home?"

"Yes."

"With Miguel and Isaiah?"

"Yes, Stephen, what happened?"

"There was an attack in Columbus Circle. Richard and I arrived, along with two police detectives, and were able to stop a group apparently sent to kill Madison Tanquerey."

"Oh, my God. Are you really alright?"

"Yes, I'm fine."

"And everyone else?"

"Richard is going to be okay, but he was shot in the neck."

Jennifer was silent, and finally said, "You were right, Stephen, about what these people are doing. And thank God you were there for Richard and Ms. Tanquerey."

Stephen continued, "The FBI showed up pretty quickly, spoke to the police, and pulled me out of there."

"Why?"

"Orders from Rich Noack. My guess is they're trying to limit, if possible at this point, public references of my involvement, and still more references to my previous work, especially given my current occupation."

"Rich is a good man."

"He is." Grant saw that they were getting closer to their destination. "Listen, I have to go. Try to relax."

She laughed at that.

Stephen said, "I know, but try. Let Miguel and Isaiah know what happened, and check out the news to see what they're saying."

"I will. Thank God you're safe."

"I'll make sure that the police have Richard covered tonight, and I'll be home. Talk to you in a bit."

Chapter 57

Imad ad-Din Zengli leaned forward in a chair, just a few feet away from the television. He stared at the screen as reports came in about a "foiled terrorist attack in New York City's Columbus Circle."

Dale Shore stood on the other side of the room, also watching.

As the reports proceeded about four terrorists killed in the attack, and one other person shot but in stable condition, Shore's shoulders sagged. He occasionally shook his head. Shore's attention eventually shifted away from the screen. Zengli stared at the television, while Shore watched Zengli.

Finally, Zengli shut off the television, sat back, and said, "How can this be?"

Shore started pacing, but did not answer.

Zengli persisted, "Do these fools realize that when they fail, they are failing Allah and his prophet?"

Shore said, "I don't think that they…"

Zengli held up a hand, making clear that Shore should stop. "No! No excuses. There are none. They have failed. I assume that they did not comprehend the magnitude of what we are doing here, or that they personally did something to offend Allah. Otherwise, they simply would not have allowed failure to happen."

Shore stopped his pacing. He appeared unsure, like he was about to say something, but in the end, decided to hold back. Finally, he asked, "What do you want to do?"

Zengli looked at Shore, and replied, "I want another victory. We need one now. And it will be you, Dale, who will give it to us."

Chapter 58

It was nearly midnight when Stephen stopped his Tahoe on the circular driveway in front of his home, and shut off the engine. He slowly got out of the vehicle, and looked up as a few flakes of snow started to fall.

The snowstorm. Supposed to get ten inches. He chuckled to himself. *I could use a snow day. But that isn't going to happen. Maybe the weathermen will get it wrong again.* There were two more funerals at St. Mark's – one tomorrow and the last on Thursday – and with Richard wounded, Stephen and Brett Matthews agreed on the phone earlier to handle things. Whatever the accumulation might be in the morning, Stephen would be heading back to Staten Island early. *No matter, I had to see Jen.*

He walked toward the front door. *Tired. Coming down from the events of the day.*

Stephen entered the house, and it was fairly dark and quiet. He expected to be greeted by Jennifer, along with Miguel and Isaiah.

He moved into the kitchen. *Anybody? Maybe they're all in bed?*

On the island in the middle of the room, there was a note. "Friends staying in the apartment for the night. Leftovers in the refrigerator. Wife in bedroom. You better make the right choice." Jennifer signed it with a heart.

Stephen and Jennifer recently had the space above the two-car garage across the circular driveway from the house made into a full apartment for guests, with a small living room, a bedroom and a bath.

Stephen walked upstairs and into the bedroom. Jennifer was under the covers, and rolled onto her side to see him as he entered.

He leaned down, and kissed her on the cheek. "Hey, beautiful, how are you?"

She smiled. "I'm fine. What about you?"

"Quite a day, to say the least. Our houseguests are staying in the apartment tonight?"

She nodded. "They'll be over for breakfast. Just how tired are you?"

He focused on her smile. "Are you wearing anything under those covers?"

She shook her head.

"I most certainly am not that tired."

"Better not be."

Shortly, Stephen moved under the blanket with his wife.

Jennifer wrapped her arms around him, and said, "I'm so glad you're home."

"So am I, Jen."

Chapter 59

Three days, even in a luxury home on the Nile River, took their toll when a group of seven people in the country illegally, holding a hostage, and standing guard, had to make sure that no one in the area caught even a whiff of anything being out of the norm. It was a mix of monotony, readiness, frustration, relaxation and boredom. But each of the CDM personnel were the best at what they did. No one faltered. Assignments rotated, with plenty of time for rest, sleep, eating, and checking and rechecking equipment. People could even shower – rarely the case on a mission like this.

But now, the awaited time arrived. At some point on this Wednesday morning, two men – Youseff Sarwar and Waqqad Rais – were supposed to come to this house. The plan was for Paige Caldwell, Charlie Driessen, Sean McEnany and company to grab the two, take a brief time for interrogation, and then take them, along with Terif Pasha, to the CDM plane and back to the U.S. to face the music for their terrorist activities.

Everyone was in position. Driessen watched out the bedroom window in the front of the house, looking down on the street, with Lucena, and his bandaged, healing shoulder, looking out a second-story window in the back of the home. On the first floor, Dicce was positioned by the back sliding glass door. In the kitchen, Axelrod drew guard duty on Pasha, with Caldwell, McEnany and West near the front door. All of the CDM team were equipped with mics and earpieces.

A little after 10:30 AM local time, a cab turned onto the road. Driessen said, "Possible targets. Taxi just pulled onto the street." He watched as the car stopped across the street from the home. "This is it, people. Stopped across the street."

The car sat running, but no one got out. Thirty seconds passed.

Driessen whispered, "Shit."

He added, "They're apparently waiting. My guess, for a signal. And since we don't know what the hell that signal is, move people!"

Caldwell led McEnany and West out the front door with guns drawn. They moved quickly, opened the driveway gate, and approached the cab.

Caldwell used her limited Arabic language skills, and yelled, "Get out of the car with your hands showing!"

The three spread apart and moved closer to the vehicle. No one got out.

The driver and the heads of two passengers in the backseat were now visible by the CDM threesome.

One of the passengers opened the door on the other side of the cab. He jumped out, and started to level a gun at the three using the top of the car as a foundation.

McEnany called out, "Gun!" He then squeezed off two shots. One bullet entered the forehead of Waqqad Rais. He tumbled backwards, dead before coming to rest on the ground.

On the second floor, Driessen had his Glock trained on the scene below. He declared, "One down! Phil, Lis, Chase, clean it out, we're going to have to move out now!"

On the street, Caldwell slipped into English. "Get out of the fucking car, now! And I want to see hands."

The back door facing her opened, and the shaking hands of Sarwar emerged first, followed by the rest of him. McEnany moved forward to grab Sarwar.

The cab driver emerged on the other side. His hands also were in the air. In Arabic, he said, "Fine, fine. I am doing as you request." He moved in front of the car.

West moved toward him. Once she spotted a gun under his light brown jacket, West pulled the trigger. The bullet hit the man's chest. He fell back against the grille of the cab, and then slid to the ground. He was in a sitting position with his eyelids fluttering when West added a bullet to the head. The taxi driver slid sideways to the street.

Driessen was now moving down the stairs, and joined Dicce and Lucena in moving to the front door. He asked, "We good?"

Dicce replied, "Clean."

Dicce and Lucena were carrying black garbage bags filled with anything that could be linked to the CDM team. Driessen opened the door, and watched as Caldwell and McEnany maneuvered Sarwar into the back of the van. Caldwell gave a thumbs up, and Driessen called to the kitchen, "Okay, Chase, let's move."

Axelrod directed Pasha, whose arms were secured behind him, forward, out the door and into the van. Pasha joined Sarwar on the floor of the vehicle. In a few seconds, both had their arms and feet bound together, and duct tape covered their mouths.

The back and side doors of the van were closed. Driessen took the driver's seat, and Caldwell the front passenger spot.

The van was out of the neighborhood, and still none of the neighbors had emerged to see what happened, or to check on the dead cab driver whose blood continued to ooze, now very slowly, from the bullet holes in his chest and head.

Chapter 60

After more than a century in northeast Ohio, the Conneaut Daily Tribune was barely hanging on in this digital age so hostile to newspapers. But publisher and editor Spencer Graham pledged to keep the newspaper going as long as he was able.

Fortunately, Graham's father made a fortune in the farm supply business, and left his son a considerable inheritance. Over much of the 62 years that Graham ran the *Trib*, it was a money-making venture. However, the newspaper dropped into the red roughly twenty years ago. Graham reluctantly added a less-than-impressive website, advertising revenues plummeted, subscriptions faltered, and staff was cut dramatically. But Graham persisted. Now at 87 years old, he was still at this desk every day, writing two daily editorials, and, with the help of an editorial staff of two, laying out the paper. He managed to keep a Washington, D.C.-based reporter and columnist on the payroll, along with two local reporters, and a sports writer. Wire stories and syndicated columnists filled up the rest of the hard copy paper and online version.

The *Trib's* aggressively conservative editorial line and the fact that its Washington columnist, Stitch Nettles, was so widely respected helped keep the paper afloat – along with a healthy subsidy from Graham's personal fortune. Graham laughed and told people, "I figure that my bank account and my life will run out at about the same time, when I turn 99. After that, I won't care what happens to the newspaper business."

It was just after 4:40 on Wednesday afternoon. At the back of the newsroom was Graham's office, up several steps from the bullpen area that ran from the front door back to the office. Graham was at his desk trying to hammer out an editorial on his computer, but he was distracted by the television coverage of President Elizabeth Sanderski's funeral. One of the local reporters and the two editorial staffers also wandered from their tasks to take in the funeral. Sanderski's body was now being carried out of the National Cathedral.

A four-door white pickup truck pulled into the parking lot in front of the *Trib's* small building. Three men got out; the driver stayed behind the wheel. Two carried dark canvas bags. They were led by Dale Shore, who pulled a gun out and held it down at his side as he entered the building. The three stopped and scanned the room. The heads of the two editorial personnel popped up to see the rare visitors. The reporter kept watching the funeral on her desktop, and Graham had his eyes glued on the television up in his office.

One of the editorial staff – a skinny, twenty-something man with brown hair, a beard and a blue shirt – stood up, and started walking toward the three. "Can I help you?"

Shore raised his gun and shot the man in the chest. The three intruders then bolted forward.

The reporter looked up and screamed. She was shot in the right eye, and her head fell back in the chair.

The other editor decided to jump under her desk. She was shot several times and never emerged from that cramped space.

Shore said, "I've got him," pointing to Graham. "Get things set up."

The other two assailants scrambled to each side of the room, and zipped open their bags.

Shore climbed the few steps and entered Graham's office. The *Trib's* editor and publisher fumbled and dropped a key ring. He was trying to get to the right key that would unlock the desk drawer where an old revolver resided. He gave up upon seeing Shore entering the office and pointing a gun.

Ever the newspaperman, Graham said, "I assume you're part of this terrorist group. Why the hell are you doing this?"

Shore simply stood pointing the weapon.

Graham persisted, "What is the point? What are you trying to do? And why?"

Again, Shore did not respond.

And then the editorial writer in Graham emerged. He proclaimed, "You know how this will end for you, right? You're going to die, and guess what, you're not going to heaven or anything like it. You'll forever be known as..."

Shore fired, and Graham fell back. The combination of the bullet in the chest, and his head striking a filing cabinet as he fell, sealed his fate.

Shore glanced at the television, and smiled. He then exited the office. His two fellow terrorists completed their tasks, and left the bags behind. As the three approached the door, Shore asked, "You're sure they are tied in to the Wi-Fi?"

One nodded and the other said, "Done."

They got back into the pickup and drove off.

A half-hour later, the mailman entered the building with a box in his hand. "Hey, folks, I have a package for you."

He paused at the lack of response. Taking a few steps forward, he saw a body on the floor. He backed out of the building, got into his mail truck, and called 911.

Five minutes later, two local police officers entered the building with their guns drawn. They searched, checked each body for any life, and called in what they found. Four more officers and two detectives arrived ten minutes later, along with the local coroner. Another five minutes, and the other *Trib* reporter arrived on the scene.

Not far over the border into northwestern Pennsylvania, Imad ad-Din Zengli waited in a dark blue van in a tucked away spot. The pickup would be abandoned there, and the five men would drive into southwestern New York.

The pickup pulled up, and the four men climbed into the van. Zengli asked, "How did it go?"

Shore answered, "Perfect."

"And during the funeral for Sanderski. That just makes it even better."

Shore pulled out a smartphone, jumped on the Internet, and entered the proper URL. He waited a few seconds, and then smiled at what he saw. "There it is." He turned the device, and showed the split screen view.

Zengli leaned closer to the screen. "Looks like we have…" He paused to count. "Yes, nine or ten. Do it."

The video stream was coming from the *Trib's* building. At four points around the newsroom – strategically positioned on a shelf, a bookcase, and two filing cabinets – sat smartphones. Two had their cameras on and each was strapped to C4.

In the van, Shore hit the phone numbers on his own screen. As each phone rang in the newsroom, the C4 was triggered. By the time the fourth bomb went off, the furniture and equipment around the room were destroyed, walls were torn, and six police officers and the other *Trib* reporter were added to the list of murdered. The two officers who originally answered the call and the coroner survived, thanks to their being in Graham's office which took far less of the concussive blasts.

Shore said, "It's done."

Zengli declared, "We have another much-needed victory, my friend. Allah be praised."

Chapter 61

When the van carrying the CDM team members and their two prisoners was roughly 40 minutes from the small airport, Sean McEnany pulled out his phone. While doing so, he announced to the others, "My friends at the airport reported no interest in the hangar or our plane early this morning. I'm going to give them a heads-up on our pending arrival."

Since they had touched down on Saturday night and headed to Pasha's location, the pro-Western group that McEnany had previously worked with maintained watch on the plane. McEnany had been checking in regularly over the last three days. Now, it was time for the final update to verify that all was clear.

McEnany finished the call, and announced, "We're good, people. Still nobody interested."

"Does that strike anyone as odd?" asked Jessica West.

McEnany started to open his mouth, but Lis Dicce beat him to it. She said, "Not really. Even if the Egyptian government knew we were here and what we were doing, what incentive would they have to interfere? After all, they don't want their fingerprints on any of the terrorist attacks in the U.S. Here's my prediction when we stop these assholes and the news comes out that these two were grabbed from Egypt: The Egyptian government will claim to have aided the American effort to stop and apprehend these terrorists. But if we had somehow failed, the government could claim ignorance, issue protests, and even demand an apology from the U.S."

Caldwell smiled in the front seat. "Sounds about right, Lis."

"Thanks." Dicce shifted her attention to Driessen. "Hey, Charlie, when we get to the hangar, I'll get inside the cockpit immediately, and get things ready."

"Sounds good," replied Driessen. "I'll be right behind you, Lis."

McEnany added, "I'll do a final rundown with my friends."

Caldwell said, "The rest of us will move our guests on board, and get them ready to answer questions once we're wheels up."

After the assignments were set for the arrival at the airfield, Dicce took back the floor. The anything-but-typical quietness that had prevailed since the Sanderski assassination was giving way to her natural chattiness. She took the opportunity to fill everyone in on the latest political struggles within the Egyptian president's office, between political parties, and the state of radical elements in the country.

Driessen was able to guide the van into the airport with nothing more than a nod at the uninterested person in some kind of uniform at the gate. As he pulled the van into the hangar, two men quickly rolled the building's doors shut.

The van came to a stop, and McEnany strained to look out the front windshield.

Driessen shut off the engine, and Dicce pulled open the vehicle's side door and jumped out. As she walked toward the aircraft, she was turned, looking back at the van. "Charlie, I'll get started."

At the same time, McEnany leaned forward and spotted a boot sticking out from behind a crate against a wall. He then looked at the five men spread out in front of them. "Lis! Get back here!"

Dicce froze for just a second, and then she moved to pull out her Glock. But it was too late.

The man directly in front of her opened fire with a submachine gun. Bullets riddled Dicce's chest and stomach. She left her feet going backwards, and then crashed to the slick floor, sliding a few inches before coming to rest.

Caldwell had taken a step out of the vehicle, and yelled, "No!"

The others standing in the hangar began firing at the van.

Caldwell retreated to use the van's door as some kind of cover, as she swung her submachine gun around.

Driessen did the same thing on the other side, as the two men that had closed the hangar doors focused their fire at him.

Inside the van, Axelrod, West, and Lucena jockeyed for some kind of position that granted cover and the ability to fire.

McEnany, however, stepped out of the van with submachine gun in hand, firing and screaming in rage. "You bastards!"

The attackers seemed to assume that they would need no cover, that surprise would be enough. And it would have, if they had only waited until their targets were clear of the van. But they failed to do that, so now they were standing in the open, unprotected.

Driessen took down the attacker who had the clearest shot at him.

Caldwell did the same on her side, shooting across and in front of McEnany. "Sean, get to cover!"

Instead, McEnany continued to move forward. He mowed down the terrorist who shot Dicce, and then turned to the left, and took down the next.

Two more were firing from the left. West emerged to stand high on the step of the van, leveled her Glock, and made an impressive shot into the head of an attacker.

The other attacker finally realized the need for cover, but as he moved, McEnany, now standing over Lis Dicce's body, pulled off another string of shots that ended the terrorist's life.

The last attacker was on Driessen's side of the van. That individual actually made it to some cover behind a workbench. He popped up a couple of times, fired, and dropped back down.

Driessen discarded the submachine gun, and pulled out his Glock 21. He steadied his aim, and waited. The terrorist's head began to move upward once again. Driessen squeezed off two shots. One found its intended target. The projectile entered the man's skull through the nose.

With the firing done, Caldwell sprinted forward. McEnany remained upright, merely looking down at Dicce. Caldwell slid to the floor, and reached out to find a pulse in Dicce's neck. But there was none. Caldwell's eyes filled with tears. She stared down at her dead colleague and friend, and then gently brushed Dicce's hair back.

Driessen arrived, and crouched down on the other side of Dicce. "Aw, shit. No." He rubbed his forehead, and then his eyes.

Lucena, West and Axelrod started to move forward to the grouping. West glanced over her shoulder, though, and stopped. Lucena looked at her. She whispered, "Go, I'll watch these shits."

McEnany turned and walked over to the place where he spotted the boot. Behind the crates were piled four dead bodies. Here were the men that McEnany had worked with before. The gunshot wounds were recent.

McEnany turned away, and walked to the back of the van. He pulled open the back doors. West was standing over Pasha and Sarwar. McEnany called out, "Chase."

Axelrod turned away from Dicce, and trotted over. "Yes?"

"Help me get these two pieces of crap on the plane."

"Right."

Driessen stood up, and declared, "I'll get everything set for takeoff." He paused. "Paige?"

She didn't look at him, but nodded.

When Caldwell finally did look up, she saw that Phil Lucena also had tears in his eyes. "Phil, why don't you make a place for Lis on board, and then we'll get her set up properly?"

In a cracked voice, he managed, "Yes, yes, of course."

As Lucena walked toward the jet, Paige looked back at Dicce. She whispered, "Lis, I'm so sorry ... so very sorry."

Fifteen minutes later, with engines ready and everyone else on board, West and Axelrod pulled open the hangar doors ever so slightly, and stepped out to look around. West said, "Really? Nothing?"

"If so, let's count our..." His voice trailed off. "Well ... it looks good to go, right?"

"Yes."

Axelrod gave a thumbs-up to Driessen and McEnany in the cockpit. He and West opened the doors the rest of the way, and then scrambled into the plane.

Less than five minutes later, the G650 accelerated down the runway, and rose into the sky. A short time later, Driessen announced, "We're clear of Egyptian airspace and at cruising altitude."

After nearly three hours in the air, Caldwell finally turned her attention away from looking out the window. The cabin was quiet. Pasha and Sarwar had been put in seats in the back, with new bindings on their hands and legs. West watched Pasha, while Axelrod guarded Sarwar.

Caldwell rose, pulled out her tactical knife, and walked to the back of the plane. She stopped in the aisle that separated the two captives. She said, "Jessica, Chase, take a break."

West moved toward the front of the cabin. Axelrod asked, "You sure?" Caldwell nodded. Chase patted her on the shoulder as he moved by.

Caldwell looked at one and then the other, as she twirled the knife. "My colleague, no, my friend, Lis Dicce, is dead. I assume those were terrorists working with you." She pointed to Pasha. "Understand, that was your last gasp."

Neither offered any response, not even a movement.

Caldwell continued, "That act alone means that everyone here wants to toss each of you out of this plane. I have little problem with that. In fact, I'll help. Or, if we want to bring your bodies back to the U.S., I can do wonders with a knife like this." She pointed it casually at each man. "Nevertheless, if you're still alive when we land, you'll eventually be executed by the U.S. government for the many more innocent people you played a part in murdering, including President Sanderski. And believe me, I will make sure I'm in attendance to see that."

Sarwar shifted in his seat first.

"Now, perhaps you really are true believers. And if that is the case, I know that you will not give us any information, and you actually look forward to death. But if you aren't complete suicidal nutcases, then there might be a way for you to actually survive all of this." She then lied. "I have been given the power to make that happen. Now, it's up to you" – she leaned down, pushed the knife's blade against Sarwar's forehead, opening a small cut – "and you" – then doing the same to Pasha's cheek.

After Caldwell withdrew the knife, each man looked down at the floor. Silence reigned for a few minutes.

Pasha actually spoke first, with Sarwar then joining in.

Caldwell held up a hand, and said "Stop." She then asked Lucena, "Phil, can you record this?"

Lucena approached and handed Caldwell a small digital recorder. She said, "Thanks."

Caldwell pulled over a rolling tray, locked the wheels, turned on the recorder, and placed it on the tray between the two men. She pointed at Pasha, and ordered, "You first." She turned to Sarwar, adding, "And then you."

Over the next 45 minutes, the two men provided a list of safe houses in the U.S. Their exact locations were fleshed out with the help of Lucena, courtesy of online maps. Training camps were revealed, one in the U.S., and others in Canada, Venezuela and Afghanistan. They served up the broad target areas that were discussed, with the two men noting that Zengli then had discretion to pick the particulars in order to fit moments and developments.

When she was finished, Caldwell moved back to the front of the cabin. Her first call was to Tank Hoard. It was 2:30 on Thursday morning in D.C., yet Hoard answered the phone on just the second ring. She apologized for not calling in earlier, but told him about losing Dicce. Caldwell provided a rundown on what had happened, and relayed the basics of what Pasha and Sarwar had just volunteered. "Lucena is sending you the recording of what they said."

Hoard concluded, "Thanks, Paige. I'm so sorry about Lis."

"I know. Thanks, Tank."

"Listen, I'll get this information over to Noack at the FBI."

"No, actually, I'll call him right now, in case he has questions about our actions that you might not be able to answer. I'll make sure he gets a hold of you when we're done."

"Good enough."

The call with Hoard ended, and the conversation with Rich Noack covered the same ground, including Noack's sympathies regarding Dicce.

When finished with Noack, Caldwell resumed staring out the window. She glanced at the time on her phone, and then leaned forward and punched in a number. When she heard a voice on the other end, she sat up a little straighter, and turned her body a bit to face the window. In a low voice, she said, "Mr. President, it's a success. Two of three were acquired, with the other terminated. They gave up key information, clearly actionable."

"Excellent," responded President Links. "And your people?"

Caldwell cleared her throat. "I lost one. Lis Dicce. She had worked with me at the Agency."

"Oh, God, Paige, I'm so sorry."

"I know."

"I assume you're not speaking in private?"

"I'm not."

Links switched gears. "You obviously filled in the right people?"

"Yes."

"Good. I'm not sure if you heard, but we had two more attacks. One yesterday and one today – well, I mean on Wednesday and another on Tuesday. The bastards took out a small newspaper in Ohio, along with some police officers, while President Sanderski's funeral was happening. It's a fucking nightmare." He paused, and then added, "Your clergy friend basically stopped the first attack in New York City."

Caldwell shook her head. "We heard, but obviously not the part about Stephen. Sir, the information we acquired might put an end to this."

"That's good to hear. Let's hope so."

"Yes, sir."

Links' voice softened, as he said, "I'm so very sorry, Paige."

"Thanks."

After that call ended, Caldwell made one more.

"Stephen, are you alright? I just heard that you stopped an attack."

Grant got up from bed, not wanting to wake Jennifer. "I'm fine." He wandered downstairs and toward the kitchen. He gave Paige a quick rundown on what had occurred at Columbus Circle.

"Thankfully, you were there. Pastor Leonard is okay?"

"Yes, he should be leaving the hospital this morning. I was going to pick him up, but it looks like Ms. Tanquerey will be handling that. What about you?"

Caldwell took a deep breath, and proceeded to tell Stephen the full story on the mission, including what had just occurred today.

Hearing about Dicce, Grant thought of her good-natured way, and how much she liked to talk. He also was reminded of uncomfortable, mixed feelings when an important mission was successful, but lives, friends, were lost in the effort. He knew that this would be different – far worse – for Paige, given that it was her team. Dicce was a friend, a colleague and her employee.

Grant decided to put aside the fact that the effort that Caldwell led very well could play the key part in stopping the current wave of terrorism plaguing the U.S. Others would commend her for that, and Grant also would at a later time. Right now, he thought she needed to hear from Stephen Grant as a friend and a pastor.

He said, "How are you handling it?" He knew she understood what he was asking.

"Handling it? That's funny."

"Paige, you and I both know that you'll play this over time and again in your mind. But my guess is that there wasn't anything you could have done differently. Right?"

She whispered, "Right."

"Lis would understand that as well. Correct?"

Paige delayed answering. Finally, she managed to say, "I can't do this right now."

"Okay, I get it. Listen, I don't know what faith Lis…"

Paige interrupted, "She's Catholic. From what she said, it seemed that she pretty much went to Mass every Sunday, when she could, with her family."

"Glad to hear that."

The reality of Lis's family just seemed to dawn on Paige. "Shit, Stephen, her husband and son. What am I going to say?"

Stephen took a deep breath. "That's going to be brutal. There's no way around that. But I know you, and I know you'll say what's appropriate."

Caldwell glanced over her shoulder. "Stephen, I really need to go. I might call later for some additional advice."

"Before you go, just listen for a few seconds. I'm going to say a quick prayer for you." He heard no protest, so Grant pushed ahead. "Father of all mercy, give strength and confidence to Your servant Paige in this time of sadness and challenge. Grant that she may know that You are near, and that she is uplifted by Your everlasting arms. Grant that she, resting on Your protection, may fear no evil, for You are with her to comfort and deliver her; through Jesus Christ, Your Son, our Lord, who lives and reigns with You and the Holy Spirit, one God, now and forever."

Paige was silent for a few seconds, and then said, "Thanks, Stephen. We'll talk later." And she ended the call. She then whispered to herself, "I actually needed that."

Caldwell then rose, and entered the cockpit. She patted Driessen on the shoulder, and said, "Charlie, go get some rest, I'll take the remainder of the flight with Sean."

Driessen glanced at both of them, and said, "Sounds good."

Caldwell settled in, and said, "Are you okay?"

McEnany's eyes stayed straight ahead. "No, of course not."

"Me, either."

"I'm mustering all of my strength to not go back there and slit both their throats."

"I was close, very close."

After several minutes of silence, Caldwell said, "They gave us information that might end this thing – at least in terms of what we're dealing with right now in the U.S."

McEnany didn't reply.

Caldwell continued, "I lied, and told them that I'd been given the power to possibly save their lives, if they coughed up what they knew."

McEnany raised an eyebrow, and finally glanced at Caldwell.

She said, "That, of course, was not on tape, and no one else heard it. So, it really didn't happen."

"Good. Because if they aren't eventually executed for what they've done, then I will kill them myself. And trust me, no one will know who did it."

"On that, I have no doubt, my friend, and I would help."

Chapter 62

When the CDM Gulfstream G650 landed at Dulles, a large contingent of FBI personnel and armored vehicles were on hand to take Teriff Pasha and Youseff Sarwar into custody.

As the two terrorists were being carted off, a short, thin man in a dark suit walked up to Paige Caldwell, with Driessen, McEnany, Axelrod, Lucena and West gathered behind her. He extended his hand, and said, "Ms. Caldwell, my name is Chris Menke. I work for the president, and he told me to express his thanks, to each one of you, for what you accomplished for our country today, and to express his deepest sympathies on the loss of Mrs. Dicce."

Caldwell replied, "Thank you, Mr. Menke."

Menke looked directly at Caldwell, and said, "Have you contacted Mrs. Dicce's family as yet?"

Caldwell shook her head. "I wanted to get rid of these two" – indicating Pasha and Sarwar – "and then I would contact her husband."

"The president believes that he should be the one to do that."

Caldwell said, "No. I'll do it. But if he were to follow up with the family, I think that would be much appreciated."

"I will let him know. Also, given the situation, I am authorized to run interference with the FBI, if you all would like to hold off on being debriefed until sometime later today. It's your decision." Caldwell turned and looked at each of her colleagues. She turned back to Menke, and said, "We appreciate that, but I think we'd each like to get this over with."

"Fair enough. I'll let them know, while also telling them to move things along. Throughout, I'll be here for whatever you might need."

Caldwell said, "Again, thanks." She turned to Driessen, and said, "Charlie, can you get everyone set up with the Bureau, while I call Lewis?" Lewis was Lis Dicce's husband.

*   *   *

Within an hour of completing the CDM debriefings, President Adam Links authorized the FBI to move against each location identified by Pasha and Sarwar.

A team of six FBI special agents moved in on a two-story, century-old home in Elizabeth, New Jersey. After sweeping through the home, they found nothing, including very little to indicate that anyone had been there, and if they had, when that was.

However, an elderly man sitting on his front porch across the street called out to the FBI personnel. The two agents who responded found him in pajamas, slippers, a bathrobe and a big parka.

The elderly man asked, "Looking for the four that were in that house?"

The first agent said, "There were four. You're sure?"

"Of course, I'm sure. All I do is sit here and look around. Can't sleep much anymore. No one visits."

"I'm sorry, sir, but can we get back to your neighbors?" asked the second agent.

"Ain't really neighbors. There was no one in there for a long time, and then suddenly, these four show up on

Tuesday morning. No, wait, Monday. It was Monday morning. And from what I saw, they didn't leave until" – he glanced at his watch – "two-and-a-half hours ago."

The first agent followed up, "They left at 6:15 this morning?"

"Exactly."

"Why are you so sure about the time?"

The old man shook his head. "Are you deaf? I just told you. All I do is sit here and watch the block. Yeah, you know, I can't sleep much anymore, and no one comes to visit."

The first agent said, "Yes, I got that. Sir, I'm going to send someone over who is going to ask for a description of these men. They'll probably try to get information from you to make some sketches."

"What makes you think they were all men?"

The second agent said, "They weren't?"

"No. Two couples. Two men and two women."

*   *   *

Caldwell, Driessen and McEnany wound up back at the CDM offices across from the Pentagon, while Lucena, West and Axelrod headed home for some rest.

The three sat in Caldwell's office, each sipping a cold beer at about nine in the morning.

Caldwell's phone buzzed. "Yes."

It was the FBI's Rich Noack. "Listen, I'm on the move, but wanted to get you this information. Our agents in New Jersey just missed four individuals at one of the safe houses. Two couples are circulating somewhere in the New York metro area. Our people asked Pasha, who is becoming more and more cooperative, and his opinion is that Zengli has a Jewish target in mind. According to Pasha, Zengli particularly hates American Jewish media outlets with links to Israel."

"Naturally," responded Caldwell.

"Given your New York duo of Grant and McEnany, I thought I'd pass this along, see if anything popped up that we haven't already thought about. We've got agents and local PDs covering an assortment of possible targets in and around the city."

"Alright, Rich, I'll pass it along."

"By the way, you guys did incredible work. Thanks. And, again, I'm so sorry about Lis."

"Thanks, Rich. Stay safe."

"Appreciate it."

Caldwell passed along what Noack said to Driessen and McEnany, and then pulled Grant up on her phone and provided him with the same information.

Grant said, "Thanks, Paige. Nothing off the top of my head, but let me think about it and talk to some others. You never know. I also have an eleven o'clock funeral."

"Right. Take care."

Caldwell looked at McEnany, who was finishing his beer. She said, "Well?"

"Okay, get up and let me at your computer."

Chapter 63

After talking to Paige Caldwell, Grant approached Richard Leonard's office at St. Mark's. With one person, the small office was adequate. A second person seated across the desk from Leonard made for a close conversation, but it still worked. However, three was one too many. Grant merely leaned against the doorframe.

Grant could see the combination of both exhaustion and relief on the faces of Leonard and Brett Matthews. *Only one funeral left. What a perverse thought.*

They had nearly two hours until the funeral. Grant decided to engage his two friends on what Paige had just mentioned. "The authorities believe that a Jewish media outlet in the city area could be a target."

Matthews' head sagged, and Leonard leaned back in his chair, making sure not to turn his head given the wound healing on his neck. At first, no one replied.

Finally, Matthews said, "A Jewish media outlet in this area? How can you possibly narrow it down?"

Grant replied, "Good question. The major targets, no doubt, are being covered by law enforcement. I'm worried about something they might be missing."

Leonard asked, "Any more information than that?"

"Zengli apparently hates Jewish media outlets with links to Israel."

"Oh, crap," declared Leonard, who leaned forward, placing his hands on his desk.

Grant replied, "What?"

"I would think it's probably nothing."

"Richard."

"Right. There's a pastor and a rabbi here on Staten Island who have a column in the local weekly, a cable access show, YouTube, and so on. They called me shortly after I arrived here to see if I might be interested in being a guest on their show. They knew of some of my work, and areas of expertise."

"And?"

"Let's just say they're pretty confrontational when it comes to radical Islam. The pastor also believes in the idea that Israel – you know, the current, actual place – is special for Christians."

Grant said, "End times stuff?"

"Yes. The two – Pastor Tim and Rabbi Dennis – often have guests on from Israel, and are interviewed by Israeli media outlets."

Writing in a local weekly and hosting a cable access show. Hmmm.

Leonard added, "However, they might have gained some national attention over the past week. A parishioner mentioned something on Sunday."

Leonard opened his laptop, jumped online, and searched their names. "Yes, here it is. Actually, it looks like they were interviewed on two, no, three, cable news shows since the church attacks."

Grant said, "Oh, great – a pastor and a rabbi. That seems to be specifically designed to generate hatred from Zengli and his group."

Matthews added, "I know them as well. They've been around for some time. I actually went on their show once. I probably won't do that again." He paused, and then said, "Something just occurred to me. I think I taped in their little studio on a Thursday morning. It stuck with me due to the odd time."

Grant stepped to the desk. "Richard, please check their website to see if they have a taping schedule."

Leonard looked up from the screen. "Yes, they do record their shows on Thursday mornings. Supposed to start in about 20 minutes."

"Shit. It might be nothing, but I don't like this. It's an easy target that would make a splash. Just what these guys like. Where's the studio?"

Leonard got up. "It's five minutes from here. I'll drive you."

"No way. Besides, you have to be here for the funeral. Where am I going?"

Leonard quickly explained.

Matthews said, "You can't go alone."

"I'm not. Richard, can you get a hold of Detectives Godfrey and Baldwin? Explain this, and see if they can get there, or if they can send someone?"

Leonard picked up his phone. "I'm on it."

Grant ran out of the church, and sprinted down the street to his Tahoe, which was waiting in front of the parsonage.

He opened the vehicle, leaned over and unlocked the small case under the passenger seat. He pulled out his Glock, checked it, loaded a cartridge, and placed the gun on the seat next to him. He started the engine, and slipped the vehicle into drive.

The expected snowstorm had never materialized, so Grant made the journey to the small building housing the offices of "Pastor Tim and Rabbi Dennis Media" in less than five minutes. He pulled into the parking lot and noted that a white van was parked oddly, across two parking spots for the disabled.

No tag hanging from the mirror. It's running. Someone behind the wheel.

He pulled into a parking space, slipped the gun between his belt and shirt in the small of his back, and put on the black jacket that went with the rest of his clergy attire. He got out of the vehicle. As he walked, another "red alert" hit. Grant kept his nose down in his phone. The woman in the van watched him, but did nothing.

I'll leave her for now, or for Godfrey and Baldwin. Got to get to the studio.

He entered the building, and saw that Pastor Tim and Rabbi Dennis were on the third floor.

The elevator was climbing.

Stairs.

By the time he entered the narrow third floor hallway, it appeared empty. But then Grant spotted the back of a jacket entering an office.

Crap.

He withdrew the gun, and ran down the hallway.

How many? Lord, grant me clarity.

Grant did not hesitate at the door. He burst in. At the far end of the room, Pastor Tim and Rabbi Dennis sat at a desk, with a nun in a habit, sitting in what appeared to be the guest's chair. Another person – the cameraman – stood to the side of the desk. The four had their hands awkwardly in the air. Fear was scrawled on the faces of Tim, Dennis and the cameraman, while tears had begun to form in the nun's eyes.

Two men had their backs to Grant. One was pointing a gun at the four on the cheap set. A woman stood sideways, leaning against a wall. Her head turned first to see Grant enter.

Three. No choice.

A calm descended on Grant – a feeling he knew from many years past.

The terrorist leaning against the wall began to raise her gun.

Grant fired off two shots. Both acquired their target, and she fell.

Next was the man pointing the gun at the four potential victims. Before he could fully turn, Grant deposited one bullet in the back of his head.

At this point, the third nearly got a shot off. But he was not quick enough.

Grant slid his aim to the left, and put three slugs in the terrorist's chest.

In less than six seconds from the first shot to the last, Stephen Grant had killed the three terrorists.

Pastor Tim, Rabbi Dennis, the cameraman and the nun were stunned. Their mouths hung open, and hands remained suspended in the air.

"Everyone okay?" Grant asked.

Each nodded ever so slightly.

"Good."

The driver.

Grant turned, and ran out of the studio.

The nun, still holding her hands in the air, turned and looked at the others. "An angel?"

Pastor Tim declared, "Praise the Lord!"

Rabbi Dennis asked, "Was he wearing a collar?"

Grant was now flying down the stairs. Upon reaching the main floor, he stopped to peek out the front door. *Van still there. One more time, Lord, please?*

With the gun held in front, Grant slowly exited the building, and called out, "I want to see hands, and then slowly get..."

The driver didn't wait. She raised a gun and shot wildly out the passenger window, slipped the van into drive, and slammed on the gas pedal.

Again, he was calm. Grant trained on the driver as the van began to turn away, and quickly fired off four shots.

Glass shattered and blood splattered in the van. The terrorist fell forward on the steering wheel. Her foot remained on the gas, and the van accelerated directly for Grant's Tahoe. The van crashed into the red SUV. Grant sprinted forward. He looked inside the van and saw that the driver had breathed her last.

As he turned away from the dead terrorist, a dark sedan sped into the parking lot. Godfrey and Baldwin jumped out. Grant reported, "This one is dead, and so are three terrorists on the third floor. When I ran out, everyone else seemed okay."

"Holy shit, Grant," declared Detective Godfrey. "Thank God, you're on our side."

Chapter 64

Trent Nguyen stopped the armored SUV ferrying Rich Noack and four other FBI agents at the rendezvous point in southwestern Virginia. The terrorist training camp – set up on some sixty acres that Teriff Pasha admitted to owning via one of his companies – was about three miles away.

Given that Noack was the supervisory agent on the scene, several agents descended upon him with updates as soon as he got out of the vehicle. He responded positively to each person, and then asked, "Do we have pictures?"

A short woman stepped forward with a tablet in her hands. "Yes, sir. The satellite images apparently confirm what Pasha told us. From what we can tell, twenty people are on the site, give or take."

"Okay, thanks. Let's pull everyone together quickly."

While that was being done, Noack made contact with two approaching aircraft. Less than a minute later, he looked out at three dozen FBI personnel. "It's a 'go' people. You know the plan. Our two helicopter teams are inbound and we're on time. Remember, assume that these guys have been trained and know what they're doing. No unnecessary chances. Stay safe. Godspeed."

Noack, Nguyen and the four other agents climbed back into the SUV. Nguyen waited as four armored, SWAT-like personnel carriers moved out first. Atop each vehicle, a hatch was open where an agent dressed like everyone else – in a dark helmet, goggles and wearing body armor, holding a Colt M4 Carbine rifle – stood, with the top part of his body exposed. A second SUV followed, with Nguyen then slipping in at the back.

The FBI caravan moved westward on a two-lane road, and then turned onto a dirt road leading into the center of the compound. As they accelerated on the dusty, bumpy trail, Noack looked over at Nguyen, and asked, "No guards?"

Nguyen shrugged. He pointed at the clock on the dashboard that said 11:58 AM. "Maybe they're heading to lunch." He smiled, as he returned his focus to the road and the vehicles in front of him.

Noack mumbled, "If only."

The vehicles broke past trees into an open area with five buildings in the middle. Noack quickly counted a dozen individuals moving toward, climbing the stairs, or on the porch of a long, one-story building.

The men, sprinkled with a few women, turned to see the dark FBI vehicles fan out and come at them. And then the sound of helicopters from the sky drew their attention upward. Two black Apache attack helicopters swept down, and began to circle the compound. The terrorists in training seemed mesmerized by the Apaches and their large guns, as well as by the armored vehicles that stopped in front of them, with FBI agents streaming out.

As the SUV came to a stop, Noack said, "What the hell?"

He got out with his gun drawn. As he walked forward, he shouted, "We are from the Federal Bureau of Investigation. Put your hands in the air."

The trainees looked around, and slowly complied.

Noack shouted to his people, "Okay, let's shut this down! Clear each building."

One individual in the main house watched through the front window. He pulled out a phone, and hit a number. He said, "They're here. They have us."

On the other end of the call, Imad ad-Din Zengli shouted, "Shit!" and then terminated the call.

The man who had been selected by Zengli to operate this training facility simply stared at the phone after Zengli had cursed and signed off.

The walls of each building had been packed with C4 explosives for this exact scenario. He watched as FBI agents moved into each building, and as two came up the stairs and another pair moved around to the back of the house in which he stood. He pulled up the number on the screen that would trigger the explosions. As the agents approached the room, he took a breath, and then exited the screen, placed the phone on a table, and put his hands on top of his head.

As the agents took him into custody, he said, "Be careful with that phone."

After the camp was secured, Nguyen walked over to where Noack was leaning against the SUV, just having finished his report to the FBI director. Noack said, "We got off easy here."

"Damn right. That guy could have blown us all to shit."

"Yet, he didn't."

They stood in silence for several seconds, taking in the scene of the FBI moving out prisoners, and more Bureau personnel arriving to disarm the explosives and sweep every inch of the buildings and area.

Nguyen added, "We also were lucky that they actually were headed to lunch."

"What?"

"Yeah, go check out the building where these shits were headed when we arrived. They were going to lunch."

"Unbelievable," declared Noack.

"Never doubt me. Even asshole terrorists have to eat."

Chapter 65

More than 6,700 miles away, the *U.S.S. Benjamin Harrison*, an Arleigh Burke-class guided missile destroyer, cruised the waters of the Arabian Sea. The crew had just heard from three CIA operatives on the ground in southern Afghanistan. They confirmed what Teriff Pasha had said, and what the other intel sources provided. The *Benjamin Harrison* possessed the exact coordinates of the training camp, and the facilities inside the compound.

The ship's skipper, Commander Alejandro Jimenez, asked, "Are the CIA boys still in communication?"

"Aye, aye, sir."

Jimenez picked up the handset, and said, "Good work, boys. You're clear?"

Over the sound of their Humvee, one of the operatives replied, "Commander, we are clear. Make it fucking rain."

Jimenez actually smiled at that. He said, "Count on it. Get home safe."

Some 10 minutes later, the warning sirens wailed on the destroyer. The first missile erupted into the air amidst fire and smoke, and over the next three minutes, a total of nine more Tomahawk missiles, each with a 1,000-pound warhead, were launched.

Each Tomahawk flew 100 to 150 feet off the ground, adjusting nearly instantaneously to changes in the terrain below, and streaking forward at some 550 mph.

From launch, the missiles would reach their targets in southwest Afghanistan in less than an hour.

Forty minutes after the first Tomahawk rocketed into the air, the call arrived at the camp from Imad ad-Din Zengli. He said, "Pasha has given us up. That probably includes your camp. It is a good idea to scatter, and reassemble later."

After the call ended, the Afghani who ran the camp and his right-hand man looked at each other. The commander said, "Zengli still is such an American. He overreacts. What would this American administration possibly do? They are afraid to act."

He stood up, walked over to the window, and looked out at the expansive camp that trained jihadists from around the world, including the United States.

The other responded, "That definitely was the case with Sanderski, but I do not know much about this Adam Links."

"True. I do not either. How different could he be, though? After all, he was Sanderski's handpicked vice president. What are the chances that she of all people would select someone with a backbone?"

The two men laughed.

Across the camp, the first Tomahawk struck. The blast shattered the window in front of the commander, and sent him tumbling across the floor. He stopped at the feet of the second terrorist. He looked up in shock. The two men merely stared at each other until the next missile fell and obliterated them. After the tenth Tomahawk did its work, all life in the terrorist camp had been extinguished.

Chapter 66

The call from Zengli came, and his message was short and direct: "We are compromised. Act now at both universities, and then go dark. I will contact you." That was it.

Each of the four men picked up a long, black canvas bag, and slung it over his shoulder.

They descended the stairs from the apartment that sat above a pub. When they exited onto the street, they turned to the right and entered a narrow alley that led to the parking lot in the back of the building.

When the last of the four entered the alley, four FBI special agents emerged at the far end, each wearing a helmet and body armor, and pointing a Colt M4 Carbine rifle. One agent called out, "Lower the bags to the ground, and put your hands on your head."

Two of the terrorists turned in the other direction, only to see two heads and rifles, each peeking around the corner of the two buildings that formed the passageway.

The agent called out again, "Don't be stupid. Do it now!"

Three of the terrorists lowered the bags, and started to raise their heads.

The fourth, however, had other ideas. He tossed the bag behind his three fellow assailants, using them as cover from the four approaching agents. He crouched and moved to unzip the bag.

The heavy-duty zipper made it across the entire bag, and the man reached inside.

The two agents leaning around the buildings moved back behind the buildings to avoid being hit by crossfire.

The four approaching agents opened fire. With three terrorists standing with hands on their heads, each agent tried to limit the potential casualties by aiming low at the crouching man.

The stream of bullets hit the three standing men in their legs, but for one projectile that entered an assailant's stomach. Each toppled down, writhing in pain. That, in turn, provided a clear shot at the terrorist pulling a submachine gun out of the bag.

The Colt M4's spewed more bullets forward.

The weapon was dropped back into the bag, as the terrorist rolled over onto the dirty pavement.

As the agents advanced, they were greeted by the man's lifeless eyes staring up at them.

Agents checked the injuries of the three still alive, with others inspecting the bags.

One said, "Shit. Not just submachine guns, but grenades."

Before the suspects were taken down, the pub had been quietly closed, along with the surrounding stores. The supervisory agent declared, "Okay, let's get the bomb squads on the van and sweeping the apartment. These shits have a tendency to rig things."

Chapter 67

By early Friday morning, all of the safe houses and camps established by Zengli to shelter and train his ghazis in the United States had been taken over by the authorities. Imad ad-Din Zengli, Dale Shore and the three members of Shore's squad were the last of this terrorist effort on the loose in the country. With the orders he had spread to go dark, Zengli could not be aware that they were the final group, nor could law enforcement be aware of that fact.

As they drove east on the backroads of northern West Virginia and Maryland, Zengli and Shore stayed in the back of their white van, knowing that their faces would be spread all across the nation. Members of Shore's squad filled up the gas tank, bought food in a convenience store, and purchased two rooms in a dumpy roadside motel.

At 2:30 AM, Shore's three men took one room, and Shore and Zengli the other. Everyone grabbed a few hours of sleep, except Zengli, who sat on his bed madly scribbling notes in a pad while watching the news on an old television. His handgun, with suppressor attached, rested next to him on the mattress.

Shore stirred at a little past 5:30.

Zengli simply said, "Everyone else has failed. We're all that's left."

Shore swung his feet around and stared at the floor. "Okay, well, then this stage of our fight is over. We need to back off, disperse, and find a way out of the country."

Zengli did not answer.

Shore continued, "I still don't know why the hell we're driving back east." He looked up and stared at the person he had followed since high school.

"We're heading east because we're not finished. We can and will make one more statement in New York City, and then do as you say."

"That makes no sense. It's just stupid. Everyone is looking for us, and we're heading to the one place where we're most likely to be captured."

It was perhaps the first time that Shore had indicated both annoyance and disappointment in his friend.

Zengli's voice remained calm. "You're questioning me?"

"In this case, yes. You're not thinking clearly."

"I'm not thinking clearly?"

"Yes, that's what I said."

The two men stared at each other.

Zengli managed a thin smile. "Alright, Dale, you feel strongly about this."

"I do."

"You insist that we not go to New York?"

"Come on, Barry, I mean, Imad, it makes no sense."

Shore's mistake in using the name "Barry" made Zengli's thin smile fade away. He picked up the gun and pointed it at Shore.

Shore leaned back and raised his hands in front of him. "Whoa, whoa, Barry, what are you doing?"

"There. You did it again. My name is no longer 'Barry.' You know that."

"Right, right, I get it. I just slipped. It was a mistake."

"Maybe. But I'm sick of everyone around me making mistakes."

Shore started looking around. "Okay, I get it."

"No, Dale, you little shit. I don't think you ever truly got it. I'm going to New York."

"Right, we're going to New York."

"No, you must have misunderstood me. I am going to New York. You are not."

Zengli pulled the trigger. The bullet entered Shore's chest, and he fell back on the bed. Zengli stood up, and looked down at Shore as blood began to spread across his shirt.

Shore whispered, "Barry, why?"

Zengli gritted his teeth, and fired five more shots into Dale Shore's body.

Zengli then methodically collected his pad and pen, as well as Shore's gun. He slipped his shoes on, scanned the room, and walked out, locking the door behind him.

He then knocked on the door of the room where his last three ghazis slept. One opened the door. Zengli said, "We leave in five minutes."

After the three men climbed into the van, the driver asked, "Where's Dale?"

Zengli merely responded, "He will not be coming with us."

Chapter 68

After their mission and losing one of their own, Paige Caldwell reminded everyone else at CDM International to stay home on Friday and rest. She also passed along the arrangements that Lis's family had established for viewing times and the funeral early the next week.

Caldwell told everyone that she would take care of the office, and she arrived 6:45 in the morning.

She stared out the office window, and sipped her coffee.

She didn't seem too surprised when a few minutes later, a voice from behind her in the doorway asked, "How are you?"

Caldwell turned, and replied, "Okay, I guess. Why are you here, Charlie?"

He merely grunted at the question, and sat down in one of the chairs across the desk from her. He also had a hot coffee in hand.

Caldwell said, "I still can't believe she's dead."

"Yeah, I know. Me either."

"Do you think our group will make it through this?"

"I have no doubt."

"I'm glad you're so sure."

"You're as sure as I am."

She did not respond to that observation.

Driessen continued, "I'm more concerned about you and Sean, not our employees."

"What does that mean?"

"I know I feel some responsibility as one of this firm's partners, but the two of you, from what I can see, are taking this very personally."

"So?"

"So, just keep in mind the full ramifications of any shit that you think has to happen."

Caldwell again chose not to respond.

A few minutes of additional silence were broken by the phone ringing on her desk. Caldwell saw no information on the screen. She said to Driessen, "Blocked." She picked up and said, "Yes."

"Paige, it's Adam."

Caldwell placed the coffee cup on her desk, and said, "Mr. President, good morning." She gave Driessen a look indicating that he should leave, but he didn't budge.

Links asked, "You're not alone?"

"No, sir. I'm with Charlie Driessen."

"Charlie? Tell him I said hello."

"I will. What can I do for you?"

"Paige, I'm going to ask you something, and you have to be completely honest."

"You have my honesty, sir."

Driessen raised an eyebrow, and took another swig of coffee.

Links said, "Good. Is your team up for another undertaking?"

Caldwell paused for the briefest moment, and then said, "Yes, sir, they are."

"Paige, you hesitated. That's not you."

"I think my hesitation is understandable, Mr. President, but don't doubt my final answer."

"Fair enough. As you know, we've cleaned up the safe houses, the camp here in Virginia, and the one in Afghanistan that Teriff Pasha gave up. In addition, the Canadians took care of the issue north of the border."

"And that leaves Venezuela."

"Yes. You know our relationship with Venezuela. I cannot drop 10 Tomahawk missiles on the camp there."

"Right."

"I'm also not keen on sending in the SEALs, for example, because if anyone is captured or, God forbid, killed, then that opens up another set of problems."

"I understand."

"Paige, that doesn't mean..."

"Mr. President, no need to explain, I know the deal. We're on our own."

"Well, you don't know the full story. The Colombians are displeased with a terrorist training camp in a neighboring country, and it, in fact, is not far from the border – a mere 20 miles. So, the Colombians are more than willing to help."

"That's refreshing."

"I agree. Here's the bottom line: We don't know if this group is going to scatter or not. Your team needs to get down to Colombia by early tonight. You'll then take the lead with support and equipment from the Colombian version of special forces. The word on this camp is that they have numbers, as well as ample arms to protect the place, including against helicopters. You'll need to get in under the cover of darkness, and take the place out by whatever means necessary."

Caldwell chuckled, and said, "Sounds like a cakewalk."

"Anything but. However, this camp is significant, and from what we've seen and heard, they have not responded to any warning that Zengli might have passed along. That's not surprising, given our current relationship with the Venezuelan regime. In fact, I've got people telling me that this camp could be under protection from the government."

"Oh, wonderful, more good news."

"I know. But there is some actual good news in that the country is a complete mess, and I'm guessing that the government isn't wasting much on actual protection. It looks like they just let them in to set up a camp. What do you think?"

"I agree that this needs to happen as quickly as possible, and we can get the job done."

"I hate to ask, Paige, especially with your loss this week."

"You were right to, Mr. President. We'll make it happen."

"Thanks, Paige."

"Of course, Adam, you'll owe me, big time."

Driessen went from raising an eyebrow to rolling his eyes.

Links replied, "I already do."

After ending the call, Caldwell said, "President Links said to pass on a hello to you."

"Great. And what else did *Adam* say?"

Caldwell ignored the sarcasm, and said, "We have another job."

Chapter 69

Normally, Stephen Grant was first to rise in the morning. But not on this Friday. Jennifer came into the bedroom, and kissed him on the forehead. She said, "Hey, sleepy head, time to get up. A Navy SEAL made breakfast, and I don't think you're supposed to be late."

"Aye, aye. What time is it?"

She glanced at the digital clock on her nightstand. "8:10."

"Wow. When was the last time I slept this late?"

"I can't recall, but obviously, you needed it."

Stephen followed Jennifer into the kitchen where Miguel Ramos had spread out an impressive breakfast of huevos rancheros, with eggs and refried beans resting on a tortilla, topped with ranchero sauce, Cotija cheese, cilantro and onion.

Stephen joined Miguel, Isaiah Green and Jennifer at the island in the middle of the kitchen. "Miguel, this looks fantastic."

"Jennifer has been such a gracious host during our stay, I thought that the least I could do was whip up my breakfast specialty."

After swallowing her first bite, Jennifer said, "There was no need for you to do anything, given what you are doing for us. Having said that, this is delicious."

Isaiah added, "Yeah, Miguel, this is pretty darn good."

Stephen chimed in, "I agree. Excellent."

Isaiah looked at Stephen and said, "Well, you've had quite a week. Stopping two terrorist attacks. Is this how things generally go around here for your typical pastor?"

Stephen merely shook his head, and continued eating.

Miguel asked, "So, we're still looking for the ringleader, this Zengli guy, and his buddy from high school, right?"

Stephen nodded, "Yes, as far as I know."

Miguel continued, "President Links seems to have a set, as opposed to Sanderski." He looked at Jennifer, and quickly added, "Oh, sorry about that, Jennifer."

She smiled and said, "No need."

Isaiah asked, "Did you ever work with him at the Agency?"

Stephen answered, "No, we actually just missed each other. I've heard that he's a good man, a straight shooter." He glanced briefly at Jennifer.

Miguel said, "Seems to be the case."

Isaiah brought the conversation back to Zengli. "I would think Zengli and whoever he has left are going deep underground, and trying to find a way out of the country."

Stephen said, "That would make the most sense."

Miguel interjected, "But we can't bet on sense prevailing with nut jobs like this."

Stephen put his fork down and leaned back in his chair. "I know. That's the problem."

Miguel asked, "Who is with Pastor Leonard today?"

"The two police detectives – Godfrey and Baldwin – have a day off, so they're spending it with him. I'm not quite sure about the weekend yet."

Isaiah said, "Good. It is hard to believe that these clowns would come back to New York, again." No one replied. He took a mouthful of huevos rancheros, and chewed while looking back and forth at Jennifer and Stephen. "Okay, I can stay through Sunday."

Miguel added, "Yeah, I can, too. We'll continue to provide some security for St. Mary's and your lovely wife, while you cover Leonard. However, I do have to get back to the university on Monday."

Isaiah added, "Yeah, back to work on Monday for me as well."

Stephen said, "Guys, there's no need for..."

Isaiah interrupted him, and said, "Let's hope there's no need. Like I've said before, that would be the best scenario. Nonetheless, it is smart."

Stephen said, "Thank you, my brothers."

Jennifer got up, and walked over to each, gave a kiss on the cheek, and said, "Thank you so much."

Miguel smiled, and said, "Not a problem." He looked at Stephen. "But from what we've heard, it might not be Jennifer who needs some security. I understand that before the two of you got married, she came to your rescue."

Isaiah nodded.

Stephen looked at his wife, who wore a mischievous grin. He asked, "You told them about that?"

Before she could answer, Miguel added, "And a few other incidents you two have been involved in."

Jennifer said, "Hey, you call these men 'brothers,' and I have no doubt about their ability to keep a secret or two."

The look on Stephen's face signaled a good-natured resignation.

Jennifer added, "And I've learned a little more about things in my husband's past that he has failed to mention."

Stephen declared, "Oh, God, help."

Chapter 70

The neon sign for the small hotel in a tired town in southwest New Jersey flashed "Vacancy." Even though the "n" and the "y" were darkened, people got the point. Well, anyone who cared did, which on this Friday night seemed to only be two couples interested in no one knowing where they were.

From the back of the van, Zengli said, "That'll work. Pull into that store first." The driver turned into the parking lot of a convenience store diagonally across the road from the hotel.

Like Zengli, the driver was born in the United States. He was about to get out when a town police car pulled up and parked two spaces away.

The officer got out, looked at the van and the driver as he opened the door to the store, and went inside.

The driver of the van turned back to look at Zengli, and asked, "What do we do? Leave?"

In a low angry voice, Zengli said, "First, turn around. Second, get your ass inside the store. Be polite. Make eye contact. Smile. Get what we need. Make small talk if needed. Pay the clerk, and get back out here. And do it all naturally. If not, we're going to have to kill the guy behind the counter and the cop. If that happens, the plan is down the toilet. Understand?"

The driver – Craig Wainwright – nodded jerkily, and got out of the vehicle. It paid that he looked so nondescript. He was slightly overweight, five feet ten inches, black hair, and facial stubble from not shaving in a few days. He wore jeans, a dark gray sweatshirt, and a black, wool jacket.

Upon entering the store, the clerk looked up from his phone and nodded. Wainwright picked up a small basket and merely said, "Hi."

He proceeded to collect several items that could be eaten in the hotel room, along with a few bottles of water. From the back of the store, Wainwright watched as the officer approached the clerk with a large coffee cup in one hand, and two glazed doughnuts in a small bag.

The clerk rang him up only for the doughnuts.

The cop said, "Thanks, Trevor."

"Good to see you, Al."

The officer exited the building, and Wainwright moved forward toward the counter.

Outside, however, the officer did not get back in his patrol car. Rather, he stood just outside the door, sipping his coffee, and apparently taking in the surrounding area.

As each item was rung up by the clerk, Wainwright's eyes kept moving to see what the cop was doing.

The officer still didn't move.

The clerk said, "That'll be $46.78."

Wainwright said, "Right." He took out a $100 bill and went to hand it to the clerk.

"Hey, man, I don't have that kind of change. You got anything smaller?"

Wainwright turned his gaze away from the officer standing outside to the clerk. "What?"

"That bill is too big. Got anything smaller?"

"Oh, yeah." He pulled back the $100 bill, and handed over two twenties and a ten. "Sorry."

"That's better. Thanks."

The clerk handed over the change, and the two bags of items. "Take it easy."

"You, too." Wainwright took a deep breath, walked toward the door, and pushed it open. As he walked by the cop, he said, "Have a nice night, officer."

The cop replied, "Yeah, you, too."

Wainwright climbed into the van, and handed the bags to the man sitting in the front passenger seat.

The officer turned his attention to the van as the engine started up. He watched it as Wainwright backed it up, and then turned toward one of the parking lot exits.

Zengli looked out the back window.

The cop finally walked over and got in his car. He pulled over to the other exit. The patrol car barely hesitated. It turned onto the road, and moved away from the store and the hotel.

Zengli proclaimed, "Looks like we are good. Go ahead, and pull into the hotel."

Chapter 71

The security covering those leaving Venezuela and entering Colombia had been stepped up in recent times. The Venezuelan socialist paradise turned out to be a socialist hellhole, and the primary flow of humanity clearly was in one direction.

Heading in the other direction, Venezuelan guards seemed largely uninterested in those entering the country. Paige Caldwell and her team of CDM personnel and a dozen Colombian special ops were counting on such lack of interest. But at this time of night, and given that there would only be two guards on duty, they would be able to deal with the situation if anyone got too nosey.

Three trucks approached and drove onto the bridge. A guard sitting in a chair next to a gate seemed annoyed that he had to get up. He came around to the driver's door, and asked. "Who are you, what's your business?"

The driver explained that they were moving construction materials and manufacturing parts for a new factory being built. He handed the guard the fake paperwork.

The guard laughed, and said, "You people are building a plant in our country?"

The driver nodded, and gave an enthusiastic, "Yes."

Clearly, the guard's glance at the paperwork was a ritual without substance. "Good luck with that. Go ahead."

The three trucks were waved through without any problems.

A thirty-minute drive followed, with the trucks pulling off the road into a wooded area less than a mile from the terrorist camp.

At Caldwell's request, most of the Colombians spoke English. The three that didn't were placed with Chase Axelrod, since Spanish was among the seven languages he spoke.

Three teams of six fanned out according to plan. Axelrod and West led one, McEnany and Lucena a second, and Caldwell and Driessen the third.

McEnany, Lucena and their four Colombian allies were charged with quietly taking down the handful of men expected to be on guard duty.

The weather in Venezuela in February normally is quite nice, with average highs in the upper seventies and lows in the mid-sixties. But tonight, it was unseasonably cool – in the upper forties. As a result, the four guards on duty in the camp were huddled around a barrel with a fire raging inside it.

McEnany and his squad watched from a cover of bushes. He whispered into his microphone, "It's too cold for these babies? I love it. If we keep it quiet, the brightness of that fire will make sure they never see us coming. Now."

The four never did see or hear anyone.

Both Lucena and McEnany grabbed a man from behind. Each shoved a knife blade into their target's neck, and pulled back and sideways.

The other two terrorists tried to react to the opponents emerging from the darkness, but to no avail. Two members of Colombian spec ops were on top of each target. One held the terrorist from behind, covering his mouth, while the other shoved a knife into the chest.

The guards were eliminated in seconds.

McEnany declared into his microphone. "Targets down. We're moving back. You are clear."

The grounds held two double story barracks, and given the fact that it was 2:30 AM, the rest of the camp was expected to be asleep. Caldwell's squad took one of the buildings, and Axelrod's had the other.

Three squad members in each assault team raised stubby-looking grenade launchers to their shoulders. The others from each group were positioned with submachine guns to cut down anyone who might emerge from the forthcoming conflagrations. Caldwell was the only one preferring to use her Glock.

Driessen held one of the launchers. In his microphone, he said, "Okay, quick countdown. 3, 2, 1, now."

The beauty of these grenade launchers wasn't just their laser rangefinders, but that they were semiautomatic, with five rounds in each magazine.

Coming from three sides, five projectiles penetrated walls or windows of each building, with the grenades detonating at a determined distance. After the initial massive explosions tore apart much of each building, setting them ablaze, each shooter dropped the empty magazine, and slipped on a new one. The same firing process took place, and the buildings crumbled.

Amazingly, emerging from one of the massive fires, a lone figure staggered forward. Caldwell steadied her Glock, and fired off two quick shots. The shadowy outline of the man fell to the ground.

Behind Caldwell and Driessen, less than forty yards away, the engine of an olive-green pickup truck started, and the vehicle began to accelerate. Its destination was a broken gate leading into thick foliage. The truck was moving away from all three teams. Besides the driver, a man sat on the passenger side of the cab, and another crouched down in the truck bed.

Caldwell said, "Shit."

Several feet away, Driessen smiled and said, "No, it's okay. Watch this."

With a new magazine inserted, he raised the grenade launcher, and tracked the target. But before he could pull the trigger, the truck erupted in an explosion, followed by a pillar of fire reaching high into the air, accompanied by the body of the terrorist who had been riding in the back of the pickup.

Driessen lowered his weapon, and said, "What the hell?"

A few seconds later, Jessica West strolled up with her RPG launcher slung over her shoulder. She patted the weapon. "I love this fucking gun."

Driessen said, "You beat me to it."

West flashed her bright smile, and said, "Damn right, I did. And you owe me a drink later for doing it."

She continued walking by, heading to the trucks that would take them back into Colombia.

Chapter 72

Saturday at St. Mark's was thankfully quiet for both Stephen Grant and Richard Leonard.

Grant had arrived early in the morning, and was able to have an iced tea while Richard drank coffee with Detectives Godfrey and Baldwin. Much of the conversation rested on Grant trying to fend off questions about his past from the two detectives, while Leonard watched with a bemused look.

Later, Stephen spoke with Paige Caldwell as she and the CDM crew flew back from their successful mission in South America.

Otherwise, much of the day was spent poking around Leonard's collection of history books, and talking with Richard on a wide range of topics, including looking back at his father, and looking forward to his future. Specifically, questions had been popping up of late in Leonard's mind about whether or not he was in the right place to serve the Lord and His Church. On that last point, Grant's advice amounted to "get clear of everything that had happened of late, let things calm down, and then think long and hard before you make any changes."

Leonard also brought up Madison Tanquerey, and said, "You know, I think I like her."

"No kidding?"

"What do you mean?"

"It's obvious that the two of you are interested in each other."

Leonard let that comment hang in the air for a while, and then said, "Me and a TV news reporter. At sem, the assumption always seemed to be that future pastors marry future deaconesses or Lutheran teachers."

Grant said, "Yeah, well, I love being married to an economist."

Leonard smiled at that remark.

That night, they ate another Italian dinner courtesy of the pizza parlor owner, and wound up watching a hockey game.

After talking with Jennifer and wishing her a restful sleep, Grant was in the guest room bed by eleven o'clock.

It was three-and-a-half hours later, when two muffled shots were fired in the street just a few houses away from the St. Mark's parsonage. Both officers in the patrol car bled from their heads.

Grant's eyes bolted open at the sounds. The second-floor guest room was in the front of the parsonage. He looked through the curtains and saw people moving toward the house.

He picked up the silver case next to the bed, clicked it open, and pulled out two handguns. He loaded a magazine into each Glock 20, and ran to Leonard's bedroom.

Though he whispered, the intensity of his voice came through clearly to Leonard. Grant said, "Richard, get up. We've got trouble."

Leonard sat up, and asked, "What is it?"

"Unwanted visitors." He held out the gun. "You still know what you're doing with this?"

Leonard hesitated, and then took the weapon. "Yes. What are we doing?"

The high ground.

"We've got the high ground, and we're not giving it up. Only two ways up here, correct? Main staircase, and the fire escape?"

"Yes."

"You're the fire escape. Don't let anyone climb it. I'll cover the stairs."

Again, Leonard hesitated.

Grant said, "Go."

While still moving awkwardly due to his bandaged neck, Leonard sprinted to the back bedroom, and moved to the window with the fire escape outside. He looked out. The terrorist on the ground looked up, raised his gun and fired. Leonard dove back as the window shattered.

*   *   *

When he heard the gunshot and window break, Grant started to move from his point of cover behind a doorframe at the side of the top of the stairs. But the front door was kicked open, and a man dressed in brown entered and fired up at Grant.

Grant moved back to cover.

*   *   *

Leonard was on the floor, and pushed his back against a dresser. He stared at the now-broken window.

He heard the shot inside the house, and said out loud, "Jesus, where's my father when I need him?"

*   *   *

At the bottom of the stairs, two men now fired away at Grant's hidden position. The doorframe and hallway wall were being chewed to pieces.

Grant looked around, and spotted a glass lamp resting on the table next to him. He pulled the plug out of the wall, grabbed the lamp, and turned his attention back to the bullets ascending from below.

He tossed the lamp in an arch down the hallway. As it flew, one of the assailants turned his aim on the flying lamp. Grant leaned out, looked down the stairs, aimed his Glock, and pulled off several shots at a man dressed in black. Two bullets penetrated flesh, and the man fell to the floor.

The man in brown refocused on Grant. Three shots narrowly missed, and Grant was back behind cover.

*   *   *

With gunfire elsewhere, Leonard remained up against the dresser.

Below, the attacker began to climb the generous stairs on the fire escape, pointing his gun at the window the entire time.

For a brief moment when a shot was not being fired, Leonard focused his attention on the window. The cold air blowing in carried with it the sounds of footsteps on the metal stairs.

Leonard rose with the gun in his hand. Standing next to the window, he called out, "You really need to stop and throw away your gun."

The climbing of the stairs quickened and grew louder.

With pleading in his voice, Leonard said, "Please, stop. Don't come any higher."

The ascent continued.

With a quiver in his voice, Leonard said, "I will shoot."

The sounds of weight coming down on metal grew closer.

Leonard gripped the gun tightly with two hands, and quickly leaned out the window. He met the terrorist's eyes,

a mere six feet away, and pulled the trigger twice. The
man dropped his gun, spun over the railing, and
plummeted to the ground.

Leonard staggered back into the room, and dropped the
gun on the floor.

*   *   *

The shooting from below suddenly stopped. Grant
looked around the corner and down the stairs.

Where the hell is he?

Grant moved down the stairs scanning with his eyes
and gun. He had a choice: look around on the main floor or
assume the shooter had made a break for it. He chose the
latter.

Grant stepped out on the front porch, and saw a man
running down the street. He jumped off the porch, and
began his pursuit.

The terrorist ran by the front of the university and then
went by the doors of St. Mark's Church and turned down
the side street. Grant arrived at the edge of the church
building, and paused before he would make the same turn.

He stepped out with his Glock pointed in front of him.
Grant scanned the darkness as best he could. He took
several steps forward.

Then a voice came from behind. "Drop it."

*Crap. Circled around the church. Who does that when
being chased?*

"I said drop it."

Grant leaned down, placed the gun on the ground, and
with his hands stretched out, he turned and saw the face of
Imad ad-Din Zengli, or Barry Hill. "Barry Hill. The so-
called mastermind."

"Imad ad-Din Zengli."

Anger him. Get him off balance. Only chance.

"Yeah, right. Where'd you get that name, Barry? Some jihadist asshole in history? And you came back here just to get revenge against a pastor who managed to piss you off. You've completely lost it. Did you really think that you were going to get away from here, or is this one of those cowardly suicide things?"

"There is nothing suicidal about this. It's part of my plan."

"Your plan? Or is this all about Allah and Muhammad?"

"Silence!" Zengli's eyes narrowed. "You're Grant."

"Yes, and I've had the pleasure in recent days of taking down some of the clowns you set loose."

"And now I will have the pleasure of eliminating you. Although, I have to admit that I did not expect you to be here tonight."

"No?"

"That's why I sent someone to your home. But I'm sure your wife will still be there, mistakenly thinking that she is safe in her home and her bed."

"What!?"

Grant could see Zengli's mad smile in the dark. "That's right. My ghazi should be there about now."

God, please no!

Richard Leonard was running in the direction of Zengli and Grant. He stopped directly in front of the main doors of St. Mark's, and called out, "Please, you don't have to do this." Leonard had left the gun on the floor in the parsonage. He simply stood on the sidewalk, with his arms at his side and palms open.

Zengli stood on the sidewalk at a corner. On the side of the church, down the street in front of him was Grant. To Zengli's left, up the other street, Leonard stood unarmed and hands open.

While still pointing the gun at Grant, Zengli turned his head when Leonard spoke. That gave Grant his lone chance. He dove for the Glock.

The adrenaline kicked up in Zengli, making him shake ever so slightly. As a result, his two shots at Grant went astray.

With the Glock in his hand, Grant rolled once on the cement. He stopped, lying flat on his back. He lifted his head up, and pointed the gun through his bent legs.

Meanwhile, as Zengli fired, Leonard sprinted forward. Like in the church on that tragic Sunday, he once again was positioning himself to tackle the assailant.

Grant fired off three shots.

Leonard plowed into Zengli, and the two men crashed to the ground. They scraped along on the sidewalk, with Zengli tumbling over the curb onto the street, and Leonard then sliding over him.

God, no.

Grant sprinted forward.

The two were face up. Zengli had two holes in his chest and one in a shoulder. Each was leaking blood. His eyes were closed, and breathing ceased.

Leonard lay motionless, and then his eyes opened.

Grant looked down, relieved, and asked, "Are you okay?"

Leonard nodded, and glanced at Zengli's body.

Grant announced, "I have to warn Jennifer." He turned to run back to the parsonage and his phone.

Leonard yelled, "Go, go!"

Chapter 73

Craig Wainwright didn't drive all the way down the street. Instead, he did a quick three-point turn, and positioned the black hatchback for a quick escape. He grabbed a bag from the backseat, and unzipped it. He pulled out a handgun, and did a quick check of the connections from the cell phone detonators to the six blocks of C4. He swung the bag over his shoulder.

The wrought-iron gate at the bottom of the driveway was locked. Wainwright scaled it, and moved quickly toward the Grant home.

Zengli had instructed him where to place the explosives up against the home.

But just after passing the pool, Wainwright was greeted by floodlights. He froze, and raised his left hand to shield his eyes. The right hand still held the gun.

A voice emanated from the other side of the light barrier.

Wainwright squinted hard, but could see no one.

Isaiah Green announced, "Son, don't make another move. I don't know what's in that bag. And I can see your gun. My advice to you is put them both down, and then get down on your knees with your hands on your head. That way, no one gets hurt."

Wainwright looked to his left and then to the right. His moves grew more frantic.

Green said, "Please settle down. Just do as I say, and…"

Wainwright screamed, "No! Allahu Akbar!" He started to run forward, and pointed the gun into the light. He fired off one shot.

And then a bullet emerged from behind the light barrier. It struck Wainwright in the chest, dropping him to the ground.

From behind the light, Green said in a low voice, "Nice shot, Miguel."

"Yeah, I guess. Damn shame."

Inside the house a few minutes later, Jennifer's phone buzzed. "Stephen, are you alright?"

"Jen, Zengli is sending someone your way. Tell Miguel and Isaiah, and …"

"Stephen, Stephen. We know. We're all okay."

"What happened?"

"The security upgrade that Sean put in worked perfectly. As for the attacker, well, Isaiah and Miguel tried to have him surrender. But he wouldn't. Miguel shot him. He's dead."

"Jen, thank God, you're safe."

"Stephen, he had a bag full of C4."

"I'm so sorry."

"Stephen, it worked like it was supposed to in a time of madness. There's no reason for you to say sorry. And while I'm shaking and can't wait until you're home, we should be thankful."

Chapter 74

At 8:00 AM on Sunday morning, President Adam Links went on television from the Oval Office. He explained to the nation that the leader of the terrorist attacks against the United States had been killed.

He touched on some very basic circumstances as to what happened and where. He noted the bravery of Pastor Richard Leonard. Links also said that he could not name the person who took down Imad ad-Din Zengli for national security reasons. But he looked in the camera and declared, "You know who you are. And you have earned the thanks and respect of every person in this nation. Thank you for your service and your bravery."

Links continued, "The same goes for the incredible performance of all of the many other hard working, brave people who stopped these terrorists and serve the American people in the FBI, the CIA, the armed forces, and numerous law enforcement agencies across the nation. We will be honoring many of these people in the coming days and weeks, just as we continue to mourn those we have lost. We thank God for the time we had them among us."

Links also talked about international partners and allies, particularly mentioning Egypt, Colombia, Canada and the government in Afghanistan, fighting off terrorist infiltrations and attacks.

A bit later, Links wrapped up, "Our nation has suffered previously unimaginable losses, including, of course, the death of President Elizabeth Sanderski and the horrific attacks on churches across the land. National security and law enforcement experts tell me that they are confident that this particular group of terrorists has been eradicated in our country. I am confident that is the case. However, we all must be vigilant. Make no mistake, we are at war, not with Islam, but with militant Islamists bent on destroying our way of life, including a clear desire to eliminate the many freedoms we enjoy, including those etched in the First Amendment – freedom of religion, freedom of speech, freedom of the press, and freedom of assembly. As president, I pledge to you that this government will not allow for the loss or diminishment of our freedoms. Each of us must be strong. Now, let us proceed with the healing of our great nation, praying for the victims and families. God bless you, and God bless America."

Chapter 75

Amazingly, the FBI and NYPD made sure that Sunday morning Divine Services at St. Mark's could be held in the church.

Pastor Brett Matthews, the Atlantic District president, presided, while Pastor Leonard was there to assist, patched up with additional bandages. He spoke with parishioners before and after each service. But he appeared distracted, and understandably so, after what he had been through during the night.

Each service was filled, and Leonard must have absentmindedly said that he was "okay" nearly one hundred times during the morning.

Attending the second service was Madison Tanquerey. Leonard only seemed to notice her presence during the distribution of Communion. After the service, she lingered in the narthex until Leonard was done talking with and being hugged – for the most part carefully – by a seemingly endless stream of churchgoers.

He came over, and said, "Madison, thanks for coming. Can you grab a seat in my office, while I just finish up with Pastor Matthews?"

She said, "Should I come back at another time? I can…"

Leonard looked into her eyes, and said, "Please, no. I'll be right in. If you can wait just a couple of more minutes."

She smiled, and said, "Of course."

A few minutes later, Leonard entered the office, and said, "I am so sorry."

She got up, and said, "Oh, no problem. I..."

She came up short as she turned in the tiny office, and found her face inches from his.

Richard said, "Madison, thank God you came today."

"I'm so glad you're alright after last night."

Each moved to embrace the other.

After several seconds, Richard drew his head back from her shoulder, and kissed her.

Madison eventually said, "I've never kissed a pastor before." She smiled.

"And I've never kissed a famous TV news reporter."

"Famous? Don't think so. But I guess this is new ground for both of us."

"I guess it is. But I like it."

Madison nodded, "Me, too."

"Let's talk. How about that dinner I owe you?"

"Well, it's not one o'clock yet, but dinner sounds good."

Chapter 76

At about the same time that the late service at St. Mark's on Staten Island was ending, a similar scene was playing out nearly 90 miles east at St. Mary's Lutheran Church.

While Pastor Grant received well wishes and thanks from most parishioners, as they vaguely knew about some of the more minor challenges he had faced of late, there were a few church members who took thinly veiled shots heading out the door. One sour-puss said, "Well, I hope we'll see more of you around here now, Pastor."

Grant smiled in response, and replied, "You can bet on it, Eugene."

Within 20 minutes of the late service's conclusion, the building was empty except for six souls, who were now in Stephen's office.

Jennifer said, "Are you sure that we can't at least buy you lunch before getting on the road?"

Isaiah said, "No, thank you, again. But I need to get back home, and I think even Miguel's wife is missing him."

Miguel added, "Yeah, how crazy is that?"

She kissed Isaiah Green and Miguel Ramos on their respective cheeks, hugged them, and whispered to each, "Thank you, and God bless you."

Pastor Zack Charmichael stepped forward, and introduced his wife, Cara.

She said, "I'm sorry we didn't get to talk, but I had a hectic week at the hospital."

Isaiah said, "I understand. By the way, your husband is a good man." Stephen noticed Zack suddenly stand a little taller. Glancing at both Miguel and Zack, Isaiah continued, "We all got to know each other a bit."

Cara smiled, and said, "Thanks. And he says the same about the two of you."

Zack shook each man's hand, and added, "By the way, I appreciate the background on Stephen. That'll come in handy."

As the three men laughed, Stephen asked Miguel and Isaiah, "Is there anyone around here that the two of you didn't tell stories to?"

Miguel replied, "No, I think we covered everyone. The church secretary – I'm sorry, what's her name again?"

Jennifer volunteered, "Barbara Tunney."

"That's right. What a nice lady. She also enjoyed hearing about the younger Stephen Grant."

Stephen said, "Oh, great. Thanks so much."

Miguel stepped toward his old friend, and said, "Hey, that's what brothers are for." The two men hugged.

Stephen did the same with Isaiah, and then said, "Thanks for what you both did."

"No need for thanks," said Isaiah.

"That's right," added Miguel. "Let's get together soon, but under happier circumstances."

"Amen to that," said Isaiah.

"Amen, my brothers," affirmed Stephen.

Chapter 77

Alexandria Rappe sat on one end of the couch in the living room in her historic home. Her daughter, Lilly, was stretched out under a blanket, resting her head on Alex's lap.

Amidst the tragedy and tumult of the previous two weeks, these two women were among the many people who suffered direct and personal loss. The man they loved – Alex's husband and Lilly's father – had been killed at the hand of terrorists.

The television was on. The two looked at the screen with distant stares.

Lilly turned slightly to look up at her mother. "Mom, I think I'm going to take this semester off. I want to be home."

Alex smiled sadly. "Is that for my benefit or yours?"

"Well, both of us, I guess."

"Would your dad have wanted you to do that?"

Lilly's eyes moistened. "I don't know."

After several minutes of silence, Lilly asked, "What are we going to do, Mom, without him?"

"Lilly, part of me doesn't know the answer to that question. But the rest of me knows, as unimaginable as it might be right now, that we will go on. We'll hopefully follow our hopes and dreams, and help others along the way, just like he would have wanted."

Alex's smartphone rumbled on the end table next to her.
Lilly said, "Oh, don't answer it. I'm so tired."

"So am I, but I have to." She glanced at the screen, and
saw that the caller's number was blocked. "Hello?"

A woman said, "Alexandria Rappe, please."

"Yes."

"I have the president of the United States for you."

Alex leaned forward a bit. Lilly sat up, and looked at her
mother.

Alex replied, "Ah, yes, of course."

Links came on the line. "Undersecretary Rappe, I am so
sorry for your loss."

"Thank you, Mr. President. It's very kind of you to say,
and to call."

"Mrs. Rappe, I've been familiar with the work that both
your husband and you have done since I arrived in this
town as a senator. Your efforts in the foreign policy arena
have been impressive. And your husband, Blake, the work
that he did as a lawyer to help refugees suffering religious
persecution in their homelands, well, that was selfless and
it made profound differences in people's lives."

"I'm   very   proud   of   my   husband   and   his
accomplishments."

"You should be. His is a terrible loss. The nation mourns
with you and your daughter, and rest assured that I have
both of you, and Blake, in my prayers."

"Tha..." Her voice broke for a moment. "Thank you so
much, Mr. President."

"I have to go now, Undersecretary Rappe. I hope that
when you're ready, we might see each other on the
campaign trail. You're working for a good man in Governor
Hamilton."

Alex leaned back on the couch with a somewhat
bewildered look. "Yes, yes, he is, Mr. President. Thank you,
again."

The call ended, and Alex turned to see her daughter staring with her mouth open.

Lilly asked, "Was that actually President Links?"

Alex nodded. "It was."

They sat in silence for several minutes. Alex finally said, "I have to make another call."

Governor Wyatt Hamilton answered quickly. "Alex, how are you?"

"We're doing as well as can be expected. I just wanted to let you know that President Links just called." She proceeded to relay much of the conversation.

After she concluded, Hamilton said, "He's a man of integrity."

"He is. I wanted to let you know that, when my daughter and I are ready, I'll be back to work with the campaign."

"That obviously would make me and our team extremely happy. Are you sure, though?"

"Yes, about as sure as I can be about anything these days."

"Come back when you're ready."

"Thanks, Wyatt. By the way, if Blake were still alive, I think he'd be pleased with one thing that has become clear to so many in this country recently."

"What's that?"

"That both political parties this year look like they're going to nominate candidates of high character and integrity."

"Thanks, Alex. That means a great deal."

"I meant every word. Take care, Wyatt."

"You, too. We'll talk soon."

Lilly smiled at her mother. "Dad would have liked that – two candidates of integrity."

Alex added, "I think he can see what's happening."

Lilly moved closer, and placed her head on her mother's shoulder.

Alex said, "Maybe before dinner we should go for a little walk."

Lilly picked up her head, looked at her mother, and then nodded. After a few seconds, she seemed to find part of her voice, whispering, "Yes, I'd like that."

Chapter 78

Multiple visitors in one day to the offices of CDM International Strategies and Security was, to say the least, a rarity. On this Monday afternoon, however, standing in the bullpen area were eight men in dark suits.

The directors of the CIA and FBI took turns making short speeches thanking each of the CDM team for what they had achieved in protecting the country over the past two weeks, but particularly for what was accomplished in both Egypt and Venezuela.

After their respective comments, Paige Caldwell, Charlie Driessen, Sean McEnany, Jessica West, Chase Axelrod and Phil Lucena stood in a line. Each director proceeded to thank each one personally, and hand over a small plaque with their names and accomplishments carved out. In addition to a top aide to each director, Rich Noack and Trent Nguyen from the FBI stood watching, along with Edward "Tank" Hoard and Aaron Rixey from the CIA.

At the end of the line, each director made additional comments about Lis Dicce, praising her bravery and commitment to her country, and assuring everyone that her husband and son would know that she received the same appreciation posthumously.

As each director was ready to leave, Caldwell moved forward to thank them for coming and for recognizing the entire CDM team.

Meanwhile, an aide for each director went around the room collecting the commendations just handed out to each person. As the CIA director's aide went to reclaim what the Agency had just awarded, Driessen said, "You're shitting me."

The aide said, "Hey, you know how it is."

With that, the two directors, their aides and the awards were gone.

Rixey and Hoard broke away from talking with McEnany, Axelrod and Lucena. Tank said, "Nice offices, Paige."

"Thanks, Tank."

"McEnany knows what he's doing."

Rixey added, "Yes, I'm uncomfortable with the fact that we can still learn a few things from him."

Caldwell said, "That's one of the reasons we love him. In addition, Lis played a key role in developing the offices and all of the security measures."

Hoard said, "She was top notch."

Caldwell nodded.

Rixey extended his hand, and said, "Thanks again for what your team accomplished. If I miss you at Lis's funeral, we'll be in touch, again, I have no doubt."

"Take care, Aaron."

Caldwell leaned back ever so slightly when Rixey uncharacteristically leaned in very close. His cheek actually brushed against her long black hair. He was barely audible. "Be very careful regarding our friend."

He turned and walked away, and Caldwell gave no sign that he had just given her a cryptic warning.

Hoard and Caldwell exchanged a quick hug. He whispered, "I'll make sure everything gets done for Lis's family."

"Thanks."

"I'll see you at the funeral."

Caldwell watched as Rixey and Hoard entered the elevator. Both turned around before the doors closed. Hoard nodded at her, while Rixey kept his head down. The doors closed.

Caldwell then wandered over to Noack and Nguyen, who were talking with Driessen and West.

Driessen immediately said, "That handing awards out and then taking them back is such crap."

"Security, Charlie," Caldwell responded.

"What do they think, we're going to take them down to the local bar, get drunk and show them off?"

Caldwell raised an eyebrow, and Driessen merely grunted in response.

"Time for us to head out as well," volunteered Noack.

Nguyen then proceeded to extend a firm handshake to each person in formal fashion. To each, he said, "Thank you for your courage. I cannot tell you how much it means to me, to my family, and to the people of this nation."

Noack stood next to Caldwell and Driessen and watched his partner. He said, "If anyone else in any other situation said that, it would be so corny I'd probably puke. But he pulls it off."

Driessen said, "Yeah, actually, he does."

Caldwell added, "He's sincere."

Noack said, "He is. And that's why we continue to call him Captain America."

Nguyen said, "You know, I'm right here and can hear you."

Noack laughed. "Got it." He offered quick handshakes and thanks to Lucena, Axelrod, and McEnany. He paused a bit longer with West, and told her, "We still miss you at the Bureau, but you're doing great work right here."

Noack turned to Driessen, and said, "Charlie, stay out of trouble."

"Funny, Noack."

Caldwell and Noack then exchanged a brief hug, and he said, "You're making a real difference. Keep it up."

Chapter 79

Stephen looked at Jennifer lying next to him in bed. She was sound asleep. He pulled the blanket up a little higher to cover her shoulder.

Don't know if "normal" is the right word yet, but today was welcome. I don't think I was ever so pleased to be stuck in my office all day, catching up on work.

As he turned back to the novel he was reading, his phone buzzed on the nightstand. "Hello."

"Stephen, this is Adam Links."

"Mr. President, how are you?"

"Good, Stephen. I'm sorry to disturb you."

"You most certainly are not disturbing me."

"I promise that this isn't going to become a regular Monday night thing. I just wanted to thank you personally for what you did last week. By my tally, you took down nine terrorists, including the one behind the entire network and plan. That at least should earn a medal of some kind."

Nine people. And then I just come home to Jen and St. Mary's, and pick up the day to day? What kind of life do you live, Grant?

Links continued, "I understand, though, why we're trying to keep your actions under wraps as much as possible, especially given your background and current line of work. Still, that thank you reference to an unnamed hero in my address yesterday was meant for you."

"Well, thank you, sir."

"I thought I lived a unique life, but you might have me beat."

"I sometimes wonder, Mr. President."

"Don't wonder too much. I appreciate all you've done, Stephen, in the service of your country, not to mention in service of the Lord. Sleep well, my friend."

"You, too, Mr. President."

The call ended, and Stephen put the phone down. He sat in bed, with the closed book in his lap.

With her eyes still shut, Jennifer asked, "Was that your friend, Adam, again?"

"Yes, apparently, this is becoming a Monday night thing."

*   *   *

Tuesday wasn't a typical weekday morning for breakfast and devotions with his clergy friends, but it worked for all four to catch up.

After reading from *For All the Saints* and ordering their respective meals, Ron, Tom and Zack simply stared at Stephen. He said, "What?"

Zack replied, "What do you mean 'what'? Give us the rundown on the past week."

"No. I can't."

"Seriously?"

"Yes, seriously."

Zack persisted, "It's obvious that you were involved at Columbus Circle, and I'm betting that you took down Zengli."

Stephen said, "First, please lower your voice. Second, I really can't get into it, especially here."

Now talking just above a whisper, Zack said, "That is not a denial, and it leaves the door open for getting into this in a more private place at another time."

Stephen shrugged. He then turned to Ron. "How are you? How did it go at St. Francis?"

"I'm surviving. As for St. Francis, people are still bewildered and upset. This runs so deep. They're shaken to the core."

Tom asked, "How is the Diocese handling matters?"

"Fine, actually. They've asked me and another priest from the North Shore to split our time with the St. Francis people until they figure out what's the next step for the parish."

Stephen asked, "Can you handle that with St. Luke's?"

"Father Burns has temporarily moved back into the rectory, and he clearly is energized. So, that's good."

The food arrived, and the conversation took a turn to less intense topics.

At one point, Tom even asked, "Anyone do anything interesting last night?"

Stephen replied, "Mainly, a quiet night at home for Jennifer and me. Interesting conversation and a novel in bed." *Hey, not a lie.*

Chapter 80

The loss of his Tahoe meant that Stephen was hitching a ride with Zack. After breakfast, they arrived at St. Mary's by 8:30.

Stephen only had time to open his MacBook Pro and hit the power button before the phone rang. Barbara wasn't in yet, so he picked up and hit the flashing line. "St. Mary's Lutheran Church."

"Stephen?"

"Yes, Richard?"

"Do you have a few minutes?"

"Sure. Everything okay?"

"I'm not sure, to be honest. I can't get the shooting out of my mind. Even given what my father did, what I've studied, knowing plenty of cops and military, I don't know what to do with this."

"I understand. That's natural, especially since you weren't trained for anything like that. You had no reason before any of this to expect that you'd be put in such a situation."

"Maybe I should have."

"What do you mean?"

"My public comments and writings on Islam – both on the history and current events – made me wonder if some kind of attack was possible."

Stephen replied, "That's not my point. You're a pastor and an academic. Thinking about the remote possibility of someone reacting violently to what you've said somewhere along the line is a theoretical exercise."

"Apparently not."

"You know what I mean. Anyway, even those who have been trained for war never know how they'll actually react to the first time in battle, never mind if they wind up having to take a life. But they had that training. They expect it, at least on a certain level. Perhaps the time to worry is when such engagements feel almost natural, and a calm even sets in."

Richard asked, "Was it ever that way for you?"

Was? Apparently, it still is.

Stephen simply answered, "At times."

Richard said, "There's more, if you don't mind."

Grant was distracted briefly by the thought that what he had done over recent days was, again, feeling natural. He refocused on the conversation. "Of course, I don't mind."

"Even before the terror attacks, I was wondering if the parish life is where I'm meant to be serving the Lord and the Church."

"You mentioned that. Nearing any decisions?"

"Given my background with the interaction between Christianity and Islam, I've been contemplating mission work."

"Where?"

"The Middle East."

"Do you have a death wish?"

"Stephen, someone needs to do this."

"I know, I know. I'm sorry. That's my immediate reaction to the idea of someone I care about taking on such risks. But you're right."

"The more I think about it, the more it makes sense. I'm praying on it, and could use your prayers as well."

"You have them. You know, I'm reminded of what someone called me once."

"What was that?"

"A 'warrior monk.'""

"Like a Templar or Hospitaller?"

Stephen smiled. "Yes, exactly. But if you go down this path that label might fit you better."

"Yes and no. Stephen, you were the warrior, and apparently, still are."

Apparently, I am. "But while it's no longer the case, thankfully, that the Church and nations take up arms together as they did during the Crusades, the Church still needs to fight to engage and spread the Good News. We're doing battle as warriors."

"Modern day spiritual knights for the Church."

"In a sense, yes. Also, it doesn't surprise me that you're thinking this way. You are your father's son – both brave and fearless in their chosen fields."

"I sure don't feel fearless these days."

Stephen decided to switch gears. "By the way, I have to ask: What's the latest with you and Ms. Tanquerey?"

"Madison attended the late service on Sunday, and we had an early dinner."

"Nice. And?"

"We have another date tonight."

"Is this something that could get serious?"

"It could. Who knows? It's just a couple of dates at this point."

"And how might Ms. Tanquerey play into your decision about where you might do the most for the Church?"

"I have no idea."

"Fair enough. I like the honesty."

Chapter 81

The digital clock crept closer to midnight on Tuesday night. Paige Caldwell continued to shift her gaze between the clock, and the cable news show flickering away on the bedroom television.

When her phone's ringer called out, she nearly jumped up to sit on the side of the bed. She looked at the screen. The number was blocked. "Yes."

"I always seem to be asking the same question when we're on the phone. I assume you're alone?"

Caldwell smiled, and said, "Why would you assume that?"

"Paige, don't mess with the president of the United States."

"Oh, yes, sir. And what about you? Is a president ever really alone?"

"Well, there are a few moments, and more so for this president."

"How are you, Adam?"

"Overall, far better than I would have expected."

"Never underestimate your inner strength. I always saw it in you."

He was silent for a moment.

Caldwell continued, "I guess my advice wasn't all that good on Wyatt Hamilton."

"I think we were right, and so is he. I see his points. There's no hard and fast right or wrong answer to my offer. It's a matter of judgment. I can't disagree with his decision. I also have no doubt that he'll continue to run a fair campaign, and keep his word to me. I know I will."

"Let's not get too carried away with all of this integrity, I might start liking politicians." There was an energy in Paige's voice.

"Well, I certainly hope so."

It was Caldwell's turn to pause.

Links said, "Paige?"

"Adam, what's the deal with this?"

"What do you mean?"

"You're the president of the United States calling me on your private line in the middle of the night."

"Yes."

"Is this really just about you needing someone you can trust so you can talk freely, and get honest responses?"

"That's part of it."

"Yes, but is that all of it?"

"No, it's not all of it. Is that alright with you?"

Paige paused, and then said, "Yes, it is."

"Okay. Good."

"So, what does that mean? What exactly are we doing, or going to do, and how?"

"I have no idea."

Caldwell smiled, and replied, "Fair enough. I like the honesty."

Chapter 82

The funeral Mass for Lis Dicce took place on Wednesday morning at the family's home parish, St. Lawrence the Martyr in Rockville, Maryland. The church was filled with a strange mix of current and former CIA, a smattering of FBI, assorted others from the federal national security apparatus, and family and friends from their neighborhood and the parish who generally had no idea what Lis did for a living.

At the conclusion of the Mass, people greeted and offered comfort to each other, while also engaging in conversation, in the parking lot and across the street where the overflow was parked in a shopping center lot. Among the comfort and conversation, CDM's Chase Axelrod, Phil Lucena, and Jessica West congregated together, while Paige Caldwell, Charlie Driessen and Sean McEnany spoke with Stephen Grant.

Sean asked, "Where's Jennifer? I thought she was driving down with you?"

"I hitched a ride with her."

"Oh, that's right. You lost your Tahoe. Does she let you drive the Jeep yet?"

"No."

"That's sad, Pastor."

"Yeah, thanks. She has a meeting in her D.C. office, but she'll make it over to the cemetery. By the way, I need a ride to the cemetery."

Caldwell said, "You can come with me. Charlie and Sean have to head back to the D.C. office."

Charlie shook Stephen's hand, and said in a low voice, "Don't let the hero-who-stopped-the-terrorists stuff go to your head."

Stephen smiled, and said, "I'll try not to, Charlie."

Sean said, "See you on Sunday."

Stephen got into the passenger seat of Paige's Mustang. She slipped into the long line of cars with their lights on following the hearse.

Paige blurted out, "President Links called me last night."

"Really? Funny, he called me on Monday night. I'm guessing Adam had something different on his mind when he called you."

"Amusing."

Stephen smiled. "I think this is the first time since I've known you, Paige, that I have managed to make you feel uncomfortable about relationships."

"Don't get used to it."

"I suppose not."

"Are you going to listen?"

"Sure."

"There's more at work here for both Adam and me."

"Interesting. And what does that mean, and how the heck would it work?"

"I asked him that."

"And?"

"President Links said he had no idea."

"Hmmm, there seems to be a lot of that going around right now with friends and relationships."

"What does that mean?"

"Nothing. Never mind."

"Okay. But what do you think about this ... whatever it is?"

"Paige, you and I know firsthand that some things don't work out that might have seemed at some point inevitable."

She remained silent at that observation.

"And then there are things that seem to come out of nowhere, and eventually feel like they were meant to be. In the end, some decisions we make work out, and some don't."

"A long time ago you mentioned that one of your fellow SEALs passed along an abbreviated philosophy for life."

"That was Mike Leonard. He's Pastor Richard Leonard's father."

"Shit, you operate in a very small world."

"Tell me about it. Anyway, Mike laid it out this way: Shit happens; have faith; stay strong; love and take care of your family; pursue excellence; help others; and enjoy the gifts."

Caldwell smiled, and said, "That's right. I like that."

Stephen said, "Yeah, it seems that a lot of people do."

Chapter 83

After the burial, Jennifer called to say that she was behind schedule, so Stephen had Paige drop him at a Starbucks just off the outer loop of the Beltway.

As he sipped a venti iced tea, Stephen started reading on his phone's Kindle app one of the new biographies of Martin Luther that had been published in advance of the approaching Reformation anniversary. He also enjoyed people-watching in places like this – particularly seeing some of the reactions to his collar.

After about an hour, Stephen was fully immersed in the book, so he didn't notice Jennifer until she was just about at the table. She leaned down and gave him a peck on the cheek. "I have news, but let me grab a coffee first. Another tea?"

"Sounds good."

Five minutes later, Jennifer leaned closer to Stephen across the small round table. She spoke just above a whisper. "Governor Wyatt Hamilton called the office, said he was in D.C. and asked if he could come by for a few minutes. He apologized for it being last minute, but a meeting was cancelled, blah, blah, and all of a sudden Yvonne and I are sitting in the conference room with Hamilton and his top advisor, Ryan Thornton, with Joe on speaker."

Jennifer, Yvonne Hudson and Joe McPhee were the three principals in an economic forecasting, analysis and consulting firm. Hudson worked in their D.C. office, with McPhee in California and Jennifer in New York.

"That's an impressive last-minute meeting."

"Right, and he asked us to join his campaign, as the entire economics team."

Stephen smiled at Jennifer's news and her excitement. "Jen, that's fantastic. Congratulations. I assume you guys said yes."

"We did."

"Great."

"Driving here, only one question popped in my head." She glanced around the store. "What does this mean relative to your late-night calls from a new friend, not to mention the relationship of your former colleague with that friend?"

"I have no idea." *There's that answer again.* "All I can suggest is that we be straightforward with everyone. Obviously, my new friend, as you put it, will know quite soon of your new position. He can judge accordingly about his phone calls."

"Well, that's simple and true."

"And if there is any problem with any of this on either end, then I'll offer a list of pastors my friend can call."

"I really hope that's not necessary. But thank you."

"If that is, well, somewhat settled, are we ready to get on the road home?"

"Absolutely."

"And given your big day and excitement, why don't you let me drive and you can relax, make calls, or whatever else you need to get done?"

Jennifer smiled. "Nice try, but not a chance. You're not driving my Jeep." The two had a running joke about Stephen not being allowed to drive Jen's former car, a red convertible Thunderbird. And when he finally did get behind the wheel, it was wrecked in a car chase.

"Okay, but we've got to buy a new car tomorrow," observed Stephen.

"And let's try not to wreck that one, too."

Chapter 84

Six months later...

In a spacious hotel suite, President Adam Links was sleeping soundly the night before he was due to officially accept the nomination at the Democratic Party's National Convention. Despite being the successor to an assassinated president, Links barely survived a sharp attack from the party's hard Left during the primaries.

He now would be squaring off against Governor Wyatt Hamilton in the general election. And heading into that campaign, it turned out voters liked both candidates, with each touting strong approval ratings.

Links awoke and sat up at the knock on the bedroom door. "Yes, come in." He leaned over and flipped on the nightstand light.

The chief of staff approached. "Mr. President, I have ... unfortunate news."

"What is it?"

"Teriff Pasha and Youseff Sarwar, sir."

"Yes? Out with it."

"Each was found dead."

"What? Both of them?"

"I was told each had four bullet wounds. Two in the head and two in the chest."

Links got up, and began walking around the room.

The chief of staff added, "Apparently, at each scene, nothing was really left behind. I was told that it was very professional."

The names and roles of Pasha and Sarwar in the terrorist attacks earlier in the year were never made public. The two men disappeared. It was assumed that anyone knowing either man would think the worst, and have no incentives to bring up the matter.

Links told his closest advisors that allowing the two to enter witness protection was the hardest and most distasteful decision he ever made in his entire life. But, as he weighed the matter, Links wound up agreeing with those arguing if word got out that Pasha and Sarwar cooperated based on certain guarantees, and those guarantees were reneged on, then it would be very difficult to get others to flip.

Only Paige, in private, made the case for executing each man. She argued passionately with Links, making clear that she was the one who originally fed the two hope for something short of execution, and that, of course, was, in her words, "total bullshit." When Links finally told her that there would be no executions or prison, but instead, witness protection, he had never seen her so infuriated. She refused to speak with him for a few weeks, and when they resumed communications, nothing was said again about the Pasha and Sarwar decision.

Links said to his chief of staff, "Very professional and no evidence?"

"Correct, sir."

Links shook his head, and his pacing slowed. Finally, he said, "I'm not exactly heartbroken, to say the least. But let's find out what the hell happened, and how the marshals screwed this up."

"Yes, Mr. President."

*   *   *

As President Adam Links spoke to his fellow Democrats and the nation, Sean McEnany parked his car away from the few street lights on a quiet road. He walked through the gates of the Catholic cemetery, and stopped in front of a headstone.

He stood in silence for nearly fifteen minutes, and then another figure approached. That person stopped next to Sean, looking down at the headstone as well.

McEnany said, "Everything okay, Paige?"

"It is, Sean. And you?"

"Better."

Another ten minutes of silence passed. Sean then stepped forward, and simply touched the stone in which the name "Lis Dicce" was carved.

He looked at Paige, and said, "I'm heading home. I might get a late start on work tomorrow."

"No worries. Safe journey."

"Thanks. You, too."

Sean walked away slowly.

Paige remained for another five minutes. "Cemeteries aren't my thing, Lis. Neither is talking to the dead. To tell the truth, it might be one of the few things that really creeps me out. I'll have to ask Stephen about the theology on this someday. But for now, I'm still sorry for what happened, and I hope you somehow rest a little easier now."

She also touched the stone.

"Good-bye, Lis."

Acknowledgments

Thank you to the members of the Pastor Stephen Grant Fellowship for their support:

Bronze Readers
Michele Behl
Mike Eagle
Sue Kreft

Readers
Robert Rosenberg

As always, thanks to my bride, Beth. I value her edits and insights, but most of all, her support and love. I also thank my two sons, David and Jonathan, for making me proud, and keeping me grounded.

Naturally, any shortcomings in my books are completely my own responsibility.

Finally, the generosity of those who have used their treasure and time to purchase and read these thrillers continues to humble this writer. As long as someone keeps reading, I'll keep writing. God bless.

Ray Keating
July 2017

About the Author

This is Ray Keating's seventh novel featuring Stephen Grant. The first was *Warrior Monk: A Pastor Stephen Grant Novel*, followed by *Root of All Evil? A Pastor Stephen Grant Novel*, *An Advent for Religious Liberty: A Pastor Stephen Grant Novel*, *The River: A Pastor Stephen Grant Novel*, *Murderer's Row: A Pastor Stephen Grant Novel*, and *Wine Into Water: A Pastor Stephen Grant Novel*.

Keating also is an author of various nonfiction books and an economist. In addition, he is a columnist with RealClearMarkets.com, and a former weekly columnist for *Newsday*, *Long Island Business News*, and the *New York City Tribune*. His work has appeared in a wide range of additional periodicals, including *The New York Times*, *The Wall Street Journal*, *The Washington Post*, *New York Post*, Los Angeles *Daily News*, *The Boston Globe*, *National Review*, *The Washington Times*, *Investor's Business Daily*, New York *Daily News*, *Detroit Free Press*, *Chicago Tribune*, *Providence Journal Bulletin*, *TheHill.com*, *Touchstone* magazine, *Towhall.com*, *Newsmax*, and *Cincinnati Enquirer*. Keating lives on Long Island with his family.

Made in the USA
Middletown, DE
14 August 2017